THE SCENE OF THE CRIME...

In Mary Bellamy's bedroom all the windows were open. An evening breeze stirred the curtains and the ranks of tulips. Dr. Harkness knelt beside the pool of rose-colored chiffon from which protruded, like rods, two legs finished with high-heeled shoes and two naked arms whose clenched hands glittered with diamonds. Diamonds were spattered across the rigid plane of the chest and shone through a hank of disarranged hair. A length of red chiffon lay across the face and this was a good thing....

Also by Ngaio Marsh
from Jove

Ngaio Marsh

FALSE SCENT

A JOVE BOOK

This Jove book contains the complete
text of the original hardcover edition.

FALSE SCENT

A Jove Book / published by arrangement with
Little, Brown and Company

PRINTING HISTORY
Little, Brown and Company edition published 1959
Three previous printings
First Jove edition / November 1981
Second printing / August 1982
Third printing / December 1984

ISBN: 0-515-08056-X

Jove books are published by The Berkley Publishing Group,
200 Madison Avenue, New York, N.Y. 10016.
The words "A JOVE BOOK" and the "J" with sunburst
are trademarks belonging to Jove Publications, Inc.

PRINTED IN THE UNITED STATES OF AMERICA

For Jemima with love

CONTENTS

FALSE SCENT

chapter one

Pardoner's Place. 9:00A.M.

WHEN SHE DIED it was as if all the love she had inspired in so
many people suddenly blossomed. She had never, of course,
realized how greatly she was loved, never known that she was
to be carried by six young men who would ask to perform this
last courtesy: to bear her on their strong shoulders, so gently
and with such dedication.

Quite insignificant people were there; her old Ninn, the
family nurse, with a face like a boot, grimly crying. And
Florence, her dresser, with a bunch of primroses, because of
all flowers they were the ones she had best loved to see on her
make-up table. And George, the stage doorkeeper at the
Unicorn, sober as sober and telling anyone who would listen
to him that there, if you liked, had been a great lady. Pinky
Cavendish in floods and Maurice, very Guardee, with a stiff
upper lip. Crowds of people whom she herself would have
scarcely remembered but upon whom, at some time, she had
bestowed the gift of her charm.

All the Knights and Dames, of course, and the

1

Management, and Timon Gantry, the great producer, who
had so often directed her. Bertie Saracen, who had created
her dresses since the days when she was a bit-part actress and
who had, indeed, risen to his present eminence in the wake of
her mounting fame. But it was not for her fame that they had
come to say goodbye to her. It was because, quite simply,
they had loved her.

And Richard? Richard was there, white and withdrawn.
And—this was an afterthought—and, of course, Charles.

Miss Bellamy paused, bogged down in her own fantasy.
Enjoyable tears started from her eyes. She often indulged
herself with plans for her funeral and she never failed to be
moved by them. The only catch was the indisputable fact that
she wouldn't live to enjoy it. She would be, as it were, cheated
of her own obsequies and she felt there was some injustice in
this.

But perhaps, after all, she *would* know. Perhaps, she
would hover ambiguously over the whole show, employing
her famous gift for making a party go without seeming to do
anything about it. Perhaps—? Feeling slightly uncomfortable, she reminded herself of her magnificent constitution
and decided to think about something else.

There was plenty to think about. The new play. Her role: a
fat part if ever she saw one. The long speech about keeping
the old chin up and facing the future with a wry smile.
Richard hadn't put it quite like that and she did sometimes
wish he would write more simply. Perhaps she would choose
her moments and suggest to him that a few homely phrases
would do the trick much more effectively than those rather
involved, rather *arid* sentences that were so bloody difficult
to memorize. What was wanted—the disreputable word
"gimmick" rose to the surface and was instantly slapped
down—what was wanted, when all was said and done, was
the cosy human touch: a vehicle for her particular genius. She
believed in humanity. Perhaps this morning would be the
right occasion to talk to Richard. He would, of course, be
coming to wish her many happy returns. Her birthday! That
had to be thought of selectively and with a certain amount of
care. She must at all costs exclude that too easy little sum

whose answer would provide her age. She had, quite literally but by dint of a yogi-like discipline, succeeded in forgetting it. Nobody else that mattered knew, except Florence, who was utterly discreet and Old Ninn who, one must face it, was getting a bit garrulous, especially when she'd taken her glass or two of port. Please God she wouldn't forget herself this afternoon.

After all it was how you felt and how you looked that mattered. She lifted her head from the pillows and turned it. There, across the room, she was, reflected in the tall glass above her dressing-table. Not bad, she thought, not half bad, even at that hour and with no make-up. She touched her face here and there, manipulating the skin above the temples and at the top of the jawline. To lift or not to lift? Pinky Cavendish was all for it and said that nowadays there was no need for the stretched look. But what about her famous triangular smile? Maintaining the lift, she smiled. The effect was still triangular.

She rang her bell. It was rather touching to think of her little household, oriented to her signal. Florence, Cooky, Gracefield, the parlourmaid, the housemaid and the odd woman: all ready in the kitchen and full of plans for the Great Day. Old Ninn, revelling in her annual holiday, sitting up in bed with her *News of the World* or perhaps putting the final touch to the bedjacket she had undoubtedly knitted and which would have to be publicly worn for her gratification. And, of course, Charles. It was curious how Miss Bellamy tended to leave her husband out of her meditations, because, after all, she was extremely fond of him. She hurriedly inserted him. He would be waiting for Gracefield to tell him she was awake and had rung. Presently he would appear, wearing a pink scrubbed look and that plum-coloured dressing-gown that did so little to help.

She heard a faint chink and a subdued rumble. The door opened and Florence came in with her tray.

"Top of the morning, dear," said Florence. "What's it feel like to be eighteen again?"

"You old fool," Miss Bellamy said and grinned at her. "It feels fine."

Florence built pillows up behind her and set the tray

across her knees. She then drew back the curtains and lit the fire. She was a pale, small woman with black dyed hair and sardonic eyes. She had been Miss Bellamy's dresser for twenty-five years and her personal maid for fifteen. "Three rousing cheers," she said, "it's a handsome-looking morning."

Miss Bellamy examined her tray. The basket-ends were full of telegrams, a spray of orchids lay across the plate and beside it a parcel in silver wrapping tied with pink ribbon.

"What's all this?" she asked, as she had asked for her last fifteen birthdays, and took up the parcel.

"The flowers are from the Colonel. He'll be bringing his present later on, as per usual, I suppose."

"I wasn't talking about the flowers," Miss Bellamy said and opened the parcel. "Florrie! Florrie, *darling*!"

Florence clattered the firearms. "Might as well get in early," she muttered, "or it'd never be noticed."

It was a chemise, gossamer fine and exquisitely embroidered.

"Come *here*!" Miss Bellamy said, fondly bullying.

Florence walked over to the bed and suffered herself to be kissed. Her face became crimson. For a moment she looked at her employer with a devotion that was painful in its intensity and then turned aside, her eyes filmed with unwilling tears.

"But it's out of this world!" Miss Bellamy marvelled, referring to the chemise. "That's all! It's just *made* my day for me." She shook her head slowly from side to side, lost in wonderment. "I can't wait," she said and, indeed, she was very pleased with it.

"There's the usual mail," Florence grunted. "More, if anything."

"Truly?"

"Outside on the trolley. Will I fetch it in here?"

"After my bath, darling, may we?"

Florence opened drawers and doors, and began to lay out the clothes her mistress had chosen to wear. Miss Bellamy, who was on a strict diet, drank her tea, ate her toast, and opened her telegrams, awarding each of them some pleased ejaculation. "Darling, Bertie! Such a sweet muddled little

4

message. And a cable, Florrie, from the Bantings in New York. Heaven of them!"

"That show's folding, I'm told," Florence said, "and small wonder. Dirty *and* dull, by all accounts. You mustn't be both."

"You don't know anything about it," Miss Bellamy absentmindedly observed. She was staring in bewilderment at the next telegram. "This," she said, "isn't true. It's just not true. My dear Florrie, *will* you listen." Modulating her lovely voice, Miss Bellamy read it aloud, "'Her birth was of the womb of morning dew and her conception of the joyous prime.'"

"Disgusting," said Florence.

"I call it rather touching. But who in the wide world is Octavius Browne?"

"Search me, love." Florence helped Miss Bellamy into a negligee designed by Bertie Saracen, and herself went into the bathroom. Miss Bellamy settled down to some preliminary work on her face.

There was a tap on the door connecting her room with her husband's and he came in. Charles Templeton was sixty years old, big and fair with a heavy belly. His eyeglass dangled over his dark red dressing-gown; his hair, thin and babyishly fine, was carefully brushed; and his face, which had the florid colouring associated with heart disease, was freshly shaved. He kissed his wife's hand and forehead and laid a small parcel before her. "A very happy birthday to you, Mary, my dear," he said. Twenty years ago, when she married him, she had told him that his voice was charming. If it was so still, she no longer noticed it or, indeed, listened very attentively to much that he said.

But she let her birthday gaiety play about him and was enchanted with her present, a diamond and emerald bracelet. It was, even for Charles, quite exceptionally magnificent, and for a fleeting moment she remembered that he, as well as Florence and Old Ninn, knew her age. She wondered if there was any intention of underlining this particular anniversary. There were some numerals that by their very appearance—stodgy and rotund—wore an air of horrid maturity. Five, for instance. She pulled her thoughts up short and showed him the telegram. "I should like to know what in the world you make of that," she said and went into the bathroom, leaving the door open. Florence came back and began to make the bed with an air of standing none of its nonsense.

"Good morning, Florence," Charles Templeton said. He put up his eyeglass and walked over to the bow window with the telegram.

"Good morning, sir," Florence woodenly rejoined. Only when she was alone with her mistress did she allow herself the freedom of the dressing-room.

"Did you," Miss Bellamy shouted from her bath, "ever see anything quite like it?"

"But it's delightful," he said, "and how very nice of Octavius."

"You don't mean to say you know who he is?"

"Octavius Browne? Of course I do. He's the old boy down below in the Pegasus Bookshop. Up at the House, but a bit before my time. Delightful fellow."

"Blow me down flat!" Miss Bellamy ejaculated, splashing luxuriously. "You mean that dim little place with a fat cat in the window."

"That's it. He specializes in pre-Jacobean literature."

"Does that account for the allusion to wombs and conceptions? Of *what* can he be thinking, poor Mr. Browne?"

"It's a quotation," Charles said, letting his eyeglass drop. "From Spenser. I bought a very nice Spenser from him last week. No doubt he supposes you've read it."

"Then, of course, I must pretend I have. I shall call on him and thank him. Kind Mr. Browne!"

"They're great friends of Richard's."

Miss Bellamy's voice sharpened a little. "Who? *They?*"

"Octavius Browne and his niece. A good-looking girl." Charles glanced at Florence and after a moment's hesitation added, "She's called Anelida Lee."

Florence cleared her throat.

"Not true!" The voice in the bathroom gave a little laugh. "A-nelly-da! It sounds like a face cream."

"It's Chaucerian."

"I suppose the cat's called Piers Plowman."

6

"No. He's out of the prevailing period. He's called Hodge."

"I've never heard Richard utter her name."

Charles said: "She's on the stage, it appears."

"Oh, *God*!"

"In the new club theatre behind Walton Street. The Bonaventure."

"You need say no more, my poor Charles. One knows the form." Charles was silent and the voice asked impatiently, "Are you still there?"

"Yes, my dear."

"How do you know Richard's so thick with them?"

"I meet him there occasionally," Charles said, and added lightly, "I'm thick with them too, Mary."

There was further silence and then the voice, delightful and gay, shouted, "Florrie! Bring me *you know what*."

Florence picked up her own offering and went into the bathroom.

Charles Templeton stared through the window at a small London square, brightly receptive of April sunshine. He could just see the flower-woman at the corner of Pardoner's Row, sitting in a galaxy of tulips. There were tulips everywhere. His wife had turned the bow window into an indoor garden and had filled it with them and with a great mass of early-flowering azaleas, brought up in the conservatory and still in bud. He examined these absent-mindedly and discovered among them a tin with a spray-gun mechanism. The tin was labelled "Slaypest" and bore alarming captions about the lethal nature of its contents. Charles peered at them through his eyeglass.

"Florence," he said, "I don't think this stuff ought to be left lying about."

"Just what I tell her," Florence said, returning.

"There are all sorts of warnings. It shouldn't be used in enclosed places. *Is* it used like that?"

"It won't be for want of my telling her if it is."

"Really, I *don't* like it. Could you lose it?"

"I'd get the full treatment meself if I did," Florence grunted.

7

"Nevertheless," Charles said, "I think you should do so."

Florence shot a resentful look at him and muttered under her breath.

"What did you say?" he asked.

"I said it wasn't so easy. She knows. She can read. I've told her." She glowered at him and then said, "I take my orders from her. Always have and always will."

He waited for a moment. "Quite so," he said. "But all the same—" and hearing his wife's voice, put the spray-gun down, gave a half-sigh and turned to confront the familiar room.

Miss Bellamy came into it wearing Florence's gift. There was a patch of sunshine in the room and she posed in it, expectant, unaware of its disobliging candour.

"Look at my smashing shift!" she cried. "Florrie's present! A new birthday suit."

She had "made an entrance," comic-provocative, skilfully French-farcical. She had no notion at all of the disservice she had done herself.

The voice that she had once called charming said, "Marvellous. How kind of Florence."

He was careful to wait a little longer before he said, "Well, darling, I shall leave you to your mysteries," and went down to his solitary breakfast.

2

There was no particular reason why Richard Dakers should feel uplifted that morning; indeed, there were many formidable reasons why he should not. Nevertheless, as he made his way by bus and on foot to Pardoner's Place, he did experience, very strongly, that upward kick of the spirit which lies in London's power of bestowal. He sat in the front seat at the prow of the bus and felt like a figurehead, cleaving the tide of the King's Road, masterfully above it, yet gloriously of it. The Chelsea shops were full of tulips and when, leaving the bus, he walked to the corner of Pardoner's

Row, there was his friend the flower-woman with buckets of them, still pouted up in buds.

"Morning, dear," said the flower-woman. "Duck of a day, innit?"

"It's a day for the gods," Richard agreed, "and your hat fits you like a halo, Mrs. Tinker."

"It's me straw," Mrs. Tinker said. "I usually seem to change to me straw on the second Sat in April."

"Aphrodite on her cockleshell couldn't say fairer. I'll take two dozen of the yellows."

She wrapped them up in green paper. "Ten bob to you," said Mrs. Tinker.

"Ruin!" Richard ejaculated, giving her eleven shillings. "Destitution! But what the hell!"

"That's right, dear, we don' care, do we? Tulips, lady? Lovely tulips."

Carrying his tulips and with his dispatch case tucked under his arm, Richard entered Pardoner's Place and turned right. Three doors along he came to the Pegasus, a bow-fronted Georgian house that had been converted by Octavius Browne into a bookshop. In the window, tilted and open, lay a first edition of Beijer and Duchartre's *Premieres Comedies Italiennes*. A little further back, half in shadow, hung a Negro marionette, very grand in striped silks. And in the watery depths of the interior Richard could just make out the shapes of the three beautifully polished old chairs, the lovely table and the vertical strata of rows and rows of books. He could see, too, the figure of Anelida Lee moving about among her uncle's treasures, attended by Hodge, their cat. In the mornings Anelida, when not rehearsing at her club theatre, helped her uncle. She hoped that she was learning to be an actress. Richard, who knew a good deal about it, was convinced that already she was one.

He opened the door and went in.

Anelida had been dusting and wore her black smock, an uncompromising garment. Her hair was tied up in a white scarf. He had time to reflect that there was a particular beauty that most pleased when it was least adorned and that Anelida was possessed of it.

"Hullo," he said. "I've brought you some tulips. Good morning, Hodge." Hodge stared at him briefly, jerked his tail, and walked away.

"How lovely! But it's not *my* birthday."

"Never mind. It's because it's a nice morning and Mrs. Tinker was wearing her straw."

"I couldn't be better pleased," said Anelida. "Will you wait while I get a pot for them? There's a green jug."

She went into a room at the back. He heard a familiar tapping noise on the stairs. Her uncle Octavius came down, leaning on his black stick. He was a tall man of about sixty-three with a shock of grey hair and a mischievous face. He had a trick of looking at people out of the corners of his eyes as if inviting them to notice what a bad boy he was. He was rather touchy, immensely learned and thin almost to transparency.

"Good morning, my dear Dakers," he said, and seeing the tulips, touched one of them with the tip of a bluish finger. "Ah," he said, "'Art could not feign more simple grace, Nor Nature take a line away.' How very lovely and so pleasantly uncomplicated by any smell. We have found something for you, by the way. Quite nice and I hope in character, but it may be a little too expensive. You must tell us what you think."

He opened a parcel on his desk and stood aside for Richard to look at the contents.

"A tinsel picture, as you see," he said, "of Madame Vestris *en travesti* in jockey's costume." He looked sideways at Richard. "Beguiling little breeches, don't you think? Do you suppose it would appeal to Miss Bellamy?"

"I don't see how it could fail."

"It's rare-ish. The frame's comtemporary. I'm afraid it's twelve guineas."

"It's mine," Richard said. "Or rather, it's Mary's."

"You're sure? Then, if you'll excuse me for a moment, I'll get Nell to make a birthday parcel of it. There's a sheet of Victorian tinsel somewhere. Nell, my dear! Would you—?"

He tapped away and presently Anelida returned with the green jug and his parcel, beautifully wrapped.

Richard put his hand on his dispatch case. "What do you suppose is in there?" he asked.

"Not—not *the* play? Not *Husbandry in Heaven?*"

"Hot from the typist." He watched her thin hands arrange the tulips. "Anelida, I'm going to show it to Mary."

"You couldn't choose a better day," she said warmly, and when he didn't answer, "What's the matter?"

"There isn't a part for her in it," he blurted out.

After a moment she said, "Well, no. But does that matter?"

"It might. If, of course, it ever comes to production. And, by the way, Timmy Gantry's seen it and makes agreeable noises. All the same, it's tricky about Mary."

"But why? I don't see—"

"It's not all that easy to explain," he mumbled.

"You've already written a new play for her and she's delighted with it, isn't she? This is something quite different."

"And better? You've read it."

"Immeasurably better. In another world. Everybody must see it."

"Timmy Gantry likes it."

"Well, there you are! It's special. Won't she see that?"

He said: "Anelida, dear, you don't really know the theatre yet, do you? Or the way actors tick over?"

"Well, perhaps I don't. But I know how close you are to each other and how wonderfully she understands you. You've told me."

"That's just it," Richard said and there followed a long silence.

"I don't believe," he said at last, "that I've ever told you exactly what she and Charles did?"

"No," she agreed. "Not exactly. But—"

"My parents, who were Australians, were friends of Mary's. They were killed in a car smash on the Grande Corniche when I was rising two. They were staying with Mary at the time. There was no money to speak of. She had me looked after by her own old nanny, the celebrated Ninn, and then, after she had married Charles, they took me over completely. I owe everything to her. I like to think that, in a way, the plays have done something to repay. And now—you see what I go and do."

Anelida finished her tulips and looked directly at him. "I'm sure it'll work out," she said gently. "All very fine, I daresay, for me to say so, but you see, you've talked so much about her, I almost feel I know her."

"I very much want you to know her. Indeed, this brings me to the main object of my pompous visit. Will you let me call for you at six and take you to see her? There's a party of sorts at half-past which I hope may amuse you, but I'd like you to meet her first. Will you, Anelida?"

She waited too long before she said, "I don't think I can. I'm—I've booked myself up."

"I don't believe you. Why won't you come?"

"But I can't. It's her birthday and it's special to her and her friends. You can't go hauling in an unknown female. *And* an unknown actress, to boot."

"Of course I can."

"It wouldn't be comely."

"What a fantastic word! And why the hell do you suppose it wouldn't be comely for the two people I like best in the world to meet each other?"

Anelida said, "I didn't know—"

"Yes, you did," he said crossly. "You must have."

"We scarcely know each other."

"I'm sorry you feel like that about it."

"I only meant—well, in point of time—"

"Don't hedge."

"Now, look here—"

"I'm sorry. Evidently I've taken too much for granted."

While they stared aghast at the quarrel that between them they had somehow concocted, Octavius came tapping back. "By the way," he said happily, "I yielded this morning to a romantic impulse, Dakers. I sent your patroness a birthday greeting: one among hundreds, no doubt. The allusion was from Spenser. I hope she won't take it amiss."

"How very nice of you, sir," Richard said loudly. "She'll be enchanted. She loves people to be friendly. Thank you for finding the picture."

And forgetting to pay for it, he left hurriedly in a miserable frame of mind.

12

3

Mary Bellamy's house was next door to the Pegasus Bookshop, but Richard was too rattled to go in. He walked round Pardoner's Place trying to sort out his thoughts. He suffered one of those horrid experiences, fortunately rare, in which the victim confronts himself as a stranger in an abrupt perspective. The process resembles that of pseudo-scientific films in which the growth of a plant, by mechanical skulduggery, is reduced from seven weeks to as many minutes and the subject is seen wavering, extending, elongating itself in response to some irresistible force until it breaks into its pre-ordained fluorescence.

The irresistible force in Richard's case had undoubtedly been Mary Bellamy. The end-product, after twenty-seven years of the treatment, was two successful West End comedies, a third in the bag, and (his hand tightened on his dispatch case) a serious play.

He owed it all, as he had so repeatedly told her, to Mary. Well, perhaps not quite all. Not the serious play.

He had almost completed his round of the little Place and, not wanting to pass the shop window, turned back. Why in the world had he gone grand and huffy when Anelida refused to meet Mary? And why *did* she refuse? Any other girl in Anelida's boots, he thought uneasily, would have jumped at that sort of invitation: the great Mary Bellamy's birthday party. A tiny, handpicked group from the topmost drawer in the London theatre. *The* Management. *The* producer. Any other girl—he fetched up short, not liking himself very much, conscious that if he followed his thoughts to their logical conclusion he would arrive at an uncomfortable position. What sort of man, he would have to ask himself, was Richard Dakers? Reality would disintegrate and he would find himself face-to-face with a stranger. It was a familar experience and one he didn't enjoy. He shook himself free of it, made a sudden decision, walked quickly to the house and rang the bell.

Charles Templeton breakfasted in his study on the ground floor. The door was open and Richard saw him there, reading

13

his *Times,* at home among his six so judiciously chosen pieces of *chinoiserie,* his three admirable pictures, his few distinguished chairs and lovely desk. Charles was fastidious about his surroundings and extremely knowledgeable. He could wait, sometimes for years, for the acquisition of a single treasure.

Richard went in. "Charles!" he said. "How are you?"

"Hullo, old boy. Come to make your devotions?"

"Am I the first?"

"The first in person. There are the usual massive offerings in kind. Mary'll be delighted to see you."

"I'll go up," Richard said, but still hovered. Charles lowered his newspaper. How often, Richard wondered, had he seen him make that gesture, dropping his eyeglass and vaguely smiling. Richard, still involved in the aftermath of his moment of truth, if that was its real nature, asked himself what he knew of Charles. How used he was to that even courtesy, that disengagement! What of Charles in other places? What of the reputedly implacable man of affairs who had built his own fortune? Or of the lover Charles must have been five and twenty years ago? Impossible to imagine, Richard thought, looking vaguely at an empty niche in the wall.

He said, "Hullo! Where's the T'ang musician?"

"Gone," Charles said.

"Gone! Where! Not broken?"

"Chipped. The peg of her lute. Gracefield did it, I think. I've given her to Maurice Warrender."

"But—even so—I mean, so often they're not absolutely perfect and you—it was your treasure."

"Not now," Charles said. "I'm a perfectionist, you know."

"That's what you say!" Richard exclaimed warmly. "But I bet it was because Maurice always coveted her. You're so absurdly generous."

"Oh nonsense," Charles said and looked at his paper. Richard hesitated. He heard himself say,

"Charles, do I ever say thank you? To you and Mary?"

"My dear fellow, what for?"

"For everything." He took refuge in irony. "For befriending the poor orphan boy, you know, among other things."

"I sincerely hope you're not making a vicarious birthday resolution."

"It just struck me."

Charles waited for a moment and then said, "You've given us a trememdous interest and very much pleasure." He again hesitated as if assembling his next sentence. "Mary and I," he said at last, "look upon you as an achievement. And now, do go and make your pretty speeches to her."

"Yes," Richard said. "I'd better, hadn't I? See you later."

Charles raised his newspaper and Richard went slowly upstairs, wishing, consciously, for perhaps the first time in his life, that he was not going to visit Miss Bellamy.

She was in her room, dressed and enthroned among her presents. He slipped into another gear as he took her to his heart in a birthday embrace and then held her at arm's length to tell her how lovely she looked.

"Darling, darling, darling!" she cried joyously. "How *perfect* of you to come. I've been hoping and hoping!"

It occurred to him that it would have been strange indeed if he hadn't performed this time-honoured observance, but he kissed her again and gave her his present.

It was early in the day and her reservoir of enthusiasm scarcely tapped. She was able to pour a freshet of praise over his tinsel picture and did so with many cries of gratitude and wonder. Where, she asked, where, *where* had he discovered the *one*, the *perfect* present.

It was an opening Richard had hoped for, but he found himself a little apprehensive nevertheless.

"I found it," he said, "at the Pegasus—or rather Octavius Browne found it for me. He says it's rare-ish."

Her triangular smile didn't fade. Her eyes continued to beam into his, her hands to press his hands.

"Ay, yes!" she cried gaily. "The old man in the bookshop! Believe it or not, darling, he sent me a telegram about my conception. Too sweet, but a little difficult to acknowledge."

"He's very donnish," Richard said. She made a comic face at him. "He *was,* in fact, a don, but he found himself out of sympathy with angry young men and set up a bookshop instead."

She propped up her tinsel picture on the dressing-table and gazed at it through half-closed eyes. "Isn't there a

15

daughter or something? I seem to have heard—"

"A niece," Richard said. Maddeningly, his mouth had gone dry.

"Ought I," she asked, "to nip downstairs and thank him? One never quite knows with that sort of person."

Richard kissed her hand. "Octavius," he said, "is not that sort of person, darling. Do nip down. He'll be enchanted. And Mary—"

"What, my treasure?"

"I thought perhaps you might be terribly kind and ask them for a drink. If you find them pleasant, that is."

She sat at her dressing-table and examined her face in the glass. "I wonder," she said, "if I *really* like that new eyeshade." She took up a heavy Venetian glass scent-spray and used it lavishly. "I hope someone gives me some really superlative scent," she said. "This is almost gone." She put it down. "For a drink?" she said. "When? Not today, of course."

"*Not* today, you think?"

She opened her eyes very wide. "My dear, we'd only embarrass them."

"Well," he murmured, "see how you feel about it."

She turned back to the glass and said nothing. He opened his dispatch case and took out his typescript.

"I've brought something," he said, "for you to read. It's a surprise, Mary." He laid it on the dressing-table. "There."

She looked at the cover page. "*Husbandry in Heaven*. A play by Richard Dakers."

"Dicky? Dicky, darling, *what* is all this?"

"Something I've kept for today," he said and knew at once that he'd made a mistake. She gave him that special luminous gaze that meant she was deeply moved. "O Dicky!" she whispered. "For me? My *dear*!"

He was panic-stricken.

"But when?" she asked him, slowly shaking her head in bewilderment. "When did you *do* it? With all the other work? I don't understand. I'm flabbergasted, Dicky!"

"I've been working on it for some time. It's—it's quite a different thing. Not a comedy. You may hate it."

"Is it the great one—at last?" she whispered. "The one that we always knew would happen? And all by yourself, Dicky?

Not even with poor stupid, old, loving me to listen?"

She was saying all the things he would least have chosen for her to say. It was appalling.

"For all I know," he said, "it may be frighteningly bad. I've got to that state where one just can't tell. Anyway, don't let's burden the great day with it."

"You couldn't have given me anything else that would make me half so happy." She stroked the typescript with both eloquent, not very young hands. "I'll shut myself away for an hour before lunch and wolf it up."

"Mary," he said desperately. "Don't be so sanguine about it. It's not your sort of play."

"I won't hear a word against it. You've written it for *me*, darling."

He was hunting desperately for some way of telling her he had done nothing of the sort when she said gaily, "All right! We'll see. I won't tease you. What were we talking about? Your funnies in the bookshop? I'll pop in this morning and see what I think of them, shall I? Will that do?"

Before he could answer two voices, one elderly and uncertain and the other a fluting alto, were raised outside in the passage:

"Happy birthday to you. Happy birthday to you.
Happy birthday, dear Mary,
Happy birthday to you."

The door opened to admit Colonel Warrender and Mr. Bertie Saracen.

—

4

Colonel Warrender was sixty years old, a bachelor and a cousin of Charles Templeton, whom, in a leaner, better-looking way, he slightly resembled. He kept himself fit, was well dressed and wore a moustache so neatly managed that it looked as if it had been ironed on his face. His manner was pleasant and his bearing soldierly.

Mr. Bertie Saracen was also immaculate, but more

adventurously so. The sleeves of his jacket were narrower and displayed a great deal of pinkish cuff. He had a Berlin-china complexion, wavy hair, blue eyes and wonderfully small hands. His air was gay and insouciant. He too was a bachelor and most understandably so.

They made a comic entrance together: Warrender good-naturedly self-conscious, Bertie Saracen revelling in his act of prima ballerina. He chassed to right and left, holding aloft his votive offering and finally laid it at Miss Bellamy's feet.

"God, what a fool I must look!" he exclaimed. "Take it, darling, quickly or we'll kill the laugh."

A spate of greetings broke out and an examination of gifts: from Warrender, who had been abroad, gloves of Grenoble, and from Bertie a miniature group of five bathing beauties and a photographer all made of balsa wood and scraps of cotton. "It's easily the nicest present you'll get," he said. "And now I must enjoy a good jeer at all the others."

He flitted about the room, making little darts at them. Warrender, a rather silent man, generally believed to entertain a long-standing and blameless adoration of Mary Bellamy, had a word with Richard, who liked him.

"Rehearsals started yet?" he asked. "Mary tells me she's delighted with her new part."

"Not yet. It's the mixture as before," Richard rejoined.

Warrender gave him a brief look. "Early days to settle into a routine, isn't it?" he said surprisingly. "Leave that to the old hands, isn't it?" He had a trick of ending his remarks with this colloquialism.

"I'm trying, on the side, to break out in a rash of serious writing."

"Are you? Good. Afford to take risks, I'd have thought."

"How pleasant," Richard exclaimed, "to hear somebody say that!"

Warrender looked at his shoes. "Never does," he said, "to let yourself be talked into things. Not that I know anything about it."

Richard thought with gratitude: "That's exactly the kind of thing I wanted to be told," but was prevented from saying so by the entrance of Old Ninn.

Old Ninn's real name was Miss Ethel Plumtree, but she was given the courtesy title of "Mrs." She had been Mary Bellamy's nurse, and from the time of his adoption by Mary and Charles, Richard's also. Every year she emerged from retirement for a fortnight to stay with her former charge. She was small, scarlet-faced and fantastically opinionated. Her age was believed to be eighty-one. Nannies being universally accepted as character parts rather than people in their own right, Old Ninn was the subject of many of Mary Bellamy's funniest stories. Richard sometimes wondered if she played up to her own legend. In her old age she had developed a liking for port and under its influence made great mischief among the servants and kept up a sort of guerilla warfare with Florence, with whom, nevertheless, she was on intimate terms. They were united, Miss Bellamy said, in their devotion to herself.

Wearing a cerise shawl and a bold floral print, for she adored bright colours, Old Ninn trudged across the room with the corners of her mouth turned down and laid a tissue paper parcel on the dressing-table.

"Happy birthday, m'," she said. For so small a person she had an alarmingly deep voice.

A great fuss was made over her. Bertie Saracen attempted Mercutian badinage and called her Nurse Plumtree. She ignored him and addressed herself exclusively to Richard.

"We don't see much of you these days," she said, and by the sour look she gave him, proclaimed her affection.

"I've been busy, Ninn."

"Still making up your plays, by all accounts."

"That's it."

"You always were a fanciful boy. Easy to see, you've never grown out of it."

Mary Bellamy had unwrapped the parcel and disclosed a knitted bed-jacket of sensible design. Her thanks were effusive, but Old Ninn cut them short.

"Four-ply," she said. "You require warmth when you're getting on in years and the sooner you face the fact the more comfortable you'll find yourself. Good morning, sir," Ninn added, catching sight of Warrender. "I dare say you'll bear me out. Well, I won't keep you."

19

With perfect composure she trudged away, leaving a complete silence behind her.

"Out of this world!" Bertie said with a shrillish laugh. "Darling Mary, here I am *sizzling* with decorative fervour. *When* are we to tuck up our sleeves and lay all our plots and plans?"

"Now, darling, if you're ready. Dicky, treasure, will you and Maurice be able to amuse yourselves? We'll scream if we want any help. Come along, Bertie."

She linked her arm in his. He sniffed ecstatically. "You smell," he said, "like all, but *all,* of King Solomon's wives *and* concubines. In spring. *En avant!*"

They went downstairs. Warrender and Richard were left together in a room that still retained the flavour of her personality, as inescapably potent as the all-pervasive aftermath of her scent.

It was an old established custom that she and Bertie arranged the house for her birthday party. Her drawing-room was the first on the left on the ground floor. It was a long Georgian saloon with a door into the hall and with folding doors leading into the dining-room. This, in its turn opened both into the hall and into the conservatory, which was her especial pride. Beyond the conservatory lay a small formal garden. When all the doors were open an impressive vista was obtained. Bertie himself had "done" the decor and had used a wealth of old French brocades. He had painted bunches of misty cabbage roses in the recesses above the doors and in the wall panels, and had found some really distinguished chandeliers. This year the flowers were to be all white and yellow. He settled down with great efficiency and determination to his task, borrowing one of Gracefield's, the butler's, aprons for the purpose. Miss Bellamy tied herself into a modish confection with a flounced bib, put on washleather gloves, and wandered happily about her conservatory, snipping off deadheads and re-arranging groups of flowerpots. She was an enthusiastic gardener. They shouted at each other from room to room, exchanging theatre shop, and breaking every now and then into stage cockney: "Whatseye, dear?" and "Coo! You wouldn't credit it!" this mode of communication being sacred to the occasion. They enjoyed themselves enormously while from under Bertie's clever fingers emerged bouquets of white and gold and wonderful garlands for the table. In this setting, Miss Bellamy was at her best.

They had been at it for perhaps half an hour and Bertie had retired to the flower-room when Gracefield ushered in Miss Kate Cavendish, known to her intimates as Pinky.

Pinky was younger than her famous contemporary and less distinguished. She had played supporting roles in many Bellamy successes and their personal relationship, not altogether to her satisfaction, resembled their professional one. She had an amusing face, dressed plainly and well, and possessed the gifts of honesty and direct thinking. She was, in fact, a charming woman.

"I'm in a tizzy," she said. "High as a rocket, darling, and in a minute I'll tell you why. Forty thousand happy returns, Mary, and may your silhouette never grow greater. Here's my offering."

It was a flask of a new scent by a celebrated maker and was called Formidable. "I got it smuggled over from Paris," she said. "It's not here yet. A lick on either lobe, I'm told, and the satellites reel in their courses."

Miss Bellamy insisted on opening it. She dabbed the stopper on her wrists and sniffed. "Pinky," she said solemnly, "it's *too* much! Darling, it opens the *floodgates*! Honestly!"

"It's good, isn't it?"

"Florrie shall put it into my spray. At once. Before Bertie can get at it. You know what he is."

"Is Bertie here?" Pinky asked quickly.

"He's in the flower-room."

"Oh."

"Why? Have you fallen out with him?"

"Far from it," Pinky said. "Only—well it's just that I'm not really meant to let my cat out of its bag as yet and Bertie's involved. But I really am, I fear, more than a little tiddly."

"*You!* I thought you never touched a thing in the morning."

"Nor I do. But this is an occasion, Mary. I've been drinking with the Management. Only two small ones, but on an empty tum: Bingo!"

Miss Bellamy said sharply, *"With the Management?"*

"That gives you pause, doesn't it?"

"And Bertie's involved?"

Pinky laughed rather wildly and said, "If I don't tell somebody I'll spontaneously combust, so I'm going to tell you. Bertie can lump it, bless him, because why, after all, shouldn't I be audibly grateful."

Mary Bellamy looked fixedly at her friend for a moment and then said, "Grateful?"

"All right. I know I'm incoherent. Here it comes. Darling: I'm to have the lead in Bongo Dillon's new play. At the Unicorn. Opening in September. Swear you won't breathe it, but it's true and it's settled and the contract's mine for the signing. My first lead, Mary. Oh *God*, I'm so happy."

A hateful and all too-familiar jolt under the diaphragm warned Miss Bellamy that she had been upset. Simultaneously she knew that somehow or another she must run up a flag of welcome, must show a responsive warmth, must override the awful, menaced, slipping feeling, the nausea of the emotions that Pinky's announcement had churned up.

"Sweetie-pie!" she said. "How wonderful!" It wasn't, she reflected, much cop as an expression of delighted congratulation from an old chum, but Pinky was too excited to pay any attention. She went prancing on about the merits of her contract, the glories of the role, the nice behaviour of the Management (Miss Bellamy's Management, as she sickeningly noted), and the feeling that at last this was going to be It. All this gave Miss Bellamy a breather. She began to make fairly appropriate responses. Presently when Pinky drew breath, she was able to say with the right touch of down-to-earth honesty:

"Pinky, this is going to be your Great Thing."

"I know it! I feel it myself," Pinky said soberly and added, "Please God, I'll have what it takes. Please God, I will."

"My dear, you will," she rejoined and for the life of her couldn't help adding, "Of course, I haven't read the play."

"The *purest* Bongo! Comedy with a twist. You know? Though I says it as shouldn't, it's right up my cul-de-sac. Bongo says he had me in mind all the time he was writing it."

Miss Bellamy laughed. "Darling! We do know our Bongo,

don't we? The number of plays he's said he'd written for me and when one looked at them—!"

With one of her infuriating moments of penetration, Pinky said, "Mary! Be pleased for me."

"But, sweetie, *naturally* I'm pleased. It sounds like a wonderful bit of luck and I hope with all my heart it works out."

"Of course, I know it means giving up my part in Richard's new one for you. But, face it, there wasn't much in it for me, was there? And nothing was really settled, so I'm not letting the side down, am I?"

Miss Bellamy couldn't help it. "My dear," she said with a kindly laugh, "we'll lose no sleep over that little problem: the part'll cast itself in two seconds."

"Exactly!" Pinky cried happily and Miss Bellamy felt one of her rare onsets of rage begin to stir. She said:

"But you were talking about Bertie, darling. Where does he come in?"

"Aha!" Pinky said maddeningly and shook her finger.

At this juncture Gracefield, the butler, arrived with a drinks tray.

Miss Bellamy controlled herself. "Come on," she said, "I'm going to break my rule, too. We *must* have a drink on this, darling."

"No, no no!"

"Yes, yes, yes. A teeny one. Pink for Pinky?"

She stood between Pinky and the drinks and poured out one stiff and one negligible gin-and-bitters. She gave the stiff one to Pinky.

"To your wonderful future, darling," she said. "Bottoms up!"

"Oh *dear!*" Pinky said. "I shouldn't."

"Never mind."

They drank.

"And Bertie?" Miss Bellamy asked presently. "Come on. You know I'm as silent as the grave."

The blush that long ago had earned Pinky her nickname appeared in her cheeks. "This really *is* a secret," she said. "Deep and deadly. But I'm sure he won't mind my telling *you*. You see, it's a part that has to be dressed up to the hilt—five changes and all of them grand as grand. Utterly beyond me and my little woman in Bayswater. Well! Bertie, being so much mixed up with the Management, has heard all about it, and do you know, darling, he's offered, *entirely* of his own accord, to do my clothes. Designs, materials, making—*everything* from Saracen. And all completely free-ers. *Isn't* that kind?"

Wave after wave of fury chased each other like electrical frequencies through Miss Bellamy's nerves and brain. She had time to think: "I'm going to throw a temperament and it's bad for me," and then she arrived at the point of climax.

The explosion was touched off by Bertie himself, who came tripping back with a garland of tuberoses twined round his person. When he saw Pinky he stopped short, looked from her to Miss Bellamy and turned rather white.

"Bertie," Pinky said. "I've split on you."

"How could you!" he said. "Oh Pinky, how could you!"

Pinky burst into tears.

"I don't know!" she stammered. "I didn't mean to, Bertie darling. Forgive me. I was high."

"Stay me with flagons!" he said in a small voice. Miss Bellamy, employing a kind of enlargement of herself that was technically one of her most telling achievements, crossed to him and advanced her face to within four inches of his own.

"You rat, Bertie," she said quietly. "You little, two-timing, double-crossing, dirty rat."

And she wound her hands in his garland, tore it off him and threw it in his face.

chapter two

Preparation for a Party

MARY BELLAMY'S temperaments were of rare occurrence but formidable in the extreme and frightening to behold. They were not those regulation theatre tantrums that seem to afford pleasure both to observer and performer; on the contrary they devoured her like some kind of migraine and left her exhausted. Their onset was sudden, their duration prolonged and their sequel incalculable.

Bertie and Pinky, both familiar with them, exchanged looks of despair. Miss Bellamy had not raised her voice, but a kind of stillness seemed to have fallen on the house. They themselves spoke in whispers. They also, out of some impulse of helpless unanimity, said the same thing at the same time.

"Mary!" they said. "Listen! Don't!"

They knew very well that they had better have held their tongues. Their effort, feeble though it was, served only to inflame her. With an assumption of calmness that was infinitely more alarming than raging hysteria she set about them, concentrating at first on Bertie.

"I wonder," she said, "what it feels like to be you. I wonder if you enjoy your own cunning. I expect you do, Bertie. I expect you rather pride yourself on your talent for cashing in on other people's generosity. On mine, for instance."

"Mary, *darling*! Please!"

"Let us," she continued, trembling slightly, "look at this thing quite calmly and objectively, shall we? I'm afraid it will not be a delicious experience, but it has to be faced."

Gracefield came in, took one look at his mistress and went out again. He had been with the family for some time.

"I am the last woman in the world," Miss Bellamy explained, "to remind people of their obligations. The last. However—"

She began to remind Bertie of his obligations. Of the circumstances under which she had discovered him—she did not, to his evident relief, say how many years ago—of how she had given him his first chance; of how, since then, he had never looked back; of how there had been agreement— "gentlemen's," she added bitterly—that he would never design for another leading lady in the Management without first consulting her. He opened his mouth, but was obliged without utterance to shut it again. Had he not, she asked, risen to his present position entirely on the wings of her patronage? Besieged as she was by the importunities of the great fashion houses, had she not stuck resolutely to him through thick and thin? And now—

She executed a gesture, Siddons-like in its tragic implications, and began to pace to and fro while Pinky and Bertie hastily made room for her to do so. Her glance lighting for a moment on Pinky she began obliquely to attack her.

"I imagine," she said, still to Bertie, "that I shall not be accused of lack of generosity. I am generally said, I think, to be a good friend. Faithful and just," she added, perhaps with some obscure recollection of Mark Antony. "Over and over again, for friendship's sake, I've persuaded the Management to cast actresses who were unable to give me adequate support."

"Now, look here...!" Pinky began warmly.

"—Over and over again. Timmy said, only the other day: 'Darling, you're sacrificing yourself on the altar of your

26

personal loyalties!' He's said, over and over again, that he wouldn't for anybody else under the sun accept the casting as it stood. Only for me..."

"What casting?" Pinky demanded. Miss Bellamy continued to address herself exclusively to Bertie.

"Only for me," Timmy said, "would he dream of taking into any production of his an artist whose spiritual home was weekly rep. in the ham-counties."

"Timmy," Pinky said dangerously, "is producing my play. It's entirely due to him and the author that I've got the part. They told the Management they wanted me."

Bertie said, "I happen to know that's perfectly true."

"Conspiracy!" Miss Bellamy shouted so loudly and suddenly that the others jumped in unison. She was ravaged by a terrible vision of Bertie, Pinky and Timmy all closeted with the Management and agreeing to say nothing to her of their plots and plans. In a Delphic fury she outlined this scene. Bertie, who had been moodily disengaging himself from the remnants of his garland, showed signs of fight. He waited his chance to cut in.

"Speaking," he began, "as a two-timing, double-crossing rat, which God knows I am *not*, I take leave to assure you, darling Mary, that you're wrecking yourself for nothing. I'm doing Pinky's gowns out of friendliness and my name isn't going to appear and I must say I'd have thought..."

He was allowed to get no further.

"It's not," Miss Bellamy said, "what you've done, both of you, but the revolting way you've done it. If you'd come to me in the first instance and said..." Then followed an exposition of what they should have said and of the generous response they would have enjoyed if they'd said it. For a moment it looked as if the row was going to degenerate into an aimless and repetitive wrangle. It would probably have done so if Pinky had not said abruptly:

"Now, look here, Mary! It's about time you faced up to yourself. You know jolly well that anything you've done for either of us has been paid back with interest. I know you've had a lot to do with my getting on the Management's short list and I'm grateful, but I also know that it's suited you very well to have me there. I'm a good foil to you. I know all your gimmicks. How you like to be fed lines. And when you dry, as nowadays you very often do, I can fill in like nobody's business. In the gentle art of letting myself be upstaged, cheated out of points and fiddled into nonentity, I've done you proud and you'll find I'm damn hard to replace."

"My *God!* My *God!* that I should have to listen to this!"

"As for Bertie..."

"Never mind, Pinky," he said quickly.

"I do mind. It's true you gave Bertie his start, but what hasn't he done for you? Your decor! Your clothes! Face it, Mary, without the Saracen Concealed Curve you'd be the Grand Old Lady of the Hip Parade."

Bertie gave a hysterical hoot of laughter and looked terrified.

"The truth is," Pinky said, "you want it both ways, Mary. You want to boss everybody and use everybody for your own ends and at the same time you want us all to wallow in your wake saying how noble and generous and wonderful you are. You're a cannibal, Mary, and it's high time somebody had the guts to tell you so."

A dead silence followed this unexampled speech.

Miss Bellamy walked to the door and turned. It was a movement with which they were familiar.

"After this," she said very slowly, dead-panning her voice to a tortured monotone, "there is only one thing for me to do and much as it hurts me, I shall do it. I shall see the Management. Tomorrow."

She opened the door. They had a brief glimpse of Charles, Warrender and Richard, irresolute in the hall, before she swept out and shut the door behind her.

The room seemed very quiet after she had gone.

"Bertie," Pinky said at last, "if I've done you any harm I'm desperately sorry. I was high. I'll never, never forgive myself."

"That's all right, dear."

"You're so *kind*. Bertie—do you think she'll—do you think she can...?"

"She'll try, dear. She'll try."

"It took everything I've got, I promise you, to give battle. Honestly, Bertie, she frightened me. She looked murderous."

"Horrid, wasn't it?"

Pinky stared absently at the great flask of the scent called Formidable. A ray of sunshine had caught it and it shone golden.

"What are *you* going to do?" she asked.

Bertie picked up a handful of tuberoses from the carpet. "Get on with me bloody flowers, dear," he said. "Get on with me bloody flowers."

2

Having effected her exit, Miss Bellamy swept like a sirocco past Richard, Warrender and her husband and continued upstairs. In her bedroom she encountered Florence, who said, "What have *you* been doing to yourself?"

"You shut up," Miss Bellamy shouted and slammed the door.

"Whatever it is, it's no good to you. Come on, dear. What's the story?"

"Bloody treachery's the story. Shut up. I don't want to tell you. My God, what friends I've got! My God, what friends!"

She strode about the room and made sounds of outrage and defeat. She flung herself on the bed and pummelled it.

Florence said, "You know what'll be the end of this—party and all."

Miss Bellamy burst into tears. "I haven't," she sobbed, "a friend in the world. Not in the whole wide world. Except Dicky."

A spasm of something that might have been chagrin twitched at Florence's mouth. "Him!" she said under her breath.

Miss Bellamy abandoned herself to a passion of tears. Florence went into the bathroom and returned with sal volatile.

"Here," she said. "Try this. Come along now, dear."

"I don't want that muck. Give me one of my tablets."

"Not now."

"Now!"

"You know as well as I do, the doctor said only at night."

"I don't care what he said. Get me one."

She turned her head and looked up at Florence. "Did you hear what I said?"

"There aren't any left. I was going to send out."

Miss Bellamy said through her teeth, "I've had enough of this. You think you can call the tune here, don't you? You think you're indispensable. You never made a bigger mistake. You're not indispensable and the sooner you realize it, the better for you. Now, get out."

"You don't mean that."

"Get out!"

Florence stood quite still for perhaps ten seconds and then left the room.

Miss Bellamy stayed where she was. Her temperament, bereft of an audience, gradually subsided. Presently she went to her dressing-table, dealt with her face and gave herself three generous shots from her scent-spray. At the fourth, it petered out. The bottle was empty. She made an exasperated sound, stared at herself in the glass and for the first time since the onset of her rage, began to think collectedly.

At half-past twelve she went down to call on Octavius Browne and Anelida Lee.

Her motives in taking this action were mixed. In the first place her temperament, having followed the classic pattern of diminishing returns, had finally worked itself out and had left her restless. She was unwilling to stay indoors. In the second, she wanted very badly to prove to herself how grossly she had been misjudged by Pinky and Bertie, and could this be better achieved than by performing an act of gracious consideration towards Richard? In the third place, she was burningly anxious to set her curiosity at rest in the matter of Anelida Lee.

On her way down she looked in at the drawing-room. Bertie, evidently, had finished the flowers and gone. Pinky had left a note saying she was sorry if she'd been too upsetting but not really hauling down her flag an inch. Miss Bellamy blew off steam to Charles, Richard and Warrender without paying much attention to their reactions. They withdrew, dismayed, to Charles's study from whence came the muted sound of intermittent conversation. Superbly dressed and gloved she let herself out and after pausing effectively for a moment in the sunshine, turned into the Pegasus.

Octavius was not in the shop. Anelida, having completed her cleaning, had a smudge across her cheek and grubby hands. She had cried a little after Richard went out in a huff and there had been no time to repair the damage. She was not looking her best.

Miss Bellamy was infinitely relieved.

She was charming to Anelida. Her husband and Richard Dakers, she said, had talked so much about the shop: it was so handy for them, funny old bookworms that they were, to have found one practically on the doorstep. She understood that Anelida was hoping to go on the stage. Anelida replied that she was working at the Bonaventure. With every appearance of infinite generosity Miss Bellamy said that, unlike most of her friends, she thought the little experimental club theatres performed a very useful function in showing plays that otherwise would never see the light of day. Anelida was quiet, well-mannered and, Miss Bellamy supposed, much overcome by the honour that was being paid her. That was the kindest interpretation to put upon her somewhat ungushing response. "Not much temperament *there*," Miss Bellamy thought and from her this was not a complimentary assessment. She grew more and more cordial.

Octavius returned from a brief shopping expedition and was a success. On being introduced by Anelida—quite prettily, Miss Bellamy had to admit—he uncovered his dishevelled head and smiled so broadly that his face looked rather like a mask of comedy.

"But what a pleasure!" he said, shaping his words with exquisite precision. "May we not exclaim '*Hic ver assiduum*' since April herself walks in at our door?"

Miss Bellamy got the general trend of this remark and her spirits rose. She thanked him warmly for his telegram and he at once looked extremely pleased with himself. "Your husband and your ward," he said, "told us of the event and I thought, you know, of the many delicious hours you have given us and of how meagre a return is the mere striking together of one's hands." He looked sideways at her. "An old

31

fogey's impulse," he said and waved it aside. He made her a little bow and put his head on one side. Anelida wished he wouldn't.

"It was *heaven* of you," said Miss Bellamy. "*So* much pleasure it gave, you can't think! And what's more I haven't thanked you for finding that *perfect* picture for Dicky to give me, nor," she improvised on the spur of the moment, "for that heavenly copy of..." Maddeningly, she had forgotten the author of Charles's purchase and of the quotation in the telegram. She marked time with a gesture indicating ineffable pleasure and then mercifully remembered. "Of Spenser," she cried.

"You admired the Spenser? I'm so very glad."

"*So* much. And now," she continued with an enchanting air of diffidence, "I'm going to ask you something that you'll think quite preposterous. I've come with an invitation. You are, I know, *great* friends of my ward's—of Dicky's—and I, like you, am a creature of impulse. I want you both—*please*—to come to my little party this evening. Drinks and a handful of ridiculous chums at half-past six. Now please be very sweet and spoil me on my birthday. Please, say yes."

Octavius turned quite pink with gratification. He didn't hear his niece who came near to him and said hurriedly, "Unk, I don't think we..."

"I have never," Octavius said, "in my life attended a theatrical party. It is something quite outside my experience. Really it's extraordinarily kind of you to think of inviting us. My niece, no doubt, is an initiate. Though not at such an exalted level, I think, Nelly, my love?"

Anelida had begun to say, "It's terribly kind..." but Miss Bellamy was already in full spate. She had taken Octavius impulsively by the hands and was beaming into his face. "You will? Now, *isn't* that *big* of you? I *was* so afraid I might be put in my place or that you would be booked up. And I'm *not*! And you *aren't*! Isn't that wonderful!"

"We are certainly, free," Octavius said. "Anelida's theatre is not open on Monday evenings. She had offered to help me with our new catalogue. I shall be enchanted."

"Wonderful!" Miss Bellamy gaily repeated. "And now I must run. *Au revoir*, both of you. Till this evening!"

She did, almost literally, run out of the shop filled with a delicious sense of having done something altogether charming. "Kind!" she thought. "That's what I've been. Kind as kind. Dicky will be so touched. And when he sees that *rather* dreary *rather* inarticulate girl in his own setting—well, if there *has* been anything, it'll peter out on the spot."

She saw the whole thing in a gratifying flash of clairvoyance: the last fumes of temperament subsided in the sunshine of her own loving-kindness. She returned to the house and found Richard in the hall.

"Darling!" she cried. "All settled! I've seen your buddies and asked them. The old fuddy-duddy's heaven, isn't he? Out of this world. And the girl's the nicest little thing. Are you pleased?"

"But," Richard said, amazed. "Are they...? Did Anelida say they'd come?"

"My dear, you don't imagine, do you, that a bit-part fill-in at the Bonaventure is going to turn down an invitation to my birthday party!"

"It's not a bit-part," Richard said. "They're doing *Pygmalion* and she's playing Eliza."

"Poor child."

He opened his mouth and shut it again.

"There's something," Miss Bellamy said, "so endlessly depressing about those clubs. Blue jeans, beards and a snack-bar, no doubt." He didn't answer and she said kindly, "Well! We mustn't let them feel too lost, must we? I'll tell Maurice and Charles to be kind. And now, sweetie, I'm off to keep my date with the Great Play."

Richard said hurriedly, "There's something I wanted to alter... Could we..."

"Darling! You're such heaven when you panic. I'll read it and then I'll put it in your study. Blessings!"

"Mary—Mary, thank you so much."

She kissed him lightly and almost ran upstairs to read his play and to telephone Pinky and Bertie. She would tell them that she couldn't bear to think of any cloud of dissonance overshadowing her birthday and she would add that she expected them at six-thirty. That would show them how ungrudging she could be. "After all," she thought, "they'll be in a tizzy because if I *did* do my stuff with the Management..." Reassured on all counts she went into her room.

Unfortunately, neither Bertie nor Pinky was at home, but she left messages. It was now one o'clock. Half an hour before luncheon in which to relax and skim through Richard's play. Everything was going, in the event, very well. "I'll put me boots up," she said to herself in stage cockney and did so on the chaise-longue in the bow-window of her room. She noticed that once again the azaleas were infected and reminded herself to spray them with Slaypest. She turned her attention, now growing languid, to the play. *Husbandry in Heaven. Not* a very good title, she thought. Wasn't it a quotation from something? The dialogue seemed to be quite unlike Dicky: a bit Sloane Square, in fact. The sort of dialogue that is made up of perfectly understandable phrases that taken together add up to a kind of egg-headed Goon show. Was it or was it not in verse? She read Dicky's description of the leading woman.

"Mimi comes on. She might be nineteen or twenty-nine. Her beauty is bone-deep. Seductive without luxury. Virginal and dangerous." "Hum!" thought Miss Bellamy. *Hodge comes out of the Prompt corner. Wolf-whistles. Gestures unmistakably and with feline intensity."*

Now, why had that line stirred up some obscure misgivings? She turned the pages. It was certainly an enormously long part.

"Mimi: Can this be April, then, or have I, so early in the day misinterpreted my directive?"

"Hell!" thought Miss Bellamy.

But she read one or two of the lines aloud and decided that they might have something. As she flipped over the pages she became more and more satisfied that Dicky had tried to write a wonderful part for her. Different. It wouldn't do, of course, but at least the loving intention was there.

The typescript tipped over and fell across her chest. Her temperaments always left her tired. Just before she dropped off she suffered one of those mysterious jolts that briefly galvanize the body. She had been thinking about Pinky. It may be fanciful to suppose that her momentary discomfort was due to a spasm of hatred rather than to any physical cause. However that may be, she fell at last into an unenjoyable doze.

Florence came in. She had the flask of scent called Formidable in her hands. She tip-toed across the room, put it on the dressing-table and stood for a moment looking at Miss Bellamy. Beyond the chaise-longue in the bay-window were ranks of tulips and budding azaleas and among them stood the tin of Slaypest. To secure it, Florence had to lean across her mistress. She did so, delicately, but Miss Bellamy, at that moment, stirred. Florence drew back and tip-toed out of the room.

Old Ninn was on the landing. She folded her arms and stared up at Florence.

"Asleep," Florence said, with a jerk of her head. "Gone to bye-byes."

"Always the same after tantrums," said Old Ninn. She added woodenly, "She'll be the ruin of that boy."

"She'll be the ruin of herself," said Florence, "if she doesn't watch her step."

3

When Miss Bellamy had gone, Anelida, in great distress, turned to her uncle. Octavius was humming a little Elizabethan catch and staring at himself in a Jacobean looking-glass above his desk.

"Captivating!" he said. "Enchanting! Upon my word, Nell, it must be twenty years since a pretty woman made much of me. I feel, I promise you, quite giddily inclined. And the whole thing—so spontaneous: so touchingly impulsive! We have widened our horizon, my love."

"Unk," Anelida said rather desperately, "you can't think, my poor blessing, what a muddle you've made."

"A *muddle*?" He looked plaintively at her and she knew she was in for trouble. "What do you mean? I accept an invitation, most graciously extended by a charming woman. Pray where is the muddle?" She didn't answer and he said,

"There are certain matters, of course, to be considered. I do not, for instance, know what clothes are proper, nowadays, for cocktail parties. In my day one would have worn..."

"It's not a matter of clothes."

"No? In any case, you shall instruct me."

"I've already told Richard I can't go to the party."

"Nonsense, my dear. Of course we can go," Octavius said. "What are you thinking of?"

"It's so hard to explain, Unky. It's just that—well, it's partly because of me being in the theatre only so very much at the bottom of the ladder—less than the dust, you know, beneath Miss B.'s chariot wheels. I'd be like a corporal in the officers' mess."

"That," said Octavius, reddening with displeasure, "seems to me to be a false analogy, if you'll forgive me for saying so, Nelly. And, my dear, when one quotes it is pleasant to borrow from reputable sources. The *Indian Love Lyrics,* in my undergraduate days, were the scourge of the drawing-rooms."

"I'm sorry."

"It would be extremely uncivil to refuse so kind an invitation," Octavius said, looking more and more like a spoilt and frustrated child. "I *want* to accept it. What is the matter with you, Anelida?"

"The truth is," Anelida said rather desperately, "I don't quite know where I am with Richard Dakers."

Octavius stared at her and experienced a moment of truth. "Now that I consider it," he said huffily, "I realize that Dakers is paying his addresses to you. I wonder that it hasn't occurred to me before. Have you taken against him?"

To her dismay Anelida found herself on the brink of tears. "No!" she cried. "No! Nothing like that—really, I mean—I mean I just don't know..." She looked helplessly at Octavius. He was, she knew, hovering on the edge of one of his rare fits of temper. His vanity had been tickled by Miss Bellamy. He had almost strutted and preened before her. Anelida, who loved him very much, could have shaken him.

"Never mind," she said. "It's not worth another thought. But I'm sorry, darling, if you're put out over your lovely party."

"I am put out," Octavius said crossly. "I want to go."

36

"And you shall go. I'll do your tie and make you look beautiful."

"My dear," Octavius said, "it is you who would have looked beautiful. It would have been a great pleasure to take you. I should have been proud."

"Oh hell!" said Anelida. She rushed at him and gave him an exasperated hug. He was much puzzled and hit her gently several times on the shoulder blades.

The shop door opened.

"Here," Octavius said over the top of Anelida's head, "is Dakers."

Coming from the sunshine into the dark shop, Richard had been given a confused impression of Anelida collaring Octavius in a high tackle. He waited for her to emerge, which she did after some fumbling with her uncle's handkerchief.

Octavius said, "If you'll excuse me, Nell. Really, one *must* get on with one's job." He nodded to Richard and limped away into his back room.

Richard was careful not to look at Anelida. "I came," he said, "first to apologize."

"Not at all. I expect I behaved badly."

"And to say how very glad I am. Mary told me you had decided for the party."

"It was terribly kind of her to come. Unk was bewitched."

"We are being polite to each other, aren't we?"

"Better than flying into rages."

"May I call for you?"

"There's no need. Really. You'll be busy with the party. Unk will be proud to escort me. He said so."

"So he well might." Richard now looked directly at Anelida. "You've been crying," he said, "and your face is dirty. Like a little girl's. Smudged."

"All right. All right. I'm going to tidy it up."

"Shall I?"

"No."

"How old are you, Anelida?"

"Nineteen. Why?"

"I'm twenty-eight."

"You've done very well," Anelida said politely, "for your age. Famous dramatist."

"Playwright."

"I think with the new one you may allow yourself to be a dramatist."

"My God, you've got a cheek," he said thoughtfully. After a moment he said, "Mary's reading it. Now."

"Was she pleased about it?"

"For the wrong reason. She thinks I wrote it for her."

"But—how could she? Still, she'll soon find out."

"As I mentioned before, you don't really know much as yet about theatre people."

Anelida said, to her own astonishment, "But I do know I can act."

"Yes," he agreed. "Of course you do. You're a good actress."

"You haven't seen me."

"That's what you think."

"*Richard!*"

"At least I've surprised you into calling me by my name."

"But *when* did you see me?"

"It slipped out. It's part of a deep-laid plan. You'll find out."

"When?"

"At the party. I'm off, now. *Au revoir,* dear Anelida."

When he had gone, Anelida sat perfectly still for quite a long time. She was bewildered, undecided and piercingly happy.

Richard, however, returned to the house with his mind made up. He went straight to Charles Templeton's study. He found Charles and Maurice Warrender there, rather solemn over a decanter of sherry. When he came in they both looked self-conscious.

"We were just talking about you," Charles said. "Have whatever it is you do have at this hour, Dicky. Lager?"

"Please. I'll get it. Should I make myself scarce so that you can go on talking about me?"

"No, no."

"We'd finished," Warrender said, "I imagine. Hadn't we, Charles?"

"I suppose we had."

Richard poured out his lager. "As a matter of fact," he said, "I sidled in with the idea of boring you with a few observations under that very heading."

Warrender muttered something about taking himself off. "Not unless you have to, Maurice," Richard said. "It arises, in a way, out of what you said this morning." He sat down and stared at his beer mug. "This is going to be difficult," he said.

They waited, Warrender looking owlish, Charles, as always, politely attentive.

"I suppose it's a question of divided allegiances," Richard said at last. "Partly that, anyway." He went on, trying to put what he wanted to say as objectively as might be. He knew that he was floundering and almost at once began to regret his first impulse.

Charles kept turning his elderly freckled hand and looking at it. Warrender sipped his sherry and shot an occasional, almost furtive, glance at Richard.

Presently Charles said, "Couldn't we come to the point?"

"I wish I could," Richard rejoined. "I'm making a mess of this, I know."

"May I have a go at it? Is this what you're trying to tell us? You think you can write a different kind of play from the sort of thing that suits Mary. You have, in fact, written one. You think it's the best thing you've done, but you're afraid Mary won't take kindly to the idea of your making a break. You've shown it to her and she's reading it now. You're afraid that she'll take it for granted that you see her in the lead. Right, so far?"

"Yes. That's it."

"But," Warrender demanded unexpectedly, "she won't like this play, what!"

"I don't think she'll like it."

"Isn't that your answer?" Charles said. "If she doesn't like it you can offer it elsewhere?"

"It isn't," Richard said, "as simple as that." And looking at these two men, each old enough to be his father, each with thirty years' experience of Mary Bellamy, he saw that he was understood.

"There's been one row already this morning," he said. "A snorter."

Warrender shot a look at Charles. "I don't know if I'm

imagining it," he said, "but I've fancied the rows come a bit oftener these days, isn't it?"

Charles and Richard were silent.

Warrender said, "Fellow's got to live his own life. My opinion. Worst thing that can happen is a man's getting himself bogged down in a mistaken loyalty. Seen it happen. Man in my regiment. Sorry business."

Charles said, "We all have our mistaken loyalties."

There was a further silence.

Richard said violently, "But—I owe everything to her. The ghastly things I began to write at school. The first shamingly hopeless plays. Then the one that rang the bell. *She* made the Management take it. We talked everything over. Everything. And now—suddenly—I don't want to. I—don't—want—to. Why? *Why?*"

"Very well," Charles said. Richard looked at him in surprise, but he went on very quickly. "Writing plays is your business. You understand it. You're an expert. You should make your own decisions."

"Yes. But Mary..."

"Mary holds a number of shares in companies that I direct, but I don't consult her about their policy or confine my interests to those companies only."

"Surely it's not the same thing."

"Isn't it?" Charles said placidly. "I think it is. Sentiment," he added, "can be a disastrous guide in such matters. Mary doesn't understand your change of policy—the worst reason in the world for mistrusting it. She is guided almost entirely by emotion."

Warrender said, "Think *she's* changed? Sorry. Charles, I've no kind of business to ask."

"She has changed," her husband said. "One does."

"You can see," Richard said, "what happened with Pinky and Bertie. How much more will she mind with me! Was there anything so terrible about what they did? The truth is, of course, that they didn't confide in her because they didn't know how she'd take it. Well—you saw how she took it."

"I suppose," Warrender began dimly, "as a woman gets older..." He faded out in a bass rumble.

"Charles," Richard said, "you may consider this a

monstrous suggestion, but have you thought, lately, that there might be anything—anything..."

"Pathological?" Charles said.

"It's so unlike her to be vindictive. *Isn't it?*" He appealed to both of them. "Well, my God, *isn't* it?"

To his astonishment they didn't answer immediately. Presently Charles said with a suggestion of pain in his voice: "The same thing has occurred to me. I—I asked Frank Harkness about it. He's looked after us both for years, as you know. He thinks she's been a bit nervy for some time, I gather, like many women of her—well, of her age. He thinks the high-pressure atmosphere of the theatre may have increased the tension. I got the impression he was understating his case. I don't mind telling you," Charles added unhappily, "it's been worrying me for some time. These—these ugly scenes."

Warrender muttered, "Vindictive," and looked as if he regretted it.

Richard cried out, "Her kindness! I've always thought she had the kindest eyes I'd ever seen in a woman."

Warrender, who seemed this morning to be bent on speaking out of character, did so now. "People," he said, "talk about eyes and mouths as if they had something to do with the way other people think and behave. Only bits of the body, aren't they? Like navels and knees and toenails. Arrangements."

Charles glanced at him with amusement. "My dear Maurice, you terrify me. So you discount our old friends the generous mouth, the frank glance, the open forehead. I wonder if you're right."

"Right or wrong," Richard burst out, "it doesn't get me any nearer a decision."

Charles put down his sherry and put up his eyeglass. "If I were you, Dicky," he said, "I should go ahead."

"Hear, hear!"

"Thank you, Maurice. Yes. I should go ahead. Offer your play in what you believe to be the best market. If Mary's upset it won't be for long, you know. You must keep a sense of perspective, my dear boy."

Colonel Warrender listened to this with his mouth slightly

open and a glaze over his eyes. When Charles had finished Warrender looked at his watch, rose and said he had a telephone call to make before luncheon. "I'll do it from the drawing-room if I may," he said. He glared at Richard. "Stick to your guns, isn't it?" he said. "Best policy." And went out.

Richard said, "I've always wondered: just how simple *is* Maurice?"

"It would be the greatest mistake," Charles said, "to underrate him."

4

In their houses and flats, all within a ten-mile radius of Pardoner's Place, the guests for Mary Bellamy's birthday party made ready to present themselves. Timon (Timmy) Gantry, the famous director, made few preparations for such festivities. He stooped from his inordinate height to the cracked glass on his bathroom wall in order to brush his hair, which he kept so short that the gesture was redundant. He had changed into a suit which he was in the habit of calling his "decent blue," and as a concession to Miss Bellamy, wore a waistcoat instead of a plum-coloured pullover. He looked rather like a retired policeman whose enthusiasm had never dwindled. He sang a snatch from *Rigoletto*, an opera he had recently directed, and remembered how much he disliked cocktail parties.

"Bell-a-*me*-a, you're a hell of a bore," he sang, improvising to the tune of "Bella Figlia:" And it was true, he reflected. Mary was becoming more and more of a tiresome girl. It would probably be necessary to quarrel with her before her new play went on. She was beginning to jib at the physical demands made upon her by his production methods. He liked to keep his cast moving rather briskly through complicated, almost fugal, patterns and Mary was not as sound in the wind as she used to be. Nor in the temper, he reflected. He rather thought that this play would be his last production for her.

"For she's not my, not my cuppa tea at all," he sang.

This led him to think of her influence on other people, particularly on Richard Dakers. "She's a succuba." he chanted. "She's an o—ogress. She devours young men alive. Nasty Mary!" He was delighted that Richard showed signs of breaking loose with his venture into serious dramatic writing. He had read *Husbandry in Heaven* to Gantry while it was still in manuscript. Gantry always made up his mind at once about a play and he did so about this one.

"If you go on writing slip-slop for Mary when you've got this sort of stuff under your thatch," he had said, "you deserve to drown in it. Parts of this thing are bloody awful and must come out. Other parts need a rewrite. Fix them and I'm ready to produce the piece."

Richard had fixed them.

Gantry shoved his birthday present for Miss Bellamy into his pocket. It was a bit of pinchbeck he'd picked up for five bob on a street stall. He bought his presents in an inverse ratio to the monetary situation of the recipients and Miss Bellamy was rich.

As he strode along in the direction of Knightsbridge, he thought with increasing enthusiasm about *Husbandry in Heaven* and of what he would do with it if he could persuade the Management to take it.

"The actors," he promised himself, "shall skip like young rams."

At Hyde Park Corner he began to sing again. At the corner of Wilton Place a chauffeur-driven car pulled up alongside him. The Management in the person of Mr. Montague Marchant, exquisitely dressed, with a gardenia in his coat, leaned from the window. His face and his hair were smooth, fair and pale, and his eyes wary.

"Timmy!" Mr. Marchant shouted. "*Look* at you! *So* purposeful! Such *devouring* strides! Come in, do, for God's sake, and let us support each other on our approach to the shrine."

Gantry said, "I wanted to see you." He doubled himself up like a camel and got into the car. It was his custom to plunge directly into whatever matter concerned him at the moment. He presented his ideas with the same ruthless precipitancy that he brought to his work in the theatre. It was a deceptive characteristic, because in Gantry impulse was subordinate to design.

He drew in his breath with an authoritative gasp. "Listen!" he said. "I have a proposition."

All the way along Sloane Street and into the King's Road he thrust Richard's play at Marchant. He was still talking, very eloquently, as they turned up Pardoner's Row. Marchant listened with the undivided though guarded attention that the Management brought to bear only on the utterances of the elect.

"You will do this," Gantry said as the car turned in to Pardoner's Place, "not for me and not for Dicky. You will do it because it's going to be a Thing for the Management. Mark my words. Here we are. Oh misery, *how* I abominate grand parties!"

"I'd have you remember," Marchant said as they went in, "that I commit myself to nothing, Timmy."

"Naturally, my dear man. But naturally. You *will* commit yourself, however, I promise you. You will."

"Mary, *darling!*" they both exclaimed and were swallowed up by the party.

Pinky and Bertie had arranged to go together. They came to this decision after a long gloomy post-luncheon talk in which they weighed the dictates of proper pride against those of professional expediency.

"Face it, sweetie-pie," Bertie had said, "if we *don't* show up she'll turn plug-ugly again and go straight to the Management. You know what a fuss Monty makes about personal relationships. 'A happy theatre is a successful theatre.' Nobody—but *nobody* can afford to cut up rough. He loathes internal strife."

Pinky, who was feeling the effects of her morning excesses, sombrely agreed. "God knows," she said, "that at this juncture I can ill afford to get myself the reputation of being difficult. After all my contract isn't signed, Bertie."

"It's as clear as daylight; magnanimity must be our watchword."

"I'll be blowed if I crawl."

"We shan't have to, dear. A pressure of the hand and a

long, long gaze into the eyeballs will carry us through."

"I resent having to."

"Never mind. Rise above. Watch me. I'm a past master at it. Gird up the loins, such as they are, and remember you're an actress." He giggled. "Looked at in the right way it'll be rather fun."

"What shall I wear?"

"Black, and no jewelry. She'll be clanking."

"I hate being at enmity, Bertie. What a beastly profession ours is. In some ways."

"It's a jungle, darling. Face it—it's a jungle."

"You," Pinky said rather enviously, "don't seem to be unduly perturbed, I must say."

"My poorest girl, little do you know. I'm quaking."

"Really? But could she actually do you any damage?"

"Can the boa constrictor," Bertie said, "consume the rabbit?"

Pinky had thought it better not to press this matter any further. They had separated and gone to their several flats, where in due course they made ready for the party.

Anelida and Octavius also made ready. Octavius, having settled for a black coat, striped trousers and the complementary details that he considered appropriate to these garments, had taken up a good deal of his niece's attention. She had managed to have a bath and was about to dress when, for the fourth time, he tapped at her door and presented himself before her, looking anxious and unnaturally tidy. "My hair," he said. "Having no unguent, I used a little olive oil. Do I smell like a salad?"

She reassured him, gave his coat a brush and begged him to wait for her in the shop. He had old-fashioned ideas about punctuality and had begun to fret. "It's five-and-twenty minutes to seven. We were asked for half-past six, Nelly."

"That means seven at the earliest, darling. Just take a furtive leer through the window and you'll see when people begin to come. And please, Unk, we can't go while I'm still in my dressing-gown, can we, now?"

"No, no, of course not. Half-past six *for* a quarter-to-seven? Or seven? I see. I see. In that case..."

He pottered downstairs.

Anelida thought, "It's a good thing I've had some practice in quick changes." She did her face and hair, and she put on a white dress that had been her one extravagance of the year, a large white hat with a black velvet crown, and new gloves. She looked in the glass, forcing herself to adopt the examining attitude she used in the theatre. "And it might as well be a first night," she thought, "the way I'm feeling." Did Richard like white? she wondered.

Heartened by the certainty of her dress being satisfactory and her hat becoming, Anelida began to daydream along time-honoured lines: She and Octavius arrived at the party. There was a sudden hush. Monty Marchant, the Management in person, would ejaculate to Timon Gantry, the great producer, "Who are they?" and Timon Gantry, with the abrupt gasp which all actors, whether they had heard it or not, liked to imitate, would reply, "I don't know but by God, I'm going to find out." The ranks would part as she and Octavius, escorted by Miss Bellamy, moved down the room to the accompaniment of a discreet murmur. They would be the cynosure of all eyes. What was a cynosure and why was it never mentioned except in reference to eyes? All eyes on Anelida Lee. And there, wrapt in admiration, would be Richard ...

At this point Anelida stopped short, was stricken with shame, had a good laugh at herself and became the prey of her own nerves.

She went to her window and looked down into Pardoner's Place. Cars were now beginning to draw up at Miss Bellamy's house. Here came a large black one with a very smart chauffeur. Two men got out. Anelida's inside somersaulted. The one with the gardenia *was* Monty Marchant and that incredibly tall, that unmistakably shabby figure *was* the greatest of all directors, Timon Gantry.

"Whoops!" Anelida said. "None of your nonsense, Cinderella." She counted sixty and then went downstairs.

Octavius was seated at his desk, reading, and Hodge was on his knee. They both looked extraordinarily smug.

"Have you come over calm?" Anelida asked.

"What? Calm? Yes," Octavius said. "Perfectly, thank you. I have been reading *The Gull's Hornbook*."

"Have you been up to something, Unk?"

He rolled his eyes round at her. "Up to something? I? What can you mean?"

"You look as if butter wouldn't melt on your whiskers."

"Really? I wonder why. Should we go?"

He displaced Hodge, who was moulting. Anelida was obliged to fetch the clothesbrush again.

"I wouldn't change you," she said, "for the Grand Cham of Tartary. Come on, darling, let's go."

5

Miss Bellamy's preparation for the party occupied the best part of ninety minutes and had something of the character of a Restoration salon, with Florence, truculently unaware of this distinction, in the role of abigail.

It followed the after-luncheon rest and, in its early stages, was conducted in the strictest privacy. She lay on her bed. Florence, unspeaking and tight-mouthed, darkened the room and produced from the bathroom sundry bottles and pots. She removed the make-up from her mistress's face, put wet pads over her eyes and began to apply a layer of greenish astringent paste. Miss Bellamy attempted to make conversation and was unsuccessful. At last she demanded impatiently, "What's the matter with *you*? Gone upstage?" Florence was silent. "Oh for heaven's *sake*!" Miss Bellamy ejaculated. "You're not holding out on me because of this morning, are you?"

Florence slapped a layer across Miss Bellamy's upper lip. "That stuff's stinging me," Miss Bellamy mumbled with difficulty. "You haven't mixed it properly."

Florence completed the mask. From behind it Miss Bellamy attempted to say, "All right, you can go to hell and sulk there," but remembering she was not supposed to speak, lay fuming. She heard Florence go out of the room. Ten minutes later she returned, stood for some time looking down on the greenish, blinded face and then set about removing the mask.

The toilet continued in icy silence, proceeding through its manifold and exacting routines. The face was scrutinized like a microscope slide. The hair was drilled. The person was subjected to masterful but tactful discipline. That which, unsubjected, declared itself centrally, was forced to make a less aggressive reappearance above the seventh rib where it was trapped, confined and imperceptibly distributed. And throughout these intimate manipulations, Florence and Miss Bellamy maintained an absolute and inimical silence. Only when they had been effected did Miss Bellamy open her door to her court.

In the past, Pinky and Bertie had attended: the former vaguely in the role of confidante, the latter to advise about the final stages of the ritual. Today they had not presented themselves and Miss Bellamy was illogically resentful. Though her initial fury had subsided, it lay like a sediment at the bottom of her thoughts and it wouldn't take much, she realized, to stir it up.

Charles was the first to arrive and found her already dressed. She wore crimson chiffon, intricately folded and draped with loose panels that floated tactfully past her waist and hips. The decolletage plunged and at its lowest point contained orchids and diamonds. Diamonds appeared again at intervals in the form of brooches and clips, flashed in stalactites from her ears and encircled her neck and wrist in a stutter of brilliance. She was indeed magnificent.

"Well?" she said and faced her husband.

"My dear!" said Charles gently. "I'm overwhelmed."

Something in his voice irritated her. "You don't like it," she said. "What's the matter with it?"

"It's quite superb. Dazzling."

Florence had opened the new bottle of scent and was pouring it into the Venetian glass atomizer. The air was thickened with effluvium so strong that it almost gave the impression of being visible. Charles made the slightest of grimaces.

"Do you think I'm overdressed, Charles?" Miss Bellamy demanded.

"I have implicit faith in your judgment," he said. "And you look glorious."

"Why did you make a face?"

48

"It's that scent. I find it a bit too much. It's—well..."

"Well! What is it?"

"I fancy indecent is the word I'm groping for."

"It happens to be the most exclusive perfume on the market."

"I don't much like the word 'perfume' but in this case it seems to be entirely appropriate."

"I'm sorry," she said in a high voice, "that you find my choice of words non-U."

"My dear Mary...!"

Florence screwed the top on the atomizer and placed it, with the three-quarters emptied bottle, on the dressing-table. She then retired to the bathroom.

Charles Templeton took his wife's hands in his and kissed them. "Ah!" he said. "That's your usual scent."

"The last dregs."

"I'll give you some more."

She made as if to pull her hands away, but he folded them between his own.

"Do something for me," he said. "Will you? I never ask you."

"My dear Charles!" she exclaimed impatiently. "What?"

"Don't use that stuff. It's vulgar, Mary. The room stinks of it already."

She stared at him with a kind of blank anger. His skin was mottled. The veins showed on his nose and his eyes were watery. It was an elderly face, and not very handsome.

"Don't be ridiculous," she said and withdrew her hands.

Warrender tapped on the door and came in. When he saw Miss Bellamy he ejaculated "What!" several times and was so clearly bowled over that her ill-humour modulated into a sort of petulant gratification. She made much of him and pointedly ignored her husband.

"You are the most fabulous, heavenly sweetie-pie," she said and kissed his ear.

He turned purple and said, "By George!"

Charles had walked over to the window. The tin of Slaypest was still there. At the same moment Florence re-entered the room. Charles indicated the tin. Florence cast up her eyes.

He said, "Mary, you do leave the windows open, don't

you, when you use this stuff on your plants?"

"Oh for heaven's *sake*!" she exclaimed. "Have you got a secret Thing about sprays? You'd better get yourself psychoed, my poor Charles."

"It's dangerous. I took the trouble to buy a textbook on these things and what it has to say is damn disquieting. l showed it to Maurice. Read it yourself, my dear, if you don't believe me. Ask Maurice. You don't think she ought to monkey about with it, do you, Maurice?"

Warrender picked up the tin and stared at the label with its red skull and crossbones and intimidating warning. "Shouldn't put this sort of stuff on the market," he said. "My opinion."

"Exactly. Let Florence throw it out, Mary."

"Put it down!" she shouted. "My God, Charles, what a bore you can be when you set your mind to it."

Suddenly she thrust the scent atomizer into Warrender's hands. "Stand there, darling," she said. "Far enough away for it not to make rivers or stain my dress. Just a delicious mist. Now! Spray madly."

Warrender did as he was told. She stood in the redolent cloud with her chin raised and her arms extended.

"Go on, Maurice," she said, shutting her eyes in a kind of ecstasy. "Go on."

Charles said, very quietly, "My God!"

Warrender stared at him, blushed scarlet, put down the scent-spray and walked out of the room.

Mary and Charles looked at each other in silence.

The whole room reeked of Formidable.

chapter three

Birthday Honours

MR. AND MRS. CHARLES TEMPLETON stood just inside their
drawing-room door. The guests, on their entry, encountered
a bevy of press photographers, while a movie outfit was
established at the foot of the stairs, completely blocking the
first flight. New arrivals smiled or looked thoughtful as the
flash lamps discovered them. Then, forwarded by the
parlourmaid in the hall to Gracefield on the threshold, they
were announced and, as it were, passed on to be neatly fielded
by their hosts.

It was not an enormous party—perhaps fifty, all told. It
embraced the elite of the theatre world and it differed in this
respect from other functions of its size. It was a little as if the
guests gave rattling good performances of themselves
arriving at a cocktail party. They did this to music, for Miss
Bellamy, in an alcove of her great saloon, had stationed a
blameless instrumental trio.

Although, in the natural course of events, they met each
other very often, there was a tendency among the guests to

express astonishment, even rapture, at this particular encounter. Each congratulated Miss Bellamy on her birthday and her superb appearance. Some held her at arm's length the better to admire. Some expressed bewilderment and others a sort of matey reverence. Then in turn they shook hands with Charles and by the particular pains the nice ones took with him, they somehow established the fact that he was not quite of their own world.

When Pinky and Bertie arrived, Miss Bellamy greeted them with magnanimity.

"*So* glad," she said to both of them, "that you decided to come." The kiss that accompanied this greeting was tinctured with forebearance and what passed with Miss Bellamy for charity. It also, in some ineffable manner, seemed to convey a threat. They were meant to receive it like a sacrament and (however reluctantly) they did so, progressing on the conveyor belt of hospitality to Charles, who was markedly cordial to both of them.

They passed on down the long drawing-room and were followed by two Dames, a Knight, three distinguished commoners, another Knight and his Lady, Montague Marchant and Timon Gantry.

Richard, filling his established role of a sort of unofficial son of the house, took over the guests as they came his way. He was expected to pilot them through the bottleneck of the intake and encourage them to move to the dining-room and conservatory. He also helped the hired barman and the housemaid with the drinks until Gracefield and the parlourmaid were able to carry on. He was profoundly uneasy. He had been out to lunch and late returning and had had no chance to speak to Mary before the first guests appeared. But he knew that all was not well. There were certain only too unmistakable signs, of which a slight twitch in Mary's triangular smile was the most ominous. "There's been another temperament," Richard thought, and he fancied he saw confirmation of this in Charles, whose hands were not quite steady and whose face was unevenly patched.

The rooms filled up. He kept looking towards the door and thinking he saw Anelida.

Timon Gantry came up to him. "I've been talking to

Monty," he said. "Have you got a typescript for him?"

"Timmy, how kind of you! Yes, of course."

"Here?"

"Yes. Mary's got one. She said she'd leave it in my old room upstairs."

"*Mary!* Why?"

"I always show her my things."

Gantry looked at him for a moment, gave his little gasp and then said, "I see I must speak frankly. Will Mary think you wrote the part for her?"

Richard said, "I—that was not my intention..."

"Because you'd better understand at once, Dicky, that I wouldn't dream of producing this play with Mary in the lead. Nor would I dream of advising the Management to back it with Mary in the lead. Nor could it be anything but a disastrous flop with Mary in the lead. Is that clear?"

"Abundantly," Richard said.

"Moreover," Gantry said, "I should be lacking in honesty and friendship if I didn't tell you it was high time you cut loose from those particular apron strings. Thank you, I would prefer whisky and water."

Richard, shaken, turned aside to get it. As he made his way back to Gantry he was aware of one of those unaccountable lulls that sometimes fall across the insistent din of a cocktail party. Gantry, inches taller than anyone else in the room, was looking across the other guests toward the door. Several of them also had turned in the same direction, so that it was past the backs of heads and through a gap between shoulders that Richard first saw Anelida and Octavius come in.

It was not until a long time afterwards that he realized his first reaction had been one of simple gratitude to Anelida for being, in addition to everything else, so very beautiful.

He heard Timon Gantry say, "Monty, look." Montague Marchant had come up to them.

"I am looking," he said. "Hard."

And indeed they all three looked so hard at Anelida that none of them saw the smile dry out on Mary Bellamy's face and then reappear as if it had been forcibly stamped there.

Anelida shook hands with her hostess, expected, perhaps,

some brief return of the morning's excessive cordiality, heard a voice say, "So kind of you to come," and witnessed the phenomenon of the triangular smile. Followed by Octavius, she moved on to Charles. And then she was face to face with Richard, who, as quickly as he could, had made his way down the room to meet them.

"Well?" Timon Gantry said.

"Well," Marchant repeated. "What is it?"

"It's an actress."

"Any good?"

"I'll answer that one," Gantry said, "a little later."

"Are you up to something?"

"Yes."

"What, for God's sake?"

"Patience, patience."

"I sometimes wonder, Timmy, why we put up with you."

"You needn't. You put up with me, dear boy, because I give the Management its particular brand of prestige."

"So you say."

"True?"

"I won't afford you the ignoble satisfaction of saying so."

"All the same, to oblige me, stay where you are."

He moved towards the group of three that was slowly making its way down the drawing-room.

Marchant continued to look at Anelida.

When Richard met Anelida and took her hand he found, to his astonishment, that he was unable to say to her any of the things that for the last ten years he had so readily said to lovely ladies at parties. The usual procedure would have been to kiss her neatly on the cheek, tell her she looked marvellous and then pilot her by the elbow about the room. If she was his lady of the moment, he would contrive to spend a good deal of time in her company and they would probably dine somewhere after the party. How the evening then proceeded would depend upon a number of circumstances, none of which seemed to be entirely appropriate to Anelida. Richard felt, unexpectedly, that his nine years seniority were more like nineteen.

Octavius had found a friend. This was Miss Bellamy's physician, Dr. Harkness, a contemporary of Octavius's

Oxford days and up at the House with him. They could be left together, happily reminiscent, and Anelida could be given her dry Martini and introduced to Pinky and Bertie, who were tending to hunt together through the party.

Bertie said rapidly, "I *do* congratulate you. *Do* swear to me on your *sacred* word of honour, *never* to wear anything but white and always, but *always* with your clever hat. *Ever!*"

"You mustn't take against Bertie," Pinky said kindly. "It's really a smashing compliment, coming from him."

"I'll bear it in mind," Anelida said. It struck her that they were both behaving rather oddly. They kept looking over her shoulder as if somebody or something behind her exerted a strange attraction over them. They did this so often that she felt impelled to follow their gaze and did so. It was Mary Bellamy at whom they had been darting their glances. She had moved further into the room and stood quite close, surrounded by a noisy group of friends. She herself was talking. But to Anelida's embarrassment she found Miss Bellamy's eyes looked straight into her own, coldly and searchingly. It was not, she was sure, a casual or accidental affair. Miss Bellamy had been watching her and the effect was disconcerting. Anelida turned away only to meet another pair of eyes, Timon Gantry's. And beside him yet another pair, Montague Marchant's, speculative, observant. It was like an inversion of her ridiculous daydream and she found it disturbing. "The cynosure of all eyes indeed! With a difference," thought Anelida.

But Richard was beside her, not looking at her, his arm scarcely touching hers, but *there*, to her great content. Pinky and Bertie talked with peculiar energy, making a friendly fuss over Anelida but conveying, nevertheless, a singular effect of nervous tension.

Presently Richard said, "Here's somebody else who would like to meet you, Anelida." She looked up at a brick-coloured Guardee face and a pair of surprised blue eyes. "Colonel Warrender," Richard said.

After his bumpy fashion, Warrender made conversation. "Everybody always shouts at these things, isn't it? Haven't got up to pitch yet but will, of course. You're on the stage, isn't it?"

"Just."

"Jolly good! What d'you think of Dicky's plays?"

Anelida wasn't yet accustomed to hearing Richard called Dicky or to being asked that sort of question in that sort of way.

She said, "Well—immensely successful, of course."

"Oh!" he said. "Successful! Awfully successful! 'Course. And I like 'em, you know. I'm his typical audience—want something gay and 'musing, with a good part for Mary. Not up to intellectual drama. Point is, though, is *he* satisfied? What d'you think? Wasting himself or not? What?"

Anelida was greatly taken aback and much exercised in her mind. Did this elderly soldier know Richard very intimately or did all Richard's friends plunge on first acquaintance into analyses of each other's inward lives for the benefit of perfect strangers? And did Warrender know about *Husbandry in Heaven*?

Again she had the feeling of being closely watched.

She said, "I hope he'll give us a serious play one of these days and I shouldn't have thought he'll be really satisfied until he does."

"Ah!" Warrender exclaimed, as if she'd made a dynamic observation. "There you are! Jolly good! Keep him up to it. Will you?"

"I!" Anelida cried in a hurry. She was about to protest that she was in no position to keep Richard up to anything, when it occurred to her, surprisingly, that Warrender might consider any such disclaimer an affectation.

"But does he need 'keeping up'?" she asked.

"Oh Lord, yes!" he said. "What with one thing and another. You must know all about that."

Anelida reminded herself she had only drunk half a dry Martini, so she couldn't possibly be under the influence of alcohol. Neither, she would have thought, was Colonel Warrender. Neither, apparently, was Miss Bellamy or Charles Templeton or Miss Kate Cavendish or Mr. Bertie Saracen. Nor, it would seem, was Mr. Timon Gantry to whom, suddenly, she was being introduced by Richard.

"Timmy," Richard was saying. "Here is Anelida Lee."

To Anelida it was like meeting a legend.

"Good evening," the so-often mimicked voice was saying. "What is there for us to talk about? I know. You shall tell me precisely why you make that 'throw-it-over-your-shoulder' gesture in your final speech and whether it is your own invention or a bit of producer's whimsy."

"Is it wrong?" Anelida demanded. She then executed the mime that is know in her profession as a double-take. Her throat went dry, her eyes started and she crammed the knuckle of her gloved hand between her separated teeth. "You haven't *seen* me!" she cried.

"But I have. With Dicky Dakers."

"Oh my God!" whispered Anelida, and this was not an expression she was in the habit of using.

"Look out. You'll spill your drink. Shall we remove a little from this barnyard cacophony? The conservatory seems at the moment to be unoccupied."

Anelida disposed of her drink by distractedly swallowing it. "Come along," Gantry said. He took her by the elbow and piloted her towards the conservatory. Richard, as if by sleight-of-hand, had disappeared. Octavius was lost to her.

"Good evening, Bunny. Good evening, my dear Paul. Good evening, Tony," Gantry said with the omniscience of M. de Charlus. Celebrated faces responded to these greetings and drifted astern. They were in the conservatory and for the rest of her life the smell of freesias would carry Anelida back to it.

"There!" Gantry said, releasing her with a little pat. "Now then."

"Richard didn't tell me. Nobody said you were in front."

"Nobody knew, dear. We came in during the first act and left before the curtain. I preferred it."

She remembered, dimly, that this kind of behavior was part of his legend.

"Why are you fussed?" Gantry inquired. "Are you ashamed of your performance?"

"No," Anelida said truthfully, and she added in a hurry, "I know it's very bad in patches."

"How old are you?"

"Nineteen."

"What else have you played?"

"Only bits at the Bonaventure."

"No *dra-mat-ic ac-ad-emy*?" he said, venomously spitting out the consonants. "No agonizing in devoted little groups? No *depicting*? No going to bed with Stanislavsky and rising with Method?"

Anelida, who was getting her second wind, grinned at him.

"I admire Stanislavsky," she said. "Intensely."

"Very well. Very well. Now, attend to me. I am going to tell you about your performance."

He did so at some length and in considerable detail. He was waspish, didactic, devastating and overwhelmingly right. For the most part she listend avidly and in silence, but presently she ventured to ask for elucidation. He answered, and seemed to be pleased.

"Now," he said, "those are all the things that were amiss with your performance. You will have concluded that I wouldn't have told you about them if I didn't think you were an actress. Most of your mistakes were technical. You will correct them. In the meantime I have a suggestion to make. Just that. No promises. It's in reference to a play that may never go into production. I believe you have already read it. You will do so again, if you please, and to that end you will come to the Unicorn at ten o'clock next Thursday morning. Hi! Monty!"

Anelida was getting used to the dreamlike situation in which she found herself. It had, in its own right, a kind of authenticity. When the Management, that bourne to which all unknown actresses aspired, appeared before her in the person of Montague Marchant, she was able to make a reasonable response. How pale was Mr. Marchant, how matt his surface, how immense his aplomb! He talked of the spring weather, of the flowers in the conservatory and, through some imperceptible gradation, of the theatre. She was, he understood, an actress.

"She's playing Eliza Doolittle," Gantry remarked.

"Of course. Nice notices," Marchant murmured and tidily smiled at her. She supposed he must have seen them.

"I've been bullying her about her performance," Gantry continued.

"What a bad man!" Marchant said lightly. "Isn't he?"

"I suggest you take a look at it."

"Now, you see, Miss Lee, he's trying to bully me."

"You mustn't let him," Anelida said.

"Oh, I'm well up to his tricks. Are you liking Eliza?"

"Very much indeed. It's a great stroke of luck for me to try my hand at her."

"How long is your season?"

"Till Sunday. We change every three weeks."

"God, yes. Club policy."

"That's it."

"I see no good reason," Gantry said, "for fiddling about with this conversation. You know the part I told you about in Dicky's new play? She's going to read it for me. In the meantime, Monty, my dear, you're going to look at the piece and then pay a call on the Bonaventure." He suddenly displayed the cockeyed charm for which he was famous. "No promises made, no bones broken. Just a certain amount of very kind trouble taken because you know I wouldn't ask it idly. Come, Monty, do say you will."

"I seem," Marchant said, "to be cornered," and it was impossible to tell whether he really minded.

Anelida said, "It's asking altogether too much—please *don't* be cornered."

"I shall tell you quite brutally if I think you've wasted my time."

"Yes, of course."

"Ah, Dicky!" Marchant said. "May I inquire if you're a party to this conspiracy?"

Richard was there again, beside her. "Conspiracy?" he said. "I'm up to my neck in it. Why?"

Gantry said, "The cloak-and-dagger business is all mine, however. Dicky's a puppet."

"Aren't we all!" Marchant said. "I need another drink. So, I should suppose, do you."

Richard had brought them. "Anelida," he asked, "what have they been cooking?"

For the third time, Anelida listened to her own incredible and immediate future.

"I've turned bossy, Richard," Gantry said. "I've gone

ahead on my own. This child's going to take a running jump at reading your wench in *Heaven*. Monty's going to have a look at the play and see her Eliza. I tell him he'll be pleased. Too bad if you think she can't make it." He looked at Anelida and a very pleasant smile broke over his face. He flipped the brim of her hat with a thumb and forefinger. "Nice hat," he said.

Richard's hand closed painfully about her arm. "Timmy!" he shouted. "You're a *splendid* fellow! *Timmy*!"

"The author, at least," Marchant said drily, "would appear to be pleased."

"In that case," Gantry proposed, "let's drink to the unknown quantity. To your bright eyes, Miss Potential."

"I may as well go down gracefully," Marchant said. "To your Conspiracy, Timmy. In the person of Anelida Lee."

They had raised their glasses to Anelida when a voice behind them said, "I don't enjoy conspiracies in my own house, Monty, and I'm afraid I'm not mad about what I've heard of this one. Do let me in on it, won't you?"

It was Miss Bellamy.

2

Miss Bellamy had not arrived in the conservatory unaccompanied. She had Colonel Warrender in attendance upon her. They had been followed by Charles Templeton, Pinky Cavendish and Bertie Saracen. These three had paused by Gracefield to replenish their glasses and then moved from the dining-room into the conservatory, leaving the door open. Gracefield, continuing his round, was about to follow them. The conglomerate of voices in the rooms behind had mounted to its extremity, but above it, high-pitched, edged with emotion, a single voice rang out: Mary Bellamy's. There, in the conservatory she was, for all to see. She faced Anelida and leant slightly towards her.

"No, no, no, my dear. That, really is not quite good enough."

A sudden lull, comparable to that which follows the

60

lowering of houselights in a crowded theatre, was broken by
the more distant babble in the further room and by the
inconsequent, hitherto inaudible, excursions of the musicians. Heads were turned towards the conservatory.
Warrender came to the door. Gracefield found himself
moved to one side; Octavius was there, face to face with
Warrender. Gantry's voice said:

"Mary. This won't do."

"I think," Octavius said, "if I may, I would like to go to my
niece."

"Not yet," Warrender said. "Do you mind?" He shut the
door and cut off the voices in the conservatory.

For a moment the picture beyond the glass walls was held.
Mary Bellamy's lips worked. Richard faced her and was
speaking. So were Charles and Gantry. It was like a scene
from a silent film. Then, with a concerted movement, the
figures of Gantry, Charles, Richard and Warrender, their
backs to their audience, hid Miss Bellamy and Anelida.

"Ah, there you are, Occy!" a jovial not quite sober voice
exclaimed. "I was going to ask you, old boy. D'you
remember..."

It was Octavius's old acquaintance, Dr. Harkness, now
rather tight. As if he had given a signal, everybody began to
talk again very loudly indeed. Charles broke from the group
and came through the glass door, shutting it quickly behind
him. He put his hand on Octavius's arm.

"It's all right, Browne, I assure you," he said. "It's nothing.
Dicky is taking care of her. Believe me, it's all right." He
turned to Gracefield. "Tell them to get on with it," he said.
"At once."

Gracefield gave his butler's inclination and moved away.

Octavius said, "But all the same I would prefer to join
Anelida."

Charles looked at him. "How would you have liked," he
said, "to have spent the greater part of your life among
aliens?"

Octavius blinked. "My dear Templeton," he said, "I don't
know. But if you'll forgive me I find myself in precisely that
situation at the moment and I should still like to go to my
niece."

"Here she is now."

The door had opened again and Anelida had come through with Richard. They were both very white. Again a single voice was heard. Miss Bellamy's. "Do you suppose for one moment that I'm taken in . . ." and again Warrender shut the door.

"Well, Nelly darling," Octavius said. "I promised to remind you that we must leave early. Are you ready?"

"Quite ready," Anelida said. She turned to Charles Templeton and offered him her hand. "I'm so sorry," she said. "We'll slip out under our own steam."

"I'm coming," Richard announced grimly.

"So there's nothing," Charles said, "to be done?"

"I'm afraid we must go," Octavius said.

"We're running late as it is," Anelida agreed. Her voice, to her own astonishment, was steady. "Good-bye," she said, and to Richard, "No, don't come."

"I am coming."

Octavius put his hand on her shoulder and turned her towards the end of the room.

As he did so a cascade of notes sounded from a tubular gong. The roar of voices again died down, the musicians stood up and began to play that inevitable, that supremely silly air:

Happy birthday *to* you,
Happy birthday *to* you . . .

The crowd in the far room surged discreetly through into the dining-room, completely blocking the exit. Richard muttered, "This way. Quick," and propelled them towards a door into the hall. Before they could reach it, it opened to admit a procession: the maids, Gracefield with magnums of champagne, Florence, Cooky, in a white hat and carrying an enormously ornate birthday cake, and Old Ninn. They walked to the central table and moved ceremoniously to their appointed places. The cake was set down. Led by Dr. Harkness the assembly broke into applause.

"Now," Richard said.

And at last they were out of the room and in the hall. Anelida was conscious for the first time of her own heartbeat. It thudded in her throat and ears. Her mouth was dry and she trembled.

Octavius, puzzled and disturbed, touched her arm. "Nelly, my love," he said, "shall we go?"

"Yes," Anelida said and turned to Richard. "Don't come any further. Goodbye."

"I'm coming with you. I've got to."

"Please not."

He held her by the wrist. "I don't insult you with apologies, Anelida, but I do beg you to be generous and let me talk to you."

"Not now. Please, Richard, not now."

"Now. You're cold and you're trembling. Anelida!" He looked into her face and his own darkened. "Never again shall she speak to you like that. Do you hear me, Anelida? Never again." She drew away from him.

The door opened. Pinky and Bertie came through. Pinky made a dramatic pounce at Anelida and laid her hand on her arm. "Darling!" she cried incoherently. "Forget it! Nothing! God, what a scene!" She turned distractedly to the stairs, found herself cut off by the cinema unit and doubled back into the drawing-room. The camera men began to move their equipment across the hall.

"*Too* much!" Bertie said. "No! *Too* much." He disappeared in the direction of the men's cloakroom.

Timon Gantry came out. "Dicky," he said, "push off. I want a word with this girl. You won't do any good while you're in this frame of mind. Off!"

He took Anelida by the shoulders. "Listen to me," he said. "You will rise above. You will not let this make the smallest difference. Go home, now, and sort yourself out. I shall judge you by this and I shall see you on Thursday. Understood?" He gave her a firm little shake and stood back.

Warrender appeared, shutting the door behind him. He glared wretchedly at Anelida and barked, "Anything I can do—realize how distressed... Isn't it?"

Octavius said, "Very kind. I don't think, however..."

Richard announced loudly, "I'll never forgive her for this. Never."

Anelida thought, "If I don't go now I'll break down." She heard her own voice, "Don't give it another thought. Come along, Unk."

She turned and walked out of the house into the familiar

square, and Octavius followed her.

"Richard," Warrender said, "I must have a word with you, boy. Come in here."

"No," Richard said, and he too went out into the square.

Gantry stood for a moment looking after him.

"I find myself," he observed, "unable, any longer, to tolerate Mary Bellamy."

A ripple of applause broke out in the dining-room. Miss Bellamy was about to cut her birthday cake.

3

Miss Bellamy was a conscientious, able and experienced actress. Her public appearances were the result of hard work as well as considerable talent, and if one principle above all others could be said to govern them, it was that which is roughly indicated in the familiar slogan "The show must go on." It was axiomatic with Miss Bellamy that whatever disrupting influences might attend her, even up to the moment when her hand was on the offstage doorknob, they would have no effect whatsoever upon her performance.

They had none on the evening of her fiftieth birthday. She remained true to type.

When the procession with the cake appeared in the dining-room beyond the glass wall of the conservatory, she turned upon the persons with whom she had been doing battle and uttered the single and strictly professional order: "Clear!"

They had done so. Pinky, Bertie, Warrender and Gantry had all left her. Charles had already gone. Only Marchant remained, according, as it were, to the script. It had been arranged that he escort Miss Bellamy and make the birthday speech. They stood together in the conservatory, watching. Gracefield opened the champagne. There was a great deal of laughter and discreet skirmishing among the guests. Glasses were distributed and filled. Gracefield and the maids returned to their appointed places. Everybody looked towards the conservatory.

"This," Marchant said, "is it. You'd better bury the temperament, sweetie, for the time being." He opened the door, adding blandly as he did so, "Bitch into them, dear."

"The hell I will," said Miss Bellamy. She shot one malevolent glance at him, stepped back, collected herself, parted her lips in their triangular smile and made her entrance.

The audience, naturally, applauded.

Marchant, who had his own line in smiles, fingered his bow-tie and then raised a deprecating hand.

"Mary, darling," he said, pitching his voice, "and everybody! Please!"

A press photographer's lamp flashed.

Marchant's speech was short, graceful, bland, and for the most part, highly appreciated. He made the point, an acceptable one to his audience, that nobody really understood the people of their wonderful old profession but they themselves. The ancient classification of "rogues and vagabonds" was ironically recapitulated. The warmth, the dedication, the loyalties were reviewed and a brief but moving reference was made to "our wonderful Mary's happy association with, he would not say Marchant and Company, but would use a more familiar and he hoped affectionate phrase—the 'Management.'" He ended by asking them all to raise their glasses and drink "to Mary."

Miss Bellamy's behaviour throughout was perfect. She kept absolutely still and even the most unsympathetic observer would scarcely have noticed that she was anything but oblivious of her audience. She was, in point of fact, attentive to it and was very well aware of the absence of Richard, Pinky, Bertie, Warrender and Gantry—to say nothing of Anelida and Octavius. She also noticed that Charles, a late arrival in his supporting role of consort, looked pale and troubled. This irritated her. She saw that Old Ninn, well to the fore, was scarlet in the face, a sure sign of intemperance. No doubt there had been port-drinking parties with Florence and Gracefield and further noggins on her own account. Infuriating of Old Ninn! Outrageous of Richard, Pinky, Bertie, Maurice and Timon to absent themselves from the speech! Intolerable, that on her birthday she should be subjected to slight after slight and deception after deception: culminating, my God, in their combined treachery over that boney girl from the bookshop! It was time to give Monty a look of misty gratitude. They were drinking her health.

She replied, as usual, very briefly. The suggestion was of thoughts too deep for words and the tone whimsical. She ended by making a special reference to the cake and said that on this occasion Cooky, if that were possible, had excelled herself and she called attention to the decorations.

There was a round of applause, during which Gantry, Pinky, Bertie and Warrender edged in through the far doorway. Miss Bellamy was about to utter her peroration, but before she could do so, Old Ninn loudly intervened. "What's a cake without candles?" said Old Ninn.

A handful of guests laughed, nervously and indulgently. The servants looked scandalized and apprehensive.

"Fifty of them," Old Ninn proclaimed. "Oh, wouldn't they look lovely!" and broke into a disreputable chuckle.

Miss Bellamy took the only possible action. She topped Old Ninn's lines by snatching up the ritual knife and plunging it into the heart of the cake. The gesture, which may have had something of the character of a catharsis, was loudly applauded.

The press photographer's lamps flashed.

The ceremony followed its appointed course. The cake was cut up and distributed. Glasses were refilled and the guests began to talk again at the tops of their voices. It was time for her to open the presents, which had already been deposited on a conveniently placed table in the drawing-room. When that had been done they would go and the party would be over. But it would take a considerable time and all her resources. In the meantime, there was Old Ninn, purple-faced, not entirely steady on her pins and prepared to continue her unspeakable act for the benefit of anyone who would listen to her.

Miss Bellamy made a quick decision. She crossed to Old Ninn, put her arm about her shoulders and gaily laughing, led her towards the door into the hall. In doing so she passed Warrender, Pinky, Bertie, and Timon Gantry. She ignored them, but shouted to Monty Marchant that she was going to powder her nose. Charles was in the doorway. She was obliged to stop for a moment. He said under his breath, "You've done a terrible thing." She looked at him with contempt.

"You're in my way. I want to go out."

"I can't allow you to go on like this."

"Get *out*!" she whispered and thrust towards him. In that overheated room her scent engulfed him like a fog.

He said loudly, "At least don't use any more of that stuff. At least don't do that. Mary, listen to me!"

"I think you must be mad."

They stared at each other. He stood aside and she went out, taking Old Ninn with her. In the hall she said, "Ninn, go to your room and lie down. Do you hear me!"

Old Ninn looked her fully in the face, drew down the corners of her mouth, and keeping a firm hold on the banister, plodded upstairs.

Neither she nor Charles had noticed Florence, listening avidly, a pace or two behind them. She moved away down the hall and a moment later Richard came in by the front door. When he saw Miss Bellamy he stopped short.

"Where have you been?" she demanded.

"I've been trying, not very successfully, to apologize to my friends."

"They've taken themselves off, it appears."

"Would you have expected them to stay?"

"I should have thought them capable of anything."

He looked at her with a sort of astonishment and said nothing.

"I've got to speak to you," she said between her teeth.

"Have you? I wonder what you can find to say."

"Now."

"The sooner the better. But shouldn't you—" he jerked his head at the sounds beyond the doors, "be in there?"

"Now."

"Very well."

"Not here."

"Wherever you like, Mary."

"In my room."

She had turned to the stairs when a press photographer, all smiles, emerged from the dining-room.

"Miss Bellamy, could I have a shot? By the door? With Mr. Dakers perhaps? It's an opportunity. Would you mind?"

For perhaps five seconds, she hesitated. Richard said something under his breath.

"It's a bit crowded in there. We'd like to run a full-page spread," said the photographer and named his paper.

"But of course," said Miss Bellamy.

Richard watched her touch her hair and re-do her mouth. Accustomed though he was to her professional technique he was filled with amazement. She put away her compact and turned brilliantly to the photographer. "Where?" she asked him.

"In the entrance I thought. Meeting Mr. Dakers."

She moved down the hall to the front door. The photographer dodged round her. "Not in full glare," she said, and placed herself.

"Mr. Dakers?" said the photographer.

"Isn't it better as it is?" Richard muttered.

"Don't pay any attention to him," she said with ferocious gaiety. "Come along, Dicky."

"There's a new play on the skids, isn't there? If Mr. Dakers could be showing it to you, perhaps? I've brought something in case."

He produced a paperbound quarto of typescript, opened it and put it in her hands.

"Just as if you'd come to one of those sure-fire laugh lines," the photographer said. "Pointing it out to him, you know? Right, Mr. Dakers?"

Richard, nauseated, said, "I'm photocatastrophic. Leave me out."

"No!" said Miss Bellamy. Richard shook his head.

"You're too modest," said the photographer. "Just a little this way. Grand."

She pointed to the opened script. "And the great big smile," he said. The bulb flashed. "Wonderful. *Thank* you," and he moved away.

"And now," she said through her teeth, "I'll talk to you."

Richard followed her upstairs. On the landing they passed

Old Ninn, who watched them go into Miss Bellamy's room. After the door had shut she stood outside and waited.

She was joined there by Florence, who had come up by the back stairway. They communicated in a series of restrained gestures and brief whispers.

"You all right, Mrs. Plumtree?"

"Why not!" Ninn countered austerely.

"You look flushed," Florence observed drily.

"The heat in those rooms is disgraceful."

"Has She come up?"

"In there."

"Trouble?" Florence asked, listening. Ninn said nothing. "It's him, isn't it? Mr. Richard? What's *he* been up to?"

"Nothing," Ninn said, "that wouldn't be a credit to him, Floy, and I'll thank you to remember it."

"Oh, dear," Florence said rather acidly. "He's a man like the rest of them."

"He's better than most."

In the bedroom Miss Bellamy's voice murmured, rose sharply and died. Richard's scarcely audible, sounded at intervals. Then both together, urgent and expostulatory, mounted to some climax and broke off. There followed a long silence during which the two women stared at each other, and then a brief unexpected sound.

"What was that!" Florence whispered.

"Was she laughing?"

"It's left off now."

Ninn said nothing. "Oh well," Florence said, and had moved away when the door opened.

Richard came out, white to the lips. He walked past without seeing them, paused at the stairhead and pressed the palms of his hands against his eyes. They heard him fetch his breath with a harsh sound that might have been a sob. He stood there for some moments like a man who had lost his bearings and then struck his closed hand twice on the newel post and went quickly downstairs.

"What did I tell you," Florence said. She stole nearer to the door. It was not quite shut. "Trouble," she said.

"None of his making."

"How do you know?"

"The same way," Ninn said, "that I know how to mind my own business."

Inside the room, perhaps beyond it, something crashed. They stood there, irresolute, listening.

4

At first Miss Bellamy had not been missed. Her party had reverted to its former style, a little more confused by the circulation of champagne. It spread through the two rooms and into the conservatory and became noisier and noisier. Everybody forgot the ceremony of opening the birthday presents. Nobody noticed that Richard, too, was absent.

Gantry edged his way towards Charles, who was in the drawing-room, and stooped to make himself heard.

"Dicky," he said, "has made off."

"Where to?"

"I imagine to do the best he can with the girl and her uncle."

Charles looked at him with something like despair. "There's nothing to be done," he said, "nothing. It was shameful."

"Where is she?"

"I don't know. Isn't she in the next room?"

"I don't know," Gantry said.

"I wish to God this show was over."

"She ought to get on with the present-opening. They won't go till she does."

Pinky had come up. "Where's Mary?" she said.

"We don't know," Charles said. "She ought to be opening her presents."

"She won't miss her cue, my dear, you may depend upon it. Don't you feel it's time?"

"I'll find her," Charles said. "Get them mustered if you can, Gantry, will you?"

Bertie Saracen joined them, flushed and carefree. "What goes on?" he inquired.

"We're waiting for Mary."

"She went upstairs for running repairs," Bertie announced and giggled. "I *am* a poet and *don't* I know it!" he added.

"Did you see her?" Gantry demanded.

"I heard her tell Monty. She's not uttering to poor wee me."

Monty Marchant edged towards them. "Monty, ducky," Bertie cried, "your speech was too poignantly right. Live forever! *Oh,* I'm so tiddly."

Marchant said, "Mary's powdering her nose, Charles. Should we do a little shepherding?"

"I thought so."

Gantry mounted a stool and used his director's voice, "Attention, the cast!" It was a familiar summons and was followed by an obedient hush. "To the table, please, everybody, and clear an entrance. Last act, ladies and gentlemen. Last act, please!"

They did so at once. The table with its heaped array of parcels had already been moved forward by Gracefield and the maids. The guests ranged themselves at both sides like a chorus in grand opera, leaving a passage to the principal door.

Charles said, "I'll just see..." and went into the hall. He called up the stairs, "Oh, Florence! Tell Miss Bellamy we're ready, will you?" and came back. "Florence'll tell her," he said.

There was a longish, expectant pause. Gantry drew in his breath with a familiar hiss.

"*I'll* tell her," Charles said, and started off for the door.

Before he could reach it they all heard a door slam and running steps on the stairway. There was a relieved murmur and a little indulgent laughter.

"First time Mary's ever missed an entrance," someone said.

The steps ran across the hall. An irregular flutter of clapping broke out and stopped.

A figure appeared in the entrance and paused there.

It was not Mary Bellamy but Florence.

Charles said, "Florence! Where's Miss Mary?"

Florence, breathless, mouthed at him. "Not coming."

"Oh God!" Charles ejaculated. "Not *now*!"

As if to keep the scene relentlessly theatrical, Florence cried out in a shrill voice,

"A doctor. For Christ's sake. Quick. Is there a doctor in the house!"

chapter four

Catastrophe

IT MIGHT BE argued that the difference between high tragedy and melodrama rests in the indisputable fact that the latter is more true to nature. People, even the larger-than-life people of the theatre, tend at moments of tension to express themselves not in unexpected or memorable phrases but in cliches.

Thus, when Florence made her entrance, one or two voices in her audience cried out, "My God, what's happened?" Bertie Saracen cried out shrilly, "Does she mean Mary?" and somebody whose identity remained a secret said in an authoritative British voice, "Quiet, everybody. No need to panic," as if Florence had called for a fireman rather than a physician.

The only person to remain untouched was Dr. Harkness, who was telling a long, inebriated story to Monty Marchant and whose voice droned on indecently in a far corner of the dining-room.

Florence stretched out a shaking hand towards Charles

Templeton. "Oh, for Christ's sake, sir!" she stammered. "Oh, for Christ's sake, come quick."

"—And this chap said to the other chap . . ." Dr. Harkness recounted.

Charles said, "Good God, what's the matter! Is it . . .?"

"It's her, sir. Come quick."

Charles thrust her aside, ran from the room and pelted upstairs.

"A doctor!" Florence said. "My God, a doctor!"

It was Marchant who succeeded in bringing Dr. Harkness into focus.

"You're wanted," he said. "Upstairs. Mary."

"Eh? Bit of trouble?" Dr. Harkness asked vaguely.

"Something's happened to Mary."

Timon Gantry said, "Pull yourself together, Harkness. You've got a patient."

Dr. Harkness had forgotten to remove his smile, but a sort of awareness now overtook him. "Patient?" he said. "Where? Is it Charles?"

"Upstairs. Mary."

"Good gracious!" said Dr. Harkness. "Very good. I'll come." He rocked slightly on his feet and remained stationary.

Maurice Warrender said to Florence, "Is it bad?"

Her hand to her mouth she nodded her head up and down like a mandarin.

Warrender took a handful of ice from a wine-cooler and suddenly thrust it down the back of Dr. Harkness's collar. "Come on," he said. Harkness let out a sharp oath. He swung round as if to protest, lost his balance and fell heavily.

Florence screamed.

"I'm a'right," Dr. Harkness said from the door. "Tripped over something. Silly!"

Warrender and Gantry got him to his feet. "I'm all *right!*" he repeated angrily. "Gimme some water, will you?"

Gantry tipped some out of the ice bucket. Dr. Harkness swallowed it down noisily and shuddered. "Beastly stuff," he said. "Where's this patient?"

From the stairhead, Charles called in an unrecognizable voice, "Harkness! *Harkness!*"

"Coming," Warrender shouted. Harkness, gasping, was led out.

Florence looked wildly round the now completely silent company, wrung her hands and followed them.

Timon Gantry said, "More ice, perhaps," picked up the wine-cooler and overtook them on the stairs.

The party was left in suspension.

In Mary Bellamy's bedroom all the windows were open. An evening breeze stirred the curtains and the ranks of tulips. Dr. Harkness knelt beside the pool of rose-coloured chiffon from which protruded, like rods, two legs finished with high-heeled shoes and two naked arms whose clenched hands glittered with diamonds. Diamonds were spattered across the rigid plane of the chest and shone through a hank of disarranged hair. A length of red chiffon lay across the face and this was a good thing.

Dr. Harkness had removed his coat. His ice-wet shirt stuck to his spine. His ear was laid against the place from which he had pulled away the red chiffon.

He straightened up, looked closely into the face, reveiled it and got to his feet.

"I'm afraid there's nothing whatever to be done," he said.

Charles said, "There must be. You don't know. There must be. Try. Try something. My God, try!"

Warrender, in his short-stepped, square-shouldered way, walked over to Harkness and looked down for a moment.

"No good," he said. "Have to face it. What?"

Charles sati on the bed and rubbed his freckled hand across his mouth. "I can't believe it's happened," he said. "It's *there*—it's *happened*. And I can't believe it."

Florence burst noisily into tears.

Dr. Harkness turned to her. "You," he said. "Florence, isn't it? Try to control yourself, there's a good girl. Did you find her like this?"

Florence nodded and sobbed out something indistinguishable.

"But she was..." Harkness glanced at Charles. "Conscious?"

Florence said, "Not to know me. Not to speak," and broke down completely.

"Were the windows open?"

Florence shook her head.

"Did you open them?"

She shook her head again. "I didn't think to—I got such a wicked shock—I didn't think..."

"I opened them," Charles said.

"First thing to be done," Warrender muttered.

Gantry, who from the time of his entry had stood motionless near the door, joined the others. "But what *was* it?" he asked. "What happened?"

Warrender said unevenly, "Perfectly obvious. She used that bloody spray thing there. I said it was dangerous. Only this morning."

"What thing?"

Warrender stooped. The tin of Slaypest lay on its side close to the clenched right hand. A trickle of dark fluid stained the carpet. "This," he said.

"Better leave it," Dr. Harkness said sharply.

"What?"

"Better leave it where it is." He looked at Gantry. "It's some damned insecticide. For plants. The tin's smothered in warnings."

"We told her," Warrender said. "Look at it."

"I said don't touch it."

Warrender straightened up. The blood had run into his face. "Sorry," he said, and then, "Why not?"

"You're a bit too ready with your hands. I'm wet as hell and half frozen."

"You were tight. Best cure, my experience."

They eyed each other resentfully. Dr. Harkness looked at Charles, who sat doubled up with his hands on his chest. He went to him. "Not too good?" he said. Timon Gantry put a hand on Charles's shoulder.

"I'm going to take you to your room, old boy. Next door, isn't it?"

"Yes," Dr. Harkness said. "But not just yet. In a minute. Good idea." He turned to Florence. "Do you know where Mr. Templeton keeps his tablets? Get them, will you? And you might bring some aspirin at the same time. Run along, now." Florence went into the dressing-room. He sat beside

Charles on the bed and took his wrist. "Steady does it," he said and looked at Gantry. "Brandy."

"I know where it is," Warrender said, and went out.

Gantry said, "What about the mob downstairs?"

"They can wait." He held the wrist a little longer and then laid Charles's hand on his knee, keeping his own over it. "We'll move you in a moment. You must let other people think for you. It's been a bad thing."

"I can't..." Charles said. "I can't..." and fetched his breath in irregular, tearing sighs.

"Don't try to work things out. Not just yet. Ah, here's Florence. Good. Now then, one of these."

He gave Charles a tablet. Warrender came back with brandy. "This'll help," Dr. Harkness said. They waited in silence.

"I'm all right," Charles said presently.

"Fine. Now, an arm each and take it steady. His room's next door. Lie down, Charles, won't you?"

Charles nodded and Warrender moved towards him. "No," Charles said quite strongly, and turned to Gantry. "I'm all right," he repeated, and Gantry very efficiently supported him through the door into his dressing-room.

Warrender stood for a moment, irresolute, and then lifted his chin and followed them.

"Get him a hot bottle," Harkness said to Florence.

When she'd gone he swallowed three aspirins, took up the bedside telephone and dialled a number.

"This is Dr. Frank Harkness. I'm speaking from Number 2 Pardoner's Place. Mr. Charles Templeton's house. There's been an accident. A fatality. Some sort of pest killer. Mrs. Templeton. Yes. About fifty people—a party. Right. I'll wait."

As he replaced the receiver Gantry came back. He stopped short when he saw Harkness. "What now?" he asked.

"I've telephoned the police."

"The *police*!"

"In cases like this," Harkness said, "one notifies the police."

"Anybody would think..."

"Anybody will think anything," Dr. Harkness grunted.

He turned back the elaborate counterpane and the blankets under it. "I don't want to call the servants," he said, "and that woman's on the edge of hysteria. This sheet'll do." He pulled it off, bundled it up and threw it to Gantry. "Cover her up, old boy, will you?"

Gantry turned white round the mouth. "I don't like this sort of thing," he said. "I've produced it often enough, but I've never faced the reality." And he added with sudden violence, "Cover her up yourself."

"All right. All right," sighed Dr. Harkness. He took the sheet, crossed the room and busied himself with masking the body. The breeze from the open windows moved the sheet, as if, fantastically, it was stirred by what it covered.

"May as well shut them, now," Dr. Harkness said and did so. "Can you straighten the bed at least?" he asked. Gantry did his best with the bed.

"Right," said Dr. Harkness, putting on his coat. "Does this door lock? Yes. Will you come?"

As they went out Gantry said, "Warrender's crocked up. Charles didn't seem to want him, so he flung a sort of poker-backed, stiff-lipped, Blimp-type temperament and made his exit. I don't know where he's gone, but in his way," Gantry said, "he's wonderful. Terrifyingly ham, but wonderful. He's upset, though."

"Serve him bloody well right. It won't be his fault if I escape pneumonia. My *head*!" Dr. Harkness said, momentarily closing his eyes.

"You were high."

"Not so high I couldn't come down."

Old Ninn was on the landing. Her face had bleached round its isolated patches of crimson. She confronted Dr. Harkness.

"What's she done to herself?" asked Old Ninn.

Dr. Harkness once more summoned up his professional manner. He bent over her. "You've got to be very sensible and good, Nanny," he said, and told her briefly what had happened.

She looked fixedly into his face throughout the recital and at the end said, "Where's Mr. Templeton?"

Dr. Harkness indicated the dressing-room.

"Who's looking after him?"

"Florence was getting him a hot bottle."

"Her!" Ninn said with a brief snort, and without another word stumped to the door. She gave it a smart rap and let herself in.

"Wonderful character," Gantry murmured.

"Remarkable."

They turned towards the stairs. As they did so a figure moved out of the shadows at the end of the landing, but they did not notice her. It was Florence.

"And now, I suppose," Dr. Harkness said as they went downstairs, "for the mob."

"Get rid of them?" Gantry asked.

"Not yet. They're meant to wait. Police orders."

"But..."

"Matter of form."

Gantry said, "At least we can boot the press off, can't we?"

"Great grief, I'd forgotten that gang!"

"Leave them to me."

The press was collected about the hall. A light flashed as Gantry and Harkness came down, and a young man who had evidently just arrived advanced hopefully. "Mr. Timon Gantry? I wonder if you could..."

Gantry, looking down from his great height, said, "I throw you one item. And one only. Miss Mary Bellamy was taken ill this evening and died some minutes ago."

"Doctor er...? Could you...?"

"The cause," Dr. Harkness said, "is at present undetermined. She collapsed and did not recover consciousness."

"Is Mr. Templeton...?"

"No," they said together. Gantry added, "And that is all, gentlemen. Good evening to you."

Gracefield appeared from the back of the hall, opened the front door and said, "Thank you, gentlemen. If you will step outside."

They hung fire. A car drew up in the Place. From it emerged a heavily built man, wearing a bowler hat and a tidy overcoat. He walked into the house.

"Inspector Fox," he said.

2

It has been said of Mr. Fox that his arrival at any scene of disturbance has the effect of a large and almost silent vacuum cleaner.

Under his influence the gentlemen of the press were tidied out into Pardoner's Place, where they lingered restively for a long time. The guests, some of whom were attempting to leave, found themselves neatly mustered in the drawing-room. The servants waited quietly in the hall. Mr. Fox and Dr. Harkness went upstairs. A constable appeared and stood inside the front door.

"I locked the door," Dr. Harkness said, with the air of a schoolboy hoping for praise. He produced the key.

"Very commendable, Doctor," said Fox comfortably.

"Nothing's been moved. The whole thing speaks for itself."

"Quite so. Very sad."

Fox laid his bowler on the bed, knelt by the sheet and turned it back. "Strong perfume," he said. He drew out his spectacles, placed them and looked closely into the dreadful face.

"You can see for yourself," Dr. Harkness said. "Traces of the stuff all over her."

"Quite so," Fox repeated. "Very profuse."

He contemplated the Slaypest but did not touch it. He rose and made a little tour of the room. He had very bright eyes for a middle-aged person.

"If it's convenient, sir," he said, "I'll have a word with Mr. Templeton."

"He's pretty well knocked out. His heart's dicky. I made him lie down."

"Perhaps you'd just have a little chat with him yourself, Doctor. Would you be good enough to say I won't keep him more than a minute? No need to disturb him; I'll come to his room. Where would it be?"

"Next door."

"Nice and convenient. I'll give you a minute with him and

80

then I'll come in. Thank you, Doctor."

Dr. Harkness looked sharply at him, but he was restoring his spectacles to their case and had turned to contemplate the view from the window.

"Pretty square, this," said Mr. Fox.

Dr. Harkness went out.

Fox quietly locked the door and went to the telephone. He dialled a number and asked for an extension.

"Mr. Alleyn?" he said. "Fox, here. It's about this case in Pardoner's Place. There are one or two little features..."

3

When Superintendent Alleyn had finished speaking to Inspector Fox, he went resignedly into action. He telephoned his wife with the routine information that he would not after all be home for dinner, summoned Detective Sergeants Bailey and Thompson with their impedimenta, rang the police surgeon, picked up his homicide bag and went whistling to the car. "A lady of the theatre," he told his subordinates, "appears to have looked upon herself as a common or garden pest and sprayed herself out of this world. She was mistaken as far as her acting was concerned. Miss Mary Bellamy. A comedienne of the naughty darling school and not a beginner. It's Mr. Fox's considered opinion that somebody done her in."

When they arrived at 2 Pardoner's Place, the tidying-up process had considerably advanced. Fox had been shown the guest list with addresses. He had checked it, politely dismissed those who had stayed throughout in what he called the reception area and mildly retained the persons who had left it "prior," to quote Mr. Fox, "to the unfortunate event." These were Timon Gantry, Pinky Canvendish, and Bertie Saracen, who were closeted in Miss Bellamy's boudoir on the ground floor. Hearing that Colonel Warrender was a relation, Mr. Fox suggested that he join Charles Templeton, who had now come down to his study. Showing every sign of reluctance but obedient to authority, Warrender did so. Dr.

Harkness had sent out for a corpse-reviver for himself and gloomily occupied a chair in the conservatory. Florence having been interviewed and Old Ninn briefly surveyed, they had retired to their sitting-room in the top story. Gracefield, the maids and the hired men had gone a considerable way towards removing the debris.

Under a sheet from her own bed on the floor of her locked room, Miss Bellamy began to stiffen.

Alleyn approached the front door to the renewed activity of the camera men. One of them called out, "Give us a break, won't you, Super?"

"All in good time," he said.

"What d'you know, Mr. Alleyn?"

"Damn all," Alleyn said and rang the bell.

He was admitted by Fox. "Sorry you've been troubled, sir," Fox said.

"I daresay. What *is* all this?"

Fox told him in a few neatly worded sentences.

"All right," Alleyn said. "Let's have a look, shall we?"

They went upstairs to Miss Bellamy's bedroom.

He knelt by the body. "Did she *bathe* in scent?" he wondered.

"Very strong, isn't it, sir?"

"Revolting. The whole room stinks of it." He uncovered the head and shoulders. "I see."

"Not very nice," Fox remarked.

"Not very." Alleyn was silent for a moment or two. "I saw her a week ago," he said, "on the last night of that play of Richard Dakers's that's been running so long. It was a flimsy, conventional comedy, but she filled it with her own kind of gaiety. And now—to this favour is she come." He looked more closely. "Could the stuff have blown back in her face? But you tell me they say the windows were shut?"

"That's right."

"The face and chest are quite thickly spattered."

"Exactly. I wondered," Fox said, "if the spray-gun mechanism on the Slaypest affair was not working properly and she turned it towards her to see."

"And it *did* work? Possible, I suppose. But she'd stop at once, and look at her. Just look, Fox. There's a fine spray

82

such as she'd get if she held the thing at arm's length and didn't use much pressure. And over that there are great blotches and runnels of the stuff, as if she'd held it close to her face and pumped it like mad."

"People do these things."

"They do. As a theory I don't fancy it. Nobody's handled the Slaypest tin? Since the event?"

"They say not," Fox said.

"Bailey'll have to go over it for dabs, of course. Damn this scent. You can't get a whiff of anything else."

Alleyn bent double and advanced his nose to the tin of Slaypest. "I know this stuff," he said. "It's about as highly concentrated as they come, and in my opinion shouldn't be let loose on the public for all the warnings on the label. The basic ingredient seems to be hexaethyl-tetra-phosphate."

"You don't say," Fox murmured.

"It's a contact poison and very persistent." He replaced the sheet, got up and examined the bank of growing plants in the bay window. "Here it is again. They've got thrips and red spider." He stared absently at Fox. "So what does she do, Br'er Fox? She comes up here in the middle of her own party wearing her best red wisp of tulle and all her diamonds and sets about spraying her azaleas."

"Peculiar," Fox said. "What I thought."

"Very rum indeed."

He wandered to the dressing-table. The central drawer was pulled out. Among closely packed ranks of boxes and pots was an open powder bowl. A piece of cotton-wool coloured with powder lay on the top of the table near a lipstick that had been imperfectly shut. Nearby was a bunch of Parma violets, already wilting.

"She *did* have a fiddle with her face," Alleyn pointed out. "She's got a personal maid, you say. The woman that found her."

"Florence."

"All right. Well, Florence would have tidied up any earlier goes at the powder and paint. And she'd have done something about these violets. Where do *they* come in? So this poor thing walks in, pulls out the drawer, does her running repairs and I should say from the smell, has a lavish wack at her scent." He sniffed the atomizer. "That's it. Quarter full and stinks like a civet cat, and here's the bottle it came from, empty. 'Formidable.' Expensive maker. 'Abominable' would be more like it. How women can use such muck passes my understanding."

"I rather fancy it," said Mr. Fox. "It's intriguing."

Alleyn gave him a look. "If we're to accept what appears to be the current explanation, she drenches her azaleas with hexa-ethyl-tetra-phosphate and then turns the spray-gun full in her own face and kills herself. D'you believe that?"

"Not when you put it like that."

"Nor I. Bailey and Thompson are down below and Dr. Curtis is on his way. Get them up here. We'll want the complete treatment. Detailed pictures of the body and the room, tell Thompson. And Bailey'll need to take her prints and search the spray-gun, the dressing-table and anything else that may produce dabs, latent or otherwise. We don't know what we're looking for, of course." The bathroom door was open and he glanced in. "Even this place reeks of scent. What's that on the floor? Broken picture." He looked more closely. "Rather nice tinsel picture. Madame Vestris, I fancy. Corner of washbasin freshly chipped. Somebody's tramped broken glass over the floor. Did she drop her pretty picture? And why in the bathroom? Washing the glass? Or what? We won't disturb it." He opened the bathroom cupboard. "The things they take!" he muttered. "The tablets. For insomnia. One with water on retiring. The unguents! The lotions! Here's some muck like green clay. Lifting mask. 'Apply with spatula and leave on for ten minutes. Do not move lips or facial muscles during treatment.' Here *is* the spatula with some nice fresh dabs. Florence's, no doubt. And in the clothes basket, a towel with greenish smears. She had the full treatment before the party. Sal volatile bottle by the handbasin. Did someone try to force sal volatile down her throat?"

"Not a chance, I should say, sir."

"She must have taken it earlier in the day. Why? Very fancy too, tarted up with a quilted cover, good Lord! All right, Fox. Away we go. I'd better see the husband."

"He's still in his study with a Colonel Warrender, who

seems to be a relative. Mr. Templeton had a heart-attack after the event. The doctor says he's subject to them. Colonel Warrender and Mr. Gantry took him into his dressing-room there, and then the Colonel broke up and went downstairs. Mr. Templeton was still lying in there when I came up, but I suggested the Colonel should take him down to the study. They didn't seem to fancy the move, but I wanted to clear the ground. It's awkward," Mr. Fox said, "having people next door to the body."

Alleyn went into the dressing room, leaving the door open. "Change of atmosphere," Fox heard him remark. "Very masculine. Very simple. Very good. Who gave him a hot bottle?"

"Florence. The doctor says the old nurse went in later, to take a look at him. By all accounts she's a bossy old cup-of-tea and likes her drop of port wine."

"This," Alleyn said, "is the house of a damn rich man. And woman, I suppose."

"He's a big name in the City, isn't he?"

"He is indeed. C. G. Templeton. He brought off that coup with Eastland Transport two years ago. Reputation of being an implacable chap to run foul of."

"The servants seem to fancy him. The cook says he must have everything just so. One slip and you're out. But well-liked. He's taken this very hard. Very shaky when I saw him but easy to handle. The Colonel was tougher."

"Either of them strike you as being the form for a woman-poisoner?"

"Not a bit like it," Fox said cheerfully.

"They tell me you never know."

"That's right. So they say."

They went out. Fox locked the door. "Not that it makes all that difference," he sighed. "The keys on this floor are interchangeable. As usual. However," he added, brightening, "I've taken the liberty of removing all the others."

"You'll get the sack one of these days. Come on." They went downstairs.

"The remaining guests," Fox said, "are in the second room on the right. They're the lot who were with deceased up to the time she left the conservatory and the only ones who went outside the reception area before the speeches began. And, by the way, sir, up to the time the speeches started, there was a photographer and a moving camera unit blocking the foot of the stairs and for the whole period a kind of bar with a man mixing drinks right by the backstairs. I've talked to the man concerned and he says nobody but the nurse and Florence went up while he was on duty. This is deceased's sitting-room. Or boudoir. The study is the first on the right."

"Where's the quack?"

"In the glasshouse with a hangover. Shall I stir him up?"

"Thank you."

They separated. Alleyn tapped on the boudoir door and went in.

Pinky sat in an armchair with a magazine, Timon Gantry was finishing a conversation on the telephone, and Bertie, petulant and flushed, was reading a rare edition of *'Tis Pity She's a Whore*. When they saw Alleyn the two men got up and Pinky put down her magazine as if she was ashamed of it.

Alleyn introduced himself. "This is just to say I'm very sorry to keep you waiting about."

Gantry said, "It's damned awkward. I've had to tell people over the telephone."

"There's no performance involved, is there?"

"No. But there's a new play going into rehearsal. Opening in three weeks. One has to cope."

"Of course," Alleyn said, "one does, indeed," and went out.

"What a superb-looking man," Bertie said listlessly, and returned to his play.

Warrender and Charles had the air of silence about them. It was not, Alleyn fancied, the kind of silence that falls naturally between two cousins united in a common sorrow; they seemed at odds with each other. He could have sworn his arrival was a relief rather than an annoyance. He noticed that the study, like the dressing-room, had been furnished and decorated by a perfectionist with restraint, judgment and a very great deal of money. There was a kind of relationship between the reserve of these two men and the setting in which he found them. He thought that they had probably been sitting there for a long time without speech. A full decanter and two untouched glasses stood between them on a small and exquisite table.

Charles began to rise. Alleyn said, "Please, don't move," and he sank heavily back again. Warrender stood up. His eyes were red and his face patched with uneven color.

"Bad business, this," he said. "What?"

"Yes," Alleyn said. "Very bad." He looked at Charles. "I'm sorry, sir, that at the moment we're not doing anything to make matters easier."

With an obvious effort Charles said, "Sit down, won't you? Alleyn, isn't it? I know your name, of course."

Warrender pushed a chair forward.

"Will you have a drink?" Charles asked.

"No, thank you very much. I won't trouble you longer than I can help. There's a certain amount of unavoidable business to be got through. There will be an inquest and, I'm afraid, a post-mortem. In addition to that we're obliged to check, as far as we're able, the events leading to the accident. All this, I know, is very distressing and I'm sorry."

Charles lifted a hand and let it fall.

Warrender said, "Better make myself scarce."

"No," Alleyn said. "I'd be glad if you waited a moment."

Warrender was looking fixedly at Alleyn. He tapped himself above the heart and made a very slight gesture towards Charles. Alleyn nodded.

"If I may," he said to Charles, "I'll ask Colonel Warrender to give me an account of the period before your wife left the party and went up to her room. If, sir, you would like to amend or question or add to anything he says, please do so."

Charles said, "Very well. Though God knows what difference it can make."

Warrender straightened his back, touched his Brigade-of-Guards tie, and made his report, with the care and, one would have said, the precision of experience.

He had, he said, been near to Mary Bellamy from the time she left her post by the door and moved through her guests towards the conservatory. She had spoken to one group after another. He gave several names. She had then joined a small party in the conservatory.

Alleyn was taking notes. At this point there was a pause.

Warrender was staring straight in front of him. Charles had not moved.

"Yes?" Alleyn said.

"She stayed in there until the birthday cake was brought in," Warrender said.

"And the other people in her group stayed there too?"

"No," Charles said. "I came out and—spoke to two of our guests who—who were leaving early."

"Yes? Did you return?"

He said wearily, "I told Gracefield, our butler, to start the business with the cake. I stayed in the main rooms until they brought it in."

Alleyn said, "Yes. And then . . . ?"

"They came in with the cake," Warrender said. "And she came out and Marchant—her management is Marchant & Company—Marchant gave the birthday speech."

"And did the other people in the conservatory come out?"

"Yes."

"With Miss Bellamy?"

Warrender said, "Not with her."

"After her?"

"No. Before. Some of them. I expect all of them except Marchant."

"You yourself, sir? What did you do?"

"I came out before she did."

"Did you stay in the main rooms?"

"No," he said. "I went into the hall for a moment." Alleyn waited. "To say goodbye," Warrender said, "to the two people who were leaving early."

"Oh yes. Who were they?"

"Feller called Browne and his niece."

"And having done that you returned?"

"Yes," he said.

"To the conservatory?"

"No. To the dining-room. That's where the speech was made."

"Had it begun when you returned?"

Still looking straight before him, Warrender said, "Finished. She was replying."

"Really? You stayed in the hall for some time then?"

"Longer," he said, "than I'd intended. Didn't realize the ceremony had begun, isn't it."

"Do you remember who the other people were? The ones who probably came out before Miss Bellamy from the conservatory?"

"Miss Cavendish and Saracen. And Timon Gantry, the producer-man. Your second-in-command went over all this and asked them to stay."

"I'd just like, if you don't mind, to sort it out for myself. Anyone else? The two guests who left early, for instance. Were they in the conservatory party?"

"Yes."

"And left...?"

"First," Warrender said loudly.

"So you caught them up in the hall. What were they doing in the hall, sir?"

"Talking. Leaving. I don't know exactly."

"You don't remember to whom they were talking?"

"I cannot," Charles said, "for the very life of me see why these two comparative strangers, who were gone long before anything happened, should be of the remotest interest to you."

Alleyn said quickly, "I know that sounds quite unreasonable, but they do at the moment seem to have been the cause of other people's behaviour."

He saw that for some reason this observation had disturbed Warrender. He looked at Alleyn as if the latter had said something outrageous and penetrating.

"You see," Alleyn explained, "in order to establish accident, one does have to make a formal inquiry into the movements of those persons who were nearest to Miss Bellamy up to the *time* of the accident."

"Oh!" Warrender said flatly. "Yes. Possibly."

"But—Mary—my wife—was *there*. Still *there*! Radiant. *There*, seen by everybody—I can't imagine..." Charles sank back in his chair. "Never mind," he murmured. "Go on."

Warrender said, "Browne and his niece had, I think, been talking to Saracen and Miss Cavendish. When I came into the hall... They were—saying goodbye to Gantry."

"I see. And nobody else was concerned in this leave-taking? In the hall?"

There was a long silence. Warrender looked as if somebody had tapped him smartly on the back of the head. His eyes started and he turned to Charles, who leant forward, grasping the arms of his chair.

"My God!" Warrender said. "Where is he? What's become of him? *Where's Richard?*"

4

Alleyn had been trained over a long period of time to distinguish between simulated and involuntary reactions in human behaviour. He was perhaps better equipped than many of his colleagues in this respect, being fortified by an instinct that he was particularly careful to mistrust. It seldom let him down. He thought now that, whereas Charles Templeton was quite simply astounded by his own forgetfulness, Warrender's reaction was much less easily defined. Alleyn had a notion that Warrender's reticence was of the formidable kind which conceals nothing but the essential.

It was Warrender, now, who produced an explanation.

"Sorry," he said. "Just remembered something. Extraordinary we should have forgotten. We're talking about Richard Dakers."

"The playwright?"

"That's the man. He's—you may not know this—he was..." Warrender boggled inexplicably and looked at his boots. "He's—he was my cousin's—he was the Templetons' ward."

For the first time since Alleyn had entered the room, Charles Templeton looked briefly at Warrender.

"Does he know about this catastrophe?" Alleyn asked.

"No," Warrender said, "he can't know. Be a shock."

Alleyn began to ask about Richard Dakers and found that they were both unwilling to talk about him. When had he last been seen? Charles remembered he had been in the conservatory. Warrender, pressed, admitted that Richard was in the hall, when Browne and his niece went away. Odd, Alleyn thought, that, as the climax of the party approached, no less than five of Miss Bellamy's most intimate friends should turn their backs on her to say goodbye to two people whom her husband had described as comparative strangers. He hinted as much.

Warrender glanced at Charles and then said, "Point of fact they're friends of Richard Dakers. His guests in a way. Naturally he wanted to see them off."

"And having done so, he returned for the speeches and the cake-cutting ceremony?"

"I—ah...Not exactly," Warrender said.

"No?"

"No. Ah, speaking out of school, isn't it, but I rather fancy there's an attraction. He—ah—he went out—they live in the next house."

"Not," Alleyn ejaculated, "*Octavius* Browne of the Pegasus?"

"Point of fact, yes," Warrender said, looking astonished.

"And Mr. Dakers went out with them?"

"After them."

"But you think he meant to join them?"

"Yes," he said woodenly.

"And is perhaps with them still?"

Warrender was silent.

"Wouldn't he mind missing the ceremony?" Alleyn asked.

Warrender embarked on an incomprehensible spate of broken phrases.

"If he's there," Charles said to Alleyn, "he ought to be told."

"I'll go," Warrender said and moved to the door.

Alleyn said, "One minute, if you please."

"What?"

"Shall we just see if he *is* there? It'll save trouble, won't it? May I use the telephone?"

He was at the telephone before they could reply and looking up the number.

"I know Octavius quite well," he said pleasantly.

"Splendid chap, isn't he?"

Warrender looked at him resentfully. "If the boy's there," he said, "I'd prefer to tell him about this myself."

"Of course," Alleyn agreed heartily. "Ah, here we are." He dialled a number. They heard a voice at the other end.

"Hullo," Alleyn said. "Is Mr. Richard Dakers there by any chance?"

"No," the voice said. "I'm sorry. He left some time ago."

"Really? How long would you say?"

The voice replied indistinguishably.

"I see. Thank you so much. Sorry to have bothered you."

He hung up. "He was only with them for a very short time," he said. "He must have left, it seems, before this thing happened. They imagined he came straight back here."

Warrender and Templeton were, he thought, at peculiar pains not to look at each other or at him. He said lightly, "Isn't that a little odd? Wouldn't you suppose he'd be sure to attend the birthday speeches?"

Perhaps each of them waited for the other to reply. After a moment Warrender barked out two words. "Lovers' tiff?" he suggested.

"You think it might be that?"

"I think," Warrender said angrily, "that whatever it was it's got nothing to do with this—this tragedy. "Good Lord, why should it!"

"I really do assure you," Alleyn said, "that I wouldn't worry you about these matters if I didn't think it was necessary."

"Matter of opinion," Warrender said.

"Yes. A matter of opinion and mine may turn out to be wrong."

He could see that Warrender was on the edge of some outburst and was restrained, it appeared, only by the presence of Charles Templeton.

"Perhaps," Alleyn said, "we might just make quite sure that Mr. Dakers didn't, in fact, come back. After all, it was a biggish party. Might he not have slipped in, unnoticed, and gone out again for some perfectly explainable reason? The servants might have noticed. If you would . . ."

Warrender jumped at this. "Certainly! I'll come out with

you." And after a moment, "D'you mind, Charles?"

With extraordinary vehemence Charles said, "Do what you like. If he comes back I don't want to see him. "I . . ." He passed an unsteady hand across his eyes. "Sorry," he said, presumably to Alleyn. "This has been a bit too much for me."

"We'll leave you to yourself," Alleyn said. "Would you like Dr. Harkness to come in?"

"No. No. No. If I might be left alone. That's all."

"Of course."

They went out. The hall was deserted except for the constable who waited anonymously in a corner. Alleyn said, "Will you excuse me for a moment?" and went to the constable.

"Anybody come in?" he asked under his breath.

"No, sir."

"Keep the press out, but admit anyone else and don't let them go again. Take the names and say there's been an accident in the vicinity and we're doing a routine check."

"Very good, sir."

Alleyn returned to Warrender. "No one's come in," he said. "Where can we talk?"

Warrender glanced at him. "Not here," he muttered, and led the way into the deserted drawing-room, now restored to order but filled with the flower-shop smell of Bertie Saracen's decorations and the faint reek of cigarette smoke and alcohol. The connecting doors into the dining-room were open and beyond them, in the conservatory, Dr. Harkness could be seen, heavily asleep in a canvas chair and under observation by Inspector Fox. When Fox saw them he came out and shut the glass door. "He's down to it," he said, "but rouseable. I thought I'd leave him as he is till required."

Warrender turned on Alleyn. "Look here!" he demanded. "What *is* all this? Are you trying to make out there's been any—any . . ." he boggled, "any hanky-panky?"

"We can't take accident as a matter-of-course."

"Why not? Clear as a pikestaff."

"Our job," Alleyn said patiently, "is to collect all the available information and present it to the coroner. At the moment we are not drawing any conclusions. Come sir," he said, as Warrender still looked mulish, "I'm sure that, as a

93

soldier, you'll recognize the position. It's a matter of procedure. After all, to be perfectly frank about it, a great many suicides as well as homicides have been rigged to look like accidents."

"Either suggestion's outrageous."

"And will, we hope, soon turn out to be so."

"But, good God, is there anything at all to make you suppose..." He stopped and jerked his hands ineloquently.

"Suppose what?"

"That it could be—either? Suicide—or murder?"

"Oh, yes," Alleyn said. "Could be. Could be."

"What? What evidence...?"

"I'm afraid I'm not allowed to discuss details."

"Why the hell not?"

"God bless my soul!" Alleyn exclaimed. "Do *consider*. Suppose it was murder—for all I know you might have done it. You can't expect me to make you a present of what may turn out to be the police case against you."

"I think you must be dotty," said Colonel Warrender profoundly.

"Dotty or sane, I must get on with my job. Inspector Fox and I propose to have a word with those wretched people we've cooped up over the way. Would you rather return to Mr. Templeton, sir?"

"My God, no!" he ejaculated with some force and then looked hideously discomfited.

"Why not?" Alleyn asked coolly. "Have you had a row with him?"

"No!"

"Well, I'm afraid it's a case of returning to him or staying with me."

"I...God damn it, I'll stick to you."

"Right. Here we go, then."

Bertie, Pinky, and Timon Gantry seemed hardly to have moved since he last saw them. Bertie was asleep in his chair and resembled an overdressed baby. Pinky had been crying. Gantry now was reading *'Tis Pity She's a Whore*. He laid it aside and rose to his feet.

"I don't want to be awkward," Gantry said, "but I take leave to ask why the hell we're being mewed up in this interminable and intolerable fashion."

He used what was known in the theatre as the Terrifying Tone. He moved towards Alleyn, who was almost his own height.

"This room," Bertie faintly complained as he opened his eyes, "would appear to be inhabited by angry giants."

"You're being mewed up," Alleyn said with some evidence of toughness, "because of death. Death, for your information, with what are known as unexplained features. I don't know how much longer you'll be here. If you're hungry, we shall arrange for food to be sent in. If you're stuffy, you may walk in the garden. If you want to talk, you may use the telephone, and the usual offices are last on the right at the far end of the hall."

There was an appreciable pause.

"And the worst of it is, Timmy angel," Bertie said, "you can't tell him the casting's gone wrong and you'll let him know if he's wanted."

Pinky was staring at Alleyn. "I never," she muttered, "could have thought to see the day."

There can be no dictator whose discomfiture will not bring some slight degree of pleasure, to his most ardent disciples. Bertie and Pinky, involuntarily, had given this reaction. There was a suggestion of repressed glee.

Gantry gave them the sort of look he would have thrown at an inattentive actor. They made their faces blank.

He drew in his breath. "So be it," he said. "One submits. Naturally. Perhaps one would prefer to know a little more, but elucidation is evidently *not* an ingredient of the Yardly mystique."

From his ramrod station inside the door, Warrender said, "Foul Play. What it amounts to. They're suggesting foul play."

"Oh my God!" cried Pinky and Bertie in unison. They turned sheet-white and began to talk at the tops of their voices. Fox took out his notebook.

Alleyn raised his hand and they petered out. "It doesn't," he said crossly, "amount to anything of the sort. The situation is precisely as I have tried to define it. There are unexplained discrepancies. They may add up to accident, suicide or homicide, and I know no better than any one of you what the answer will be. And now, if you please, we will try to arrive at a few possibly unimportant facts."

To his surprise he found himself supported.

Timon Gantry said, "We're being emotional and tedious. Pay no attention. Your facts?"

Alleyn said patiently, "Without any overtones or suggestions of criminal intention, I would rather like to trace exactly the movements of the group of people who were in conversation with Miss Bellamy during the last ten minutes or so of her life. You have all heard, *ad nauseam*, I daresay, of police routine. This is an example of it. I know you were all with her in the conservatory. I know each one of you, before the climax of her party, came out into the hall with the intention, Colonel Warrender tells me, of saying goodbye to two comparative strangers, who for some reason that has not yet been divulged, were leaving just before this climax. Among you was Mr. Richard Dakers, Miss Bellamy's ward. Mr. Dakers left the house on the heels of those two guests. His reason for doing so may well be personal and, from my point of view, completely uninteresting. *But I've got to clear him up*. Now, then. Any of you know why they left and why he left?"

"Certainly," Gantry said promptly. "He's catched with Anelida Lee. No doubt he wanted to see more of her."

"At that juncture? All right!" Alleyn added quickly. "We leave that one, do we? We take it that there was nothing remarkable about Octavius Browne and his niece sweeping out of the party, do we, and that it was the most natural thing in the world for Miss Bellamy's ward to turn his back on her and follow them? Do we? Or do we?"

"Oh Lord, Lord, *Lord*!" Bertie wavered. "The way you put things."

Pinky said, "I *did* hear the uncle remind her that they had to leave early."

"Did he say why?"

"No."

"Had any of you met them before?"

Silence.

"None of you? Why did you all feel it necessary to go into

the hall to say goodbye to them?"

Pinky and Bertie looked at each other out of the corners of their eyes and Warrender cleared his throat. Gantry appeared to come to a decision.

"I don't usually discuss this sort of thing outside the theatre," he said, "but under the circumstances I suppose I'd better tell you. I've decided to hear Miss Lee read the leading role in..." he hesitated fractionally, "in a new play."

"Really? Wonderful luck for her," Alleyn said. "What play?"

"*Oops!*" Bertie said involuntarily.

"It's called *Husbandry in Heaven*."

"By...?"

Warrender barked, "Does it matter?"

"Not that I know," Alleyn murmured. "Why should it? Let's find out."

Pinky said boldly, "I don't see a bit why it should matter. We all heard about it."

"Did you?" Alleyn asked. "When? At the party?"

She blushed scarlet. "Yes. It was mentioned there."

"In the conservatory?"

Bertie said in a hurry, "Mentioned. Just mentioned."

"And we haven't had the author's name yet, have we?"

Pinky said, "It's a new play by Dicky Dakers, isn't it, Timmy?"

"Yes, dear," Gantry agreed and refrained with some difficulty, Alleyn thought, from casting his eyes up to heaven. "In the hall I had a word with her about reading the part for me," he said.

"Right. And," Alleyn pursued, "might that not explain why Dakers also wanted to have a further word with Miss Lee?"

They agreed feverishly.

"Strange," he continued, "that this explanation didn't occur to any of you."

Bertie laughed musically. "Weren't we sillies?" he asked. "Fancy!"

"Perhaps you *all* hurtled into the hall in order to offer your congratulations to Miss Lee?"

"That's right!" Bertie cried, opening his eyes very wide.

"So we did! And anyway," he added, "I wanted the loo. That was really why I came out. Anything else was purely incidental. I'd forgotten."

"Well," Alleyn remarked, "since you're all so bad at remembering your motives I suppose I'd better go on cooking them up for you."

Pinky Cavendish made a quick expostulatory movement with her hands. "Yes?" Alleyn asked her. "What is it?"

"Nothing. Not really. Only—I wish you wouldn't make one feel shabby," Pinky said.

"Do I? I'm sorry about that."

"Look!" she said. "We're all of us shocked and horrified about Mary. She was our friend—a great friend. No, Timmy, please let me. She was tricky and temperamental and exacting and she said and did things that we'd rather forget about now. The important thing to remember is that one way or another, at one time or another, we've all loved her. You couldn't help it," Pinky said, "or I couldn't. Perhaps I should only speak for myself."

Alleyn asked gently, "Are you trying to tell me that you are protecting her memory?"

"You might put it like that," Pinky said.

"Nonsense, dear," Gantry said impatiently. "It doesn't arise."

Alleyn decided to dig a little further.

"The farewells being accomplished," he said, "and the two guests departed, what did you all do? Miss Cavendish?"

"Oh dear! What *did* I do? I know! I tried to nip upstairs, but the camera men were all over the bottom steps so I returned to the party."

"Mr. Saracen?"

"The gents. Downstairs. Last, as you've observed, on the right. Then I beetled back, bright as a button, for the speeches."

"Mr. Gantry?"

"I returned to the drawing-room, heard the speeches, and helped Templeton clear the way for the..." he jibbed for a moment, "for what would have been the last scene. The opening of the presents."

"Colonel Warrender?"

Warrender was staring at some part of the wall above Alleyn's head. "Went back," he said.

"Where?"

"To the party."

"Oo!" Bertie said.

"Yes, Mr. Saracen?"

"Nothing," Bertie said hurriedly. "Pay no attention."

Alleyn looked round at them all. "Tell me," he said, "hasn't Richard Dakers, up till now, written his plays exclusively for Miss Bellamy? Light comedies? *Husbandry in Heaven* doesn't suggest a light comedy."

He knew by their silence that he had struck home. Pinky's face alone would have told him as much. It was already too late when Warrender said defensively, "No need to put all his eggs in one basket, isn't it?"

"Exactly," Gantry agreed.

"Did Miss Bellamy hold this view?"

"I still fail to understand . . ." Warrender began, but Bertie Saracen cried out in a sort of rage:

"I really *don't* see, I don't for the *life* of me see why we should fiddle and fuss and fabricate. Honestly! It's all very well to be nice about poor Mary's memory and Dicky's dilemma and everybody madly loving everybody else, but sooner or later Mr. Alleyn's going to find out and then we'll all look peculiar and I for one *won't* and I'm sorry, Timmy, but I'm going to spill beans and unbag cats galore and announce in a ringing head tone that Mary minded like *hell* and that she made a scene in the conservatory and insulted the girl and Dicky left in a rage and why not, because suppose somebody *did* do something frightful to Mary, it couldn't be Dicky because Dicky flounced out of the house while Mary was still fighting fit and cutting her cake. And one other thing. I don't know why Colonel Warrender should go all cagey and everything but he didn't go straight back to the party. He went out. At the front door. I *saw* him on my way back from the loo. Now then!"

He had got to his feet and stood there, blinking, but defiant.

Gantry said, "*Oh*, well!" and flung up his hands.

Pinky said, "I'm on Bertie's side."

But Warrender, purple in the face, advanced upon Bertie.

"Don't touch me!" Bertie shouted angrily.

"You little rat!" Warrender said and seized his arm.

Bertie gave an involuntary giggle. "That's what she called me," he said.

"Take," Warrender continued between his teeth, "that damned impertinent grin off your face and hold your tongue, sir, or by God I'll give you something to make you."

He grasped Bertie with his left hand. He had actually drawn back his right and Alleyn had moved in, when a voice from the door said: *"Will somebody be good enough to tell me what goes on in this house?"*

Warrender lowered his hand and let Bertie go, Gantry uttered a short oath and Pinky, a stifled cry. Alleyn turned.

A young man with a white face and distracted air confronted him in the doorway.

"Thank God!" Bertie cried. "Dicky!"

chapter five

Questions of Adherence

THE MOST NOTICEABLE thing about Richard Dakers was his agitation. He was pale, his face was drawn and his hands were unsteady. During the complete silence that followed Bertie's ejaculation, Richard stood where he was, his gaze fixed with extraordinary concentration upon Colonel Warrender. Warrender, in his turn, looked at him with, as far as his soldierly blueprint of a face could express anything, the same kind of startled attention. In a crazy sort of way, each might have been the reflection of the other.

Warrender said, "Can I have a word with you, old boy? Shall we...?"

"No!" Richard said quickly and then, "I'm sorry. I don't understand. What's that dammed bobby doing in the hall? What's happened? Where's everybody? Where's Mary?"

Alleyn said, "One moment," and went to him. "You're Mr. Richard Dakers, aren't you? I'm from Scotland Yard—Alleyn.... At the moment I'm in charge of a police inquiry here. Shall we find somewhere where I can tell you why?"

"I'll tell him," Warrender said.

"I think not," Alleyn rejoined and opened the door. "Come along," he said and looked at the others. "You will stay here, if you please."

Richard put his hand to his head. "Yes. All right. But—why?" Perhaps out of force of habit he turned to Timon Gantry. "Timmy?" he said. "What *is* this?"

Gantry said, "We must accept authority, Dicky. Go with him."

Richard stared at him in amazement and walked out of the room, followed by Alleyn and Fox.

"In here, shall we?" Alleyn suggested and led the way into the deserted drawing-room.

There, he told Richard, as briefly as possible and without emphasis, what had happened. Richard listened distractedly, making no interruption but once or twice wiping his hand over his face as if a cobweb lay across it. When Alleyn had finished he said haltingly, "Mary? It's happened to Mary? How can I possibly believe it?"

"It is hard, isn't it?"

"But—*how*? How did it happen? With the plant spray?"

"It seems so."

"But she's used it over and over again. For a long time. Why did it happen now?" He had the air, often observable in people who have suffered a shock, of picking over the surface of the matter and distractedly examining the first thing he came upon. "Why now?" he repeated and appeared scarcely to attend to the answer.

"That's one of the things we've got to find out."

"Of course," Richard said, more, it seemed, to himself than to Alleyn, "it *is* dangerous. We were always telling her." He shook his head impatiently. "But—I don't see—she went to her room just after the speeches and . . ."

"Did she? How do you know?"

Richard said quickly, "Why because . . ." and then, if possible, turned whiter than he had been before. He looked desperately at Alleyn, seemed to hover on the edge of an outburst and then said, "She must have. You say she was found there."

"Yes. She was found there."

"But why? Why would she use the plant spray at that moment? It sounds so crazy."

"I know. Very strange."

Richard beat his hands together. "I'm sorry," he said, "I can't get hold of myself. I'm sorry."

Looking at him, Alleyn knew that he was in that particular state of emotional unbalance when he would be most vulnerable to pressure. He was a nice-looking chap, Alleyn thought. It was a sensitive face and yet, obscurely, it reminded him of one much less sensitive. But whose?

He said, "You yourself have noticed two aspects of this tragic business that are difficult to explain. Because of them and because of normal police procedure I have to check as fully as possible the circumstances surrounding the event."

"Do you?" Richard asked vaguely and then seemed to pull himself together. "Yes. Very well. What circumstances?"

"I'm told you left the house before the birthday speeches. Is that right?"

Unlike the others, Richard appeared to feel no resentment or suspicion. "I?" he said. "Oh, yes, I think I did. I don't think they'd started. The cake had just been taken in."

"Why did you leave, Mr. Dakers?"

"I wanted to talk to Anelida," he said at once and then: "Sorry. You wouldn't know. Anelida Lee. She lives next door and . . ." He stopped.

"I do know that Miss Lee left early with her uncle. But it must have been a very important discussion, mustn't it? To take you away at that juncture?"

"Yes. It was. To me. It was private," Richard added. "A private matter."

"A long discussion?"

"It didn't happen."

"Not?"

"She wasn't—available." He produced a palpable understatement. "She wasn't—feeling well."

"You saw her uncle?"

"Yes."

"Was it about her part in your play—*Husbandry in Heaven*, isn't it?—that you wanted to talk to her?"

Richard stared at him and for the first time seemed to take

alarm. "Who told you about that?" he demanded.

"Timon Gantry."

"*He* did!" Richard exclaimed and then, as if nothing could compete with the one overriding shock, added perfunctorily, "How extraordinary." But he was watching Alleyn now with a new awareness. "It was partly to do with that," he muttered.

Alleyn decided to fire point-blank. "Was Miss Bellamy displeased with the plans for this new play?" he asked. Richard's hands made a sharp involuntary movement which was at once checked. His voice shook.

"I told you this was a private matter," he said. "It is entirely private."

"I'm afraid there is very little room for privacy in a police inquiry."

Richard surprised him by suddenly crying out, "*You think she did it herself!* She didn't! I can't believe it! Never!"

"Is there any reason why she should?"

"No! My God, no! *No!*"

Alleyn waited for a little, visited, as was not unusual with him, by a distaste for this particular aspect of his job.

He said, "What did you do when Miss Lee couldn't receive you?"

Richard moved away from him, his hands thrust down in his pockets. "I went for a walk," he said.

"Now, look here," Alleyn said, "you must see that this is a very odd story. Your guardian, as I believe Miss Bellamy was, reaches the top moment of her birthday party. You leave her cold, first in pursuit of Miss Lee and then to go for a stroll round Chelsea. Are you telling me that you've been strolling ever since?"

Without turning, Richard nodded.

Alleyn walked round him and looked him full in the face.

"Mr. Dakers," he said. "Is that the truth? It's now five to nine. Do you give me your word that from about seven o'clock when you left this house you didn't return to it until you came in, ten minutes ago?"

Richard, looking desperately troubled, waited for so long that to Alleyn the scene became quite unreal. The two of them were fixed in the hiatus-like figures in a suspended film sequence.

"Are you going to give me an answer?" Alleyn said at last.

"I—I—don't—think—I did actually—just after—she was..." A look of profound astonishment came into Richard's face. He crumpled into a faint at Alleyn's feet.

2

"He'll do," Dr. Harkness said, relinquishing Richard's pulse. He straightened up and winced a little in the process. "You say he's been walking about on an empty stomach and two or three drinks. The shock coming on top of it did the trick for him, I expect. In half an hour he won't be feeling any worse than I do and that's medium to bloody awful. Here he comes."

Richard had opened his eyes. He stared at Dr. Harkness and then frowned. "Lord, I'm sorry," he said. "I passed out, didn't I?"

"You're all right," Dr. Harkness said. "Where's this sal volatile, Gracefield?"

Gracefield presented it on a tray. Richard drank it down and let his head fall back. They had put him on a sofa there in the drawing-room. "I was talking to somebody," he said. "That man—God, yes! Oh God."

"It's all right," Alleyn said, "I won't worry you. We'll leave you to yourself for a bit."

He saw Richard's eyes dilate. He was looking past Alleyn towards the door. "Yes," he said loudly. "I'd rather be alone."

"What is all this?"

It was Warrender. He shut the door behind him and went quickly to the sofa. "What the devil have you done to him? Dicky, old boy..."

"No!" Richard said with exactly the same inflexion as before. Warrender stood above him. For a moment, apparently, they looked at each other. Then Richard said, "I forgot that letter you gave me to post. I'm sorry."

Alleyn and Fox moved, but Warrender anticipated them, stooping over Richard and screening him.

"If you don't mind," Richard said, "I'd rather be by myself. I'm all right."

"And I'm afraid," Alleyn pointed out, "that I must remind

you of instructions, Colonel Warrender. I asked you to stay with the others. Will you please go back to them?"

Warrender stood like a rock for a second or two and then, without another word, walked out of the room. On a look from Alleyn, Fox followed him.

"We'll leave you," Alleyn said. "Don't get up."

"No," Dr. Harkness said. "Don't. I'll ask them to send you in a cup of tea. Where's that old Nanny of yours? She can make herself useful. Can you find her, Gracefield?"

"Very good, sir," Gracefield said.

Alleyn, coolly picking up Richard's dispatch case, followed Gracefield into the hall.

"Gracefield."

Gracefield, frigid, came to a halt.

"I want one word with you. I expect this business has completely disorganized your household and I'm afraid it can't be helped. But I think it may make things a little easier in your department if you know what the form will be."

"Indeed, sir?"

"In a little while a mortuary van will come. It will be better if we keep everybody out of the way at that time. I don't want to worry Mr. Templeton more than I can help, but I shall have to interview people and it would suit us all if we could find some place that would serve as an office for the purpose. Is that possible?"

"There is Mr. Richard's old study, sir, on the first floor. It is unoccupied."

"Splendid. Where exactly?"

"The third on the right along the passage, sir."

"Good." Alleyn glanced at the pallid and impassive face. "For your information," he said, "it's a matter of clearing up the confusion that unfortunately always follows accidents of this sort. The further we can get, now, the less publicity at the inquest. You understand?"

"Quite so, sir," said Gracefield with a slight easing of manner.

"Very well. And I'm sorry you'll be put to so much trouble."

Gracefield's hand curved in classic acceptance. There was a faint crackle.

"Thank you, Gracefield."

"Thank you very much, sir," said Gracefield. "I will inform Mrs. Plumtree and then ascertain if your room is in order." He inclined his head and mounted the stairs.

Alleyn raised a finger and the constable by the front door came to him.

"What happened," he asked, "about Mr. Dakers? As quick and complete as you can."

"He arrived, sir, about three minutes after you left your instructions, according to which I asked for his name and let on it was because of an accident. He took it up it was something about a car. He didn't seem to pay much attention. He was very excited and upset. He went upstairs and was there about eight to ten minutes. You and Mr. Fox were with the two gentlemen and the lady in that little room, sir. When he came down he had a case in his hand. He went to the door to go out and I advised him it couldn't be done. He still seemed very upset, sir, and that made him more so. He said, 'Good God, what is all this?' and went straight to the room where you were, sir."

"Good. Thank you. Keep going."

"Sir," said the constable.

"And Philpott."

"Sir?"

"We've sent for another man. In the meantime I don't want any of the visitors in the house moving about from room to room. Get them all together in the drawing-room and keep them there, including Colonel Warrender and Mr. Templeton, if he's feeling fit enough. Mr. Dakers can stay where he is. Put the new man on the door and you keep observation in the dining-room. We can't do anything about the lavatory, I suppose, but everywhere else had better be out of bounds. If Colonel Warrender wants to go to the lavatory, you go with him."

"Sir."

"And ask Mr. Fox to join me upstairs."

The constable moved off.

A heavy thumping announced the descent of Old Ninn. She came down one step at a time. When she got to the bottom of the stairs and saw Alleyn she gave him a look and continued on her way. Her face was flaming and her mouth drawn down. For a small person she emanated an astonishingly heavy aura of the grape.

"Mrs. Plumtree?" Alleyn asked.

"Yes," said Old Ninn. She halted and looked into his face. Her eyes, surprisingly, were tragic.

"You're going to look after Mr. Richard, aren't you?"

"What's he been doing to himself?" she asked, as if Richard had been playing roughly and had barked his knee.

"He fainted. The doctor thinks it was shock."

"Always takes things to heart," Old Ninn said.

"Did you bring him up?"

"From three months." She continued to look fixedly at Alleyn. "He was a good child," she said, as if he was abusing Richard, "and he's grown into a good man. No harm in him and never was."

"An orphan?" Alleyn ventured.

"Father and mother killed in a motor accident."

"How very sad."

"You don't," Old Ninn said, "feel the want of what you've never had."

"And of course Miss Bellamy—Mrs. Templeton—took him over."

"She," Old Ninn said, "was a different type of child altogether. If you'll excuse me I'll see what ails him." But she didn't move at once. She said very loudly, "Whatever it is it'll be no discredit to him," and then stumped heavily and purposefully on to her charge.

Alleyn waited for a moment, savouring her observations. There has been one rather suggestive remark, he thought.

Dr. Harkness came out of the drawing-room, looking very wan.

"He's all right," he said, "and I wish I could say as much for myself. The secondary effects of alcoholic indulgence are the least supportable. By the way, can I go out to the car for my bag? It's just opposite the house. Charles Templeton's my patient, you know, and I'd like to run him over. Just in case. He's had a bad knock over this."

"Yes, of course," Alleyn said and nodded to the constable

108

at the door. "Before you go, though—was Mrs. Templeton your patient too?"

"She was," Harkness agreed and looked wary.

"Would you have expected anything like this? Supposing it to be a case of suicide?"

"No. I wouldn't."

"Not subject to fits of depression? No morbid tendencies? Nothing like that?"

Harkness looked at his hands. "It wasn't an equable disposition," he said carefully. "Far from it. She had 'nervous' spells. The famous theatrical temperament, you know."

"No more than that?" Alleyn persisted.

"Well—I don't like discussing my patients and never do, of course, but..."

"I think you may say the circumstances warrant it."

"I suppose so. As a matter of fact I have been a bit concerned. The temperaments had become pretty frequent and increasingly violent. Hysteria, really. Partly the time of life, but she was getting over that. There was some occasion for anxiety. One or two little danger signals. One was keeping an eye on her. But nothing suicidal. On the contrary. What's more, you can take my word for it she was the last woman on earth to disfigure herself. The last."

"Yes," Alleyn said. "That's a point, isn't it? I'll see you later."

"I suppose you will," Harkness said disconsolately, and Alleyn went upstairs. He found that Miss Bellamy's room now had the familiar look of any area given over to police investigation: something between an improvised laboratory and a photographer's studio with its focal point that unmistakable sheeted form on the floor.

Dr. Curtis, the police surgeon, had finished his examination of the body. Sergeant Bailey squatted on the bathroom floor employing the tools of his trade upon the tinsel picture, and as Alleyn came in, Sergeant Thompson, whistling between his teeth, uncovered Mary Bellamy's terrible face and advanced his camera to within a few inches of it. The bulb flashed.

Fox was seated at the dressing-table completing his notes.

"Well, Dr. Curtis?" Alleyn asked.

"Well, now," Curtis said. "It's quite a little problem, you know. I can't see a verdict of accident, Alleyn, unless the coroner accepts the idea of her presenting this spray-gun thing at her own face and pumping away like mad at it to see how it works. The face is pretty well covered with the stuff. It's in the nostrils and mouth and all over the chest and dress."

"Suicide?"

"I don't see it. Have to be an uncommon determined effort. Any motive?"

"Not so far, unless you count a suspected bout of tantrums, but I don't yet know about that. I don't see it, either. Which leaves us with homicide. See here, Curtis. Suppose I picked up that tin of Slaypest, pointed it at you and fell to work on the spray-gun—what'd you do?"

"Dodge."

"And if I chased you up?"

"Either collar you low or knock it out of your hands or bolt, yelling blue murder."

"Exactly. But wouldn't the immediate reaction, particularly in a woman, be to throw up her arms and hide her face?"

"I think it might, certainly. Yes."

"Yes," said Fox, glancing up from his notes.

"It wasn't hers. There's next to nothing on the hands and arms. And look," Alleyn went on, "at the actual character of the spray. Some of it's fine, as if delivered from a distance. Some, on the contrary, is so coarse that it's run down in streaks. Where's the answer to that one?"

"I don't know," said Dr. Curtis.

"How long would it take to kill her?"

"Depends on the strength. This stuff is highly concentrated. Hexa-ethyl-tetra-phosphate of which the deadly ingredient is TEPP: tetra-ethyl-pyro-phosphate. Broken down, I'd say, with some vehicle to reduce the viscosity. The nozzle's a very fine job: designed for indoor use. In my opinion the stuff shouldn't be let loose on the market. If she got some in the mouth, and it's evident she did, it might only be a matter of minutes. Some recorded cases mention nausea and convulsions. In others, the subject has dropped down insensible and died a few seconds later."

Fox said, "When the woman—Florence—found her, she was on the floor in what Florence describes as a sort of fit."

"I'll see Florence next," Alleyn said.

"And when Dr. Harkness and Mr. Templeton arrived she was dead," Fox concluded.

"Where *is* Harkness?" Dr. Curtis demanded. "He's pretty damn casual, isn't he? He ought to have shown up at once."

"He was flat-out with a hangover among the exotics in the conservatory," Alleyn said. "I stirred him up to look at Mr. Richard Dakers, who was in a great tizzy before he knew there was anything to have a tizzy about. When I talked to him he fainted."

"What a mob!" Curtis commented in disgust.

"Curtis, if you've finished here I think you'll find your colleague in reasonably working order downstairs."

"He'd better be. Everything is fixed now. I'll do the p.m. tonight."

"Good. Fox, you and I had better press on. We've got an office. Third on the right from here."

They found Gracefield outside the door looking scandalized.

"I'm very sorry, I'm sure, sir," he said, "but the keys on this landing appear to have been removed. If you require to lock up . . ."

"'T, 't!" Fox said and dived in his pocket. "Thoughtless of me! Try this one."

Gracefield coldly accepted it. He showed Alleyn into a small pleasantly furnished study and left Fox to look after himself, which he did very comfortably.

"Will there be anything further, sir?" Gracefield asked Alleyn.

"Nothing. This will do admirably."

"Thank you, sir."

"Here," Fox said, "are the other keys. They're interchangeable, which is why I took the liberty of removing them."

Gracefield received them without comment and retired.

"I always seem to hit it off better," Fox remarked, "with the female servants."

"No doubt they respond more readily to your unbridled body-urge," said Alleyn.

"That's one way of putting it, Mr. Alleyn," Fox primly conceded.

"And the other is that I tipped that antarctic monument. Never mind. You'll have full play in a minute with Florence. Take a look at this room. It was Mr. Richard Dakers's study. I suppose he now inhabits a bachelor flat somewhere, but he was adopted and brought up by the Templetons. Here you have his boyhood, adolescence and early maturity in microcosm. The usual school groups on one wall. Note the early dramatic interest. On the other three, his later progress. O.U.D.S. Signed photographs of lesser lights succeeded by signed photographs of greater ones. Sketches from unknown designers followed by the full treatment from famous designers and topped up by Saracen. The last is for a production that opened three years ago and closed last week. Programme of Command Performance. Several framed photographs of Miss Mary Bellamy, signed with vociferous devotion. One small photograph of Mr. Charles Templeton. A calender on the desk to support the theory that he left the house a year ago. Books from E. Nesbit to Samuel Beckett. *Who's Who in the Theatre* and *Spotlight* and cast an eye at this one, will you?"

He pulled out a book and showed it to Fox. "*Handbook of Poisons by a Medical Practitioner*. Bookplate: '*Ex Libris* C. H. Templeton.' Let's see if the medical practitioner has anything to say about pest killers. Here we are. Poisons of Vegetable Origin. Tobacco. Alkaloid of." He read for a moment or two. "Rather scanty. Only one case quoted. Gentleman who swallowed nicotine from a bottle and died quietly in thirty seconds after heaving a deep sigh. Warnings about agricultural use of. And here are the newer concoctions including HETP and TEPP. Exceedingly deadly and to be handled with the greatest care. Ah, well!"

He replaced the book.

"That'll be the husband's," Fox said. "Judging by the bookplate."

"The husband's. Borrowed by the ward and accessible to all and sundry. For what it's worth. Well, Foxkin, that about completes our tour of the room. Tabloid history of the tastes and career of Richard Dakers. Hullo! Look here, Fox."

He was stooping over the writing desk and had opened the blotter.

"This looks fresh," he said. "Green ink. Ink on desk dried up and anyway, blue."

There was a small Georgian glass above the fireplace. Alleyn held the blotting-paper to it and they looked at the reflected image:

"I e ck to y at it w u d e o se my te ding I n't n ven a rible shock that I tget t rted t tl'm sure t ll e ter if we do t me t. l c t hin clea now ut at ast I now. I'll n for e your tr ment of An d this after on I ould ave been told everything from the beginning. R."

Alleyn copied this fragmentary message on a second sheet of paper, carried the blotter back to the desk and very carefully removed the sheet in question.

"We'll put the experts on to this," he said, "but I'm prepared to take a sporting chance on the result, Br'er Fox. Are you?"

"I'd give it a go, Mr. Alleyn."

"See if you can find Florence, will you? I'll take a flying jump while you're at it."

Fox went out. Alleyn put his copy of the message on the desk and looked at it.

The correct method of deciphering and completing a blotting-paper impression is by measurement, calculation and elimination but occasionally, for persons with a knack, the missing letters start up vividly in the mind and the scientific method is thus accurately anticipated. When he was on his game, Alleyn possessed this knack and he now made use of it. Without allowing himself any second thoughts, he wrote rapidly within the copy and stared with disfavour at the result. He then opened Richard Daker's dispatch case and found it contained a typescript of a play, *Husbandry in*

Heaven. He flipped the pages over and came across some alterations in green ink and in the same hand as the letter.

"Miss Florence Johnson," said Fox, opening the door and standing aside with something of the air of a large sporting dog retrieving a bird. Florence, looking not unlike an apprehensive fowl, came in.

Alleyn saw an unshapely little woman, with a pallid, tear-stained face and hair so remorselessly dyed that it might have been a raven wig. She wore that particular air of disillusionment that is associated with the Cockney and she reeked of backstage.

"The Superintendent," Fox told her, "just wants to hear the whole story like you told it to me. Nothing to worry about."

"Of course not," Alleyn said. "Come and sit down. We won't keep you long."

Florence looked as if she might prefer to stand, but compromised by sitting on the edge of the chair Fox had pushed forward.

"This has been a sad business for you," Alleyn said.

"That's right," Florence said woodenly.

"And I'm sure you must want to have the whole thing cleared up as soon and as quietly as possible."

"Clear enough, isn't it? She's dead. You can't have it much clearer than that."

"You can't indeed. But you see it's our job to find out why."

"Short of seeing it happen you wouldn't get much nearer, would you? If you can read, that is."

"You mean the tin of Slaypest?"

"Well, it wasn't perfume," Florence said impertinently. "They put that in bottles." She shot a glance at Alleyn and seemed to undergo a slight change of temper. Her lips trembled and she compressed them. "It wasn't all that pleasant," she said. "Seeing what I seen. Finding her like that. You'd think I might be let alone."

"So you will be if you behave like a sensible girl. You've been with her a long time, haven't you?"

"Thirty years, near enough."

"You must have got along very well to have stayed together all that time."

Florence didn't answer and he waited. At last she said, "I knew her ways."

"And you were fond of her?"

"She was all right. Others might have their own ideas. I knew 'er. Inside out. She'd talk to me like she wouldn't to others. She was all right."

It was, Alleyn thought, after its fashion, a tribute.

He said, "Florence, I'm going to be very frank indeed with you. Suppose it wasn't an accident. You'd want to know, wouldn't you?"

"It's no good you thinking she did it deliberate. She never! Not she. Wouldn't."

"I didn't mean suicide."

Florence watched him for a moment. Her mouth, casually but emphatically painted, narrowed into a scarlet thread.

"If you mean murder," she said flatly, "that's different."

"You'd want to know," he repeated. "Wouldn't you?"

The tip of her tongue showed for a moment in the corner of her mouth. "That's right," she said.

"So do we. Now, Inspector Fox has already asked you about this, but never mind, I'm asking you again. I want you to tell me in as much detail as you can remember just what happened from the time when Miss Bellamy dressed for her party up to the time you entered her room and found her—as you did find her. Let's start with the preparations, shall we?"

She was a difficult subject. She seemed to be filled with some kind of resentment and everything had to be dragged out of her. After luncheon, it appeared, Miss Bellamy rested. At half-past four Florence went in to her. She seemed to be "much as usual."

"She hadn't been upset by anything during the day?"

"Nothing," Florence muttered, after a further silence, "to matter."

"I only ask," Alleyn said, "because there's a bottle of sal volatile left out in the bathroom. Did you give her sal volatile at any stage?"

"This morning."

"What was the matter, this morning? Was she faint?"

Florence said, "Overexcited."

"About what?"

"I couldn't say," Florence said, and shut her mouth like a trap.

"Very well," he said patiently. "Let's get on with the preparation for the party. Did you give her a facial treatment of some kind?"

She stared at him. "That's correct," she said. "A mask."

"What did she talk about, Florence?"

"Nothing. You don't with that stuff over your face. Can't."

"And then."

"She make up and dressed. The two gentlemen came in and I went out."

"That would be Mr. Templeton and—who?"

"The Colonel."

"Did either of them bring her Parma violets?"

She stared at him. "Vi'lets? Them? No. She didn't like vi'lets."

"There's a bunch on her dressing-table."

"I never noticed," she said. "I don't know anything about vi'lets. There wasn't any when I left the room."

"And you saw her again—when?"

"At the party."

"Well, let's hear about it."

For a second or two he thought she was going to keep mum. She had the least eloquent face he had ever seen. But she began to speak as if somebody had switched her on. She said that from the time she left her mistress and during the early part of the cocktail party she had been with Mrs. Plumtree in their little sitting room. When the gong sounded they went down to take their places in the procession. After the speeches were over Old Ninn had dropped her awful brick about candles. Florence recounted the incident with detachment, merely observing that Old Ninn was, in fact, very old and sometimes forgot herself. "Fifty candles," Florence said grimly. "What a remark to pass!" It was the only piece of comment, so far, that she had proffered. She had realized, Alleyn gathered, that her mistress had been upset and thinking she might be wanted had gone into the hall. She heard her mistress speak for a moment to Mr. Templeton, something about him asking her not to use her scent. Up to here Florence's statement had been about as emotional as a grocery list, but at this point she appeared to boggle. She looked sideways at Alleyn, seemed to lose her bearings and came to a stop.

Alleyn said, "That's all perfectly clear so far. Then did Miss Bellamy and the nanny—Mrs. Plumtree, isn't it?—go upstairs together?"

Florence, blankly staring, said, "No."

"They didn't? What happened exactly?"

Ninn, it appeared, had gone first.

"Why? What delayed Miss Bellamy?"

"A photographer come butting in."

"He took a photograph of her, did he?"

"That's right. By the front door."

"Alone?"

"*He* came in. The chap wanted him in too."

"Who?"

Her hands ground together in her lap. After waiting for a moment he asked, "Don't you want to answer that one?"

"I want to know," Florence burst out, "if it's murder. If it's murder I don't care who it was, I want to see 'er righted. Never mind who! You can be mistaken in people, as I often told her. Them you think nearest and dearest are likely as not the ones that you didn't ought to trust. What I told her. Often and often."

How vindictive, Alleyn wondered, was Florence? Of what character, precisely, was her relationship with her mistress? She was looking at him now, guardedly but with a kind of arrogance. "What I want to know," she repeated, "is it murder?"

He said, "I believe it may be."

She muttered, "You ought to know: being trained to it. They tell you the coppers always know."

From what background had Florence emerged nearly thirty years ago into Miss Bellamy's dressing-room? She was speaking now like a Bermondsey girl. Fly and wary. Her voice, hitherto negative and respectable, had ripened into strong Cockney.

Alleyn decided to take a long shot. He said, "I expect you know Mr. Richard Dakers very well, don't you?"

"Hardly help meself, could I?"

"No, indeed. He was more like a son than a ward to her, I daresay."

Florence stared at him out of two eyes that closely resembled, and were about as eloquent as, boot-buttons.

"Acted like it," she said. "If getting nothing but the best goes for anything. And taking it as if it was 'is right."

"Well," Alleyn said lightly, "he's repaid her with two very successful plays, hasn't he?"

"Them! What'd they have been without her? See another actress in the lead! Oh dear! What a change! She *made* them, he couldn't have touched it on 'is own. She'd have breathed life into a corpse," Florence said and then looked sick.

Alleyn said, "Mr. Dakers left the house before the speeches, I understand?"

"He did. What a way to behave!"

"But he came back, didn't he?"

"He's back now," she said quickly. "You seen 'im, didn't you?" Gracefield, evidently, had talked.

"I don't mean now. I mean between the time he first left before the speeches and the time when he returned about half an hour ago. Wasn't there another visit in between?"

"That's right," she said under her breath.

"Before the birthday speech?"

"That's right."

"Take the moment we're discussing. Mrs. Plumtree had gone upstairs, Miss Bellamy was in the hall. You had come out to see if she needed you." He waited for a moment and then took his gamble. "Did he walk in at the front door? At that moment?"

He thought she was going to say "No"; she seemed to be struggling with some kind of doubt. Then she nodded.

"Did he speak to Miss Bellamy?" She nodded again.

"What about, do you know?"

"I didn't catch. I was at the other end of the hall."

"What happened then?"

"They were photographed and then they went upstairs."

"And you?"

"I went up. By the back stairs," said Florence.

"Where to?"

"I went along to the landing."

"And did you go in to her?"

"Mrs. Plumtree was on the landing," Florence said abruptly. Alleyn waited. "They was talking inside—him and the Lady. So I didn't disturb her."

"And you could hear them talking?"

She said angrily, "What say we could? We weren't snooping, if that's what you mean. We didn't hear a word. She laughed—once."

"And then?"

"He came out and went downstairs."

"And did you go in to Miss Bellamy?"

"No," Florence said loudly.

"Why not?"

"I didn't reckon she'd want me."

"But why?"

"I didn't reckon she would."

"Had you," he asked without emphasis, "had a row of some sort with Miss Bellamy?"

She went very white. "What are you getting at?" she demanded and then, "I told you. I understood her. Better than anyone."

"And there'd been no trouble between you?"

"No!" she said loudly.

He decided not to press this point. "So what did you do?" he asked. "You and Mrs. Plumtree?"

"Stayed where we was. Until..."

"Yes?"

"Until we heard something."

"What was that?"

"Inside her room. Something. Kind of a crash."

"What was it, do you think?"

"I wouldn't know. I was going in to see, whether or no, when I heard Mr. Templeton in the hall. Calling. I go down to the half-landing," Florence continued, changing her tense for the narrative present. "He calls up, they're waiting for her. So I go back to fetch her. And . . ." for the first time her voice trembled. "And I walk in."

"Yes," Alleyn said. "Before we go on, Florence, will you tell me this? Did Mr. Richard at this time seem at all upset?"

"That's right," she said, again with that air of defiance.

"When he arrived?" She nodded. "I see. And when he came out of Miss Bellamy's room?"

And now there was no mistaking Florence's tone. It was one of pure hatred.

" 'Im? 'E looked ghasterly. 'E looked," said Florence, "like death."

3

As if, by this one outburst, she had bestowed upon herself some kind of emotional bloodletting, Florence returned to her earlier manner—cagey, grudging, implicitly resentful. Alleyn could get no more from her about Richard Dakers's behaviour. When he suggested, obliquely, that perhaps Old Ninn might be more forthcoming, Florence let fall a solitary remark. "Her!" she said. "You won't get her to talk. Not about him!" and refused to elaborate.

He had learned to recognize the point at which persistence defeats its own end. He took her on to the time where she entered the bedroom and discovered her mistress. Here, Florence exhibited a characteristic attitude towards scenes of violence. It was, he thought, as if she recognized in her own fashion their epic value and was determined to do justice to the current example.

When she went into the room, Mary Bellamy was on her knees, her hands to her throat and her eyes starting. She had tried to speak but had succeeded only in making a terrible retching noise. Florence had attempted to raise her, to ask her what had happened, but her mistress, threshing about on the floor, had been as unresponsive to these ministrations as an animal in torment. Florence had thought she heard the word "doctor." Quite beside herself, she had rushed out of the room and downstairs. "Queer," she said. That was what she had felt. "Queer." It was "queer" that at such a moment she should concern herself with Miss Bellamy's nonappearance at her party. It was "queer" that a hackneyed theatre phrase should occur to her in such a crisis but it had and she remembered using it, "Is there a doctor in the house?" though, of course, she knew, really that Dr. Harkness was one of the guests. On the subject of Dr. Harkness she was violent.

"Him! Nice lot of help he give, I *don't* think! Silly with what he'd taken and knew it. Couldn't make up his mind where he was or what he was wanted for till the Colonel shoved ice down his neck. Even then he was stupid-like and had to be pushed upstairs. For all we know," Florence said, " 'e might of saved 'er. For all we know! But when 'e got there it was over and in my opinion 'e's got it on 'is conscience for the rest of 'is days. And that's no error. Dr. Harkness!"

Alleyn asked her to describe, in detail, the state of the room when she first went into it. She remembered nothing but her mistress and when he pressed her to try, he thought she merely drew on what she saw after she returned.

He said, "We've almost finished, but there's one question I must ask you. Do you know of anyone who had cause to wish for her death?"

She thought this over, warily. "There's plenty," she said, "that was jealous of her and there's some that acted treacherous. Some that called themselves friends."

"In the profession?" Alleyn ventured.

"Ah! Miss Kate Cavendish, who'd never have got further than Brighton Pier in the off-season without the Lady hadn't looked after 'er! Mr. Albert Smith, pardon the slip, I should of said Saracen. But for her 'e'd of stuck behind 'is counter in the Manchester department. Look what she done for them and how do they pay 'er back? Only this morning!"

"What happened this morning?"

"Sauce and treachery was what happened."

"That doesn't really answer my question, does it?"

She stood up. "It's all the answer you'll get. You know

your own business best, I suppose. But if she's been murdered, there's only one that had the chance. Why waste your time?"

"Only one?" Alleyn said. "Do you really think so?"

For the first time she looked frightened, but her answer was unexpected. "I don't want what I've said to go no further," she said with a look at Fox, who had been quietly taking notes. "I don't fancy being quoted, particularly in some quarters. There's some that'd turn very nasty if they knew what I said."

"Old Ninn?" Alleyn suggested. "For one?"

"Smart," Florence said with spirit, "aren't you? All right. Her for one. She's got her fancy like I had mine. Only mine," Florence said, and her voice was desolate, "mine's gone where it won't come back, and that's the difference." A spasm of something that might have been hatred crossed her face and she cried out with violence, "I'll never forgive her! Never. I'll be even with her no matter what comes out of it, see if I'm not. Clara Plumtree!"

"But what did she do?"

He thought she was going to jib, but suddenly it all came out. It had happened, she said, after the tragedy. Charles Templeton had been taken to his dressing-room and Ninn had appeared on the landing while Florence was taking him a hot bottle. Florence herself had been too agitated to tell her what had happened in any detail. She had given Mr. Templeton the bottle and left him. He was terribly distressed and wanted to be left alone. She had returned to the landing and seen Dr. Harkness and Timon Gantry come out of the bedroom and speak to Mrs. Plumtree, who had then gone into the dressing-room. Florence herself had been consumed with a single overwhelming desire.

"I wanted to see after *her*. I wanted to look after my Lady. I knew what she'd have liked me to do for her. The way they'd left her! The way she looked! I wasn't going to let them see her like that and take her away like that. I knew her better than anybody. She'd have wanted her old Floy to look after her."

She gave a harsh sob but went on very doggedly. She had

gone to the bedroom door and found it locked. This, Alleyn gathered, had roused a kind of fury in her. She had walked up and down the landing in an agony of frustration and had then remembered the communicating door between the bedroom and dressing-room. So she had stolen to the door from the landing into the dressing-room and had opened it very carefully, not wishing to disturb Mr. Templeton. She had found herself face to face with Mrs. Plumtree.

It must, Alleyn thought, have been an extraordinary scene. The two women had quarrelled in whispers. Florence had demanded to be allowed to go through into the bedroom. Mrs. Plumtree had refused. Then Florence had told her what she wanted to do.

"I told her! I told her I was the only one to lay my poor girl out and make her look more like herself. She said I couldn't. She said she wasn't to be touched by doctor's orders. *Doctor's orders!* I'd of pulled her away and gone through. I'd got me hands on 'er to do it, but it was too late."

She turned to Fox. "He'd come in. He was coming upstairs. She said, 'That's the police. D'you want to get yourself locked up?' I had to give over and I went to my room."

"I'm afraid she was right, Florence."

"*Are* you! That shows how much you know! *I* wasn't to touch the body! Me! Me, that loved her. All right! So what was Clara Plumtree doing in the bedroom? Now!"

"What!" Fox ejaculated. "In the bedroom? Mrs. Plumtree?"

"Ah!" Florence cried out in a kind of triumph. "Her! She'd been in there herself and let her try and deny it!"

Alleyn said, "How do you know she'd been in the bedroom?"

"How? Because I heard the tank filling and the basin tap running in the bathroom beyond. She'd been in there doing what it was my right to do. Laying her hands on my poor girl."

"But why do you suppose this? Why?"

Her lips trembled and she rubbed her hand across them. "*Why! Why!* I'll tell you why. Because she smelt of that scent.

123

Smelt of it, I tell you, so strong it would sicken you. So if you're going to lock anybody up, you can start on Clara Plumtree."

Her mouth twisted. Suddenly she burst into tears and blundered out of the room.

Fox shut the door after her and removed his spectacles. "A tartar," he observed.

"Yes," Alleyn agreed. "A faithful, treacherous, jealous, pig-headed tartar. You never know how they'll cut up in a crisis. Never. And I fancy, for our pains, we've got a brace of them in this party."

As if to confirm this opinion there was a heavy single bang on the door. It swung violently open and there, on the threshold, was Old Ninn Plumtree with P.C. Philpott, only less red-faced than herself, towering in close attendance.

"Lay a finger on me, young man," Old Ninn was saying, "and I'll make a public example of you."

"I'm sure I'm very sorry, sir," said Philpott. "The lady insists on seeing you and short of taking her in charge I don't seem to be able to prevent it."

"All right, Philpott," Alleyn said. "Come in, Ninn. Come in."

She did so. Fox resignedly shut the door. He put a chair behind Ninn, but she disregarded it. She faced Alleyn over her own folded arms. To look in his face she was obliged to tilt her own acutely backwards and in doing so gave out such an astonishingly potent effluvium that she might have been a miniature volcano smouldering with port and due to erupt. Her voice was sepulchral and her manner truculent.

"I fancied," she said, "I knew a gentleman when I saw one and I hope you're not going to be a disappointment. Don't answer me back. I prefer to form my own opinion."

Alleyn did not answer her back.

"That Floy," Old Ninn continued, "has been at you. A bad background, if ever there was one. What's bred in the child comes out in the woman. Don't believe a word of what she tells you. What's she been saying about the boy?"

"About Mr. Dakers?"

"Certainly. A man to you, seem he may; to me who knows

him inside out, he's a boy. Twenty-eight and famous, I daresay, but no more harm in him than there ever has been, which is never. Sensitive and fanciful, yes. Not practical, granted. Vicious, fiddle! Now. What's that Floy been putting about?"

"Nothing very terrible, Ninn."

"Did she say he was ungrateful? Or bad-mannered?"

"Well..."

"He's nothing of the sort. What else?"

Alleyn was silent. Old Ninn unfolded her arms. She laid a tiny gnarled paw on Alleyn's hand. "Tell me what else," she said, glaring into his face, "I've got to know. Tell me."

"*You* tell *me*," he said and put his hand over hers. "What was the matter between Mr. Richard and Mrs. Templeton? It's better I should know. What was it?"

She stared at him. Her lips moved but no sound came from them.

"You saw him," Alleyn said, "when he came out of her room. What was the matter? Florence told us..."

"*She* told you! *She* told you that!"

"I'd have found out, you know. Can you clear it up for us? Do, if you can."

She shook her head in a very desolate manner. Her eyes were glazed with tears and her speech had become uncertain. He supposed she had fortified herself with an extra glass before tackling him and it was now taking full effect.

"I can't say," she said indistinctly. "I don't know. One of her tantrums. A tyrant from the time she could speak. The boy's never anything but good and patient." And after a moment she added quite briskly, "Doesn't take after *her* in that respect. More like the father."

Fox looked up from his notes. Alleyn remained perfectly still. Old Ninn rocked very slightly on her feet and sat down.

"Mr. Templeton?" Alleyn said.

She nodded two or three times with her eyes shut. "You may well say so," she murmured, "you—may—well..." Her voice trailed into silence and she dozed.

Fox opened his mouth and Alleyn signalled him and he shut it again. There was a considerable pause. Presently Old

Ninn gave a slight snore, moved her lips and opened her eyes.

Alleyn said, "Does Mr. Richard know about his parentage?"

She looked fixedly at him. "Why shouldn't he?" she said. "They were both killed in a motor accident and don't you believe anything you're told to the contrary. Name of Dakers." She caught sight of Fox and his notebook. "Dakers," she repeated and spelt it out for him.

"Thank you very much," said Fox.

Alleyn said, "Did you think Mr. Richard looked very much upset when he came out of her room?"

"She had the knack of upsetting him. He takes things to heart."

"What did he do?"

"Went downstairs. Didn't look at me. I doubt if he saw me."

"Florence," Alleyn said, "thought he looked like death."

Ninn got to her feet. Her little hands clutched at his arm. "What's she mean? What's she been hinting? Why didn't she say what I heard? After she went downstairs? I told her. Why didn't she tell you?"

"What did you hear?"

"She knows! I told her. I didn't think anything of it at the time and now she won't admit it. Trying to lay the blame on the boy. She's a wicked girl and always has been."

"What did you hear?"

"I heard the Lady using that thing. The poison thing. Hissing. *Heard* it! She killed herself," Ninn said. "Why, we'll never know and the sin's on her head forever. She killed herself."

4

There was a long pause during which Ninn showed signs of renewed instability. Fox put his arm under hers. "Steady does it," he said comfortably.

"That's no way to talk," she returned sharply and sat down again.

"Florence," Alleyn said, "tells us Miss Bellamy was incapable of any such thing."

The mention of Florence instantly restored her.

"Florence said this and Florence said that," she barked. "And did Florence happen to mention she fell out with her lady and as good as got her notice this morning? Did she tell you that?"

"No," Alleyn murmured, "she didn't tell us that."

"Ah! There you are, you see!"

"What did you do after Mr. Richard left the room and went downstairs? After Florence had gone and after you'd heard the spray?"

She had shut her eyes again and he had to repeat his questions. "I retired," she said with dignity, "to my room."

"When did you hear of the catastrophe?"

"There was a commotion. Floy with a hot bottle on the landing having hysterics. I couldn't get any sense out of her. Then the doctor came out and told me."

"And after that, what did you do?"

He could have sworn that she made a considerable effort to collect herself and that his question had alarmed her. "I don't remember," she said and then added, "Went back to my room." She had opened her eyes and was watching him very warily.

"Are you sure, Ninn? Didn't you have a look at Mr. Templeton in the dressing-room?"

"I've forgotten. I might have. I believe I did. You can't think of everything," she added crossly.

"How was he? How did you find him?"

"How would you expect him to be?" she countered. "Very low. Didn't speak. Upset. Naturally. With his trouble, it might have been the death of him. The shock and all."

"How long were you in the dressing-room?"

"I don't remember. Till the police came and ordered everybody about."

"Did you," Alleyn asked her, "go into the bedroom?"

She waited for a long time. "No," she said at last.

"Are you sure? You didn't go through into the bathroom or begin to tidy the room?"

"No."

"Or touch the body?"

"I didn't go into the bedroom."

"And you didn't let Florence go in either?"

"What's she been telling you?"

"That she wanted to go in and that you—very properly—told her that the doctor had forbidden it."

"She was hysterical. She's a silly girl. Bad in some ways."

"Did Mr. Templeton go into the bedroom?"

"He had occasion," she said with great dignity, "to pass through it in order to make use of the convenience. That is not forbidden, I hope?"

"Naturally not."

"Very well then," she stifled a hiccough and rose. "I'm going to bed," she said loudly, and as there was nothing further to be collected from her, they let her out.

Fox offered assistance but was rebuffed. She tacked rapidly towards the door.

He opened it quickly.

There, on the landing, looking remarkably uncomfortable, was Richard Dakers.

5

He had been caught, it was evident, in the act of moving away from the door. Now, he stood stock-still an uncomfortable smile twitching at the corner of his mouth. Old Ninn stopped short when she saw him, appeared to get her bearings and went up to him.

"Ninn," he said, looking past her at Alleyn and speaking with most unconvincing jauntiness, "what *have* you been up to!"

She stared into his face. "Speak up for yourself," she said. "They'll put upon you if you don't."

"Hadn't you better go to bed? You're not yourself, you know."

"Exactly," Ninn said with hauteur. "I'm going."

She made off at an uncertain gait towards the backstairs. Alleyn said, "Mr. Dakers, what are you doing up here?"

"I wanted to get into my room."

"I'm afraid we're occupying it at the moment. But if there's anything you need..."

"Oh God!" Richard cried out. "Is there to be no end to these indignities? No! No, there's nothing I need. Not now. I wanted to be by myself in my room where I could make some attempt to think."

"You had it all on your own in the drawing-room," Fox said crossly. "Why couldn't you think down there? How did you get past the man on duty, sir?"

"He was coping with a clutch of pressmen at the front door and I nipped up the backstairs."

"Well," Alleyn said, "you'd better nip down again to where you came from and if you're sick of the drawing-room, you can join the party next door, Unless, of course, you'd like to stay and tell us your real object in coming up here."

Richard opened his mouth and shut it again. He then turned on his heels and went downstairs. He was followed by Fox, who returned looking portentous. "I gave that chap in the hall a rocket," he said. "They don't know the meaning of keeping observation these days. Mr. Dakers is back in the drawing-room. Why do you reckon he broke out, sir?"

"I think," Alleyn said, "he may have remembered the blotting-paper."

"Ah, there is that. May be. Mrs. Plumtree wasn't bad value, though, was she?"

"Not bad. But none of it proves anything, of course," Alleyn said. "Not a damn thing."

"Floy getting the sack's interesting. If true."

"It may be a recurrent feature of their relationship, for all we know. What about the sounds they both heard in the bedroom?"

"Do we take it," Fox asked, "that Floy's crash came before Mrs. Plumtree's hiss?"

"I suppose so. Yes."

"And that Florence retired after the crash?"

"While Ninn remained for the hiss. Precisely."

"The inference being," Fox pursued, "that as soon as Mr. Dakers left her, the lady fell with a deafening crash on the four-pile carpet."

"And then sprayed herself all over with Slaypest."

"Quite so, Mr. Alleyn."

"I prefer a less dramatic reading of the evidence."

"All the same, it doesn't look very pleasant for Mr. Dakers." And as Alleyn didn't reply, "D'you reckon Mrs. Plumtree was talking turkey when she let out about his parentage?"

"I think it's at least possible that she believes it."

"Born," Fox speculated, "out of wedlock and the parents subsequently married?"

"Your guess is as good as mine. Wait a bit." He took down the copy of *Who's Who in the Theatre*. "Here we are. Bellamy. Sumptuous entry. Birth, not given. Curtis says fifty. Married 1932, Charles Gavin Templeton. Now, where's the playwright? Dakers, Richard. Very conservative entry. Born 1931. Educated Westminster and Trinity. List of three plays. That's all. Could be, Foxkin. I suppose we can dig it out if needs must."

Fox was silent for a moment. "There is this," he then said. "Mrs. Plumtree was alone on the landing after Florence went downstairs?"

"So it seems."

"And she says she heard deceased using the Slaypest. What say she went in and used it herself? On deceased."

"All right. Suppose she did. Why?"

"Because of the way deceased treated her ward or son or whatever he is? Went in and let her have it and then made off before Florence came back."

"Do you like it?"

"Not much," Fox grunted. "What about this story of Mrs. Plumtree going into the bedroom and rearranging the remains?"

"She didn't. The body was as Harkness and Gantry left it. Unless Harkness is too much hungover to notice."

"It might be something quite slight."

"What, for pity's sake?"

"God knows," Fox said. "Could you smell scent on Mrs. P?"

"I could smell nothing but rich old tawny port on Mrs. P."

"Might be a blind for the perfume. Ah, forget it!" Fox said disgustedly. "It's silly. How about this crash they heard after Mr. Dakers left the room?"

"Oh that. That was the lady pitching Madame Vestris into the bathroom."

"Why?"

"Professional jealousy? Or perhaps it was his birthday present to her and she was taking it out on the Vestris."

"Talk about conjecture! We do nothing else," Fox grumbled. "All right. So what's the next step, sir?"

"We've got to clear the ground. We've got to check, for one thing, Mr. Bertie Saracen's little outburst. And the shortest way with that one, I suppose, is to talk to Anelida Lee."

"Ah, yes. You know the young lady, don't you, Mr. Alleyn?"

"I've met her in her uncle's bookshop. She's a charming girl. I know Octavius quite well. I tell you what, Foxkin, you go round the camp, will you? Talk to the butler. Talk to the maids. Pick up anything that's offering on the general setup. Find out the pattern of the day's events. Furious Floy suggested a dust-up of some sort with Saracen and Miss Cavendish. Get the strength of it. And see if you can persuade the staff to feed the troops. Hullo—what's that?"

He went out into the passage and along to the landing. The door of Miss Bellamy's room was open. Dr. Curtis and Dr. Harkness stood just inside it watching the activities of two white-coated men. They had laid Miss Bellamy's body on a stretcher and had neatly covered it in orthodox sheeting. P.C. Philpott from the half-landing said, "O.K. chaps," and the familiar progress started. They crossed the landing, changed the angle of their burden and gingerly began the descent. Thus Miss Bellamy made her final journey downstairs. Alleyn heard a subdued noise somewhere above him. He moved to a position from which he could look up the narrower flight of stairs to the second-floor landing. Florence was there, scarcely to be seen in the shadows, and the sound he had heard was of her sobbing.

Alleyn followed the stretcher downstairs. He watched the mortuary van drive away, had a final word with his colleagues, and went next door to call on Octavius Browne.

Octavius, after hours, used his shop as his sitting-room. With the curtains drawn, the lamp on his reading table glowing and the firelight shining on his ranks of books, the room was enchanting. So, in his way, was Octavius, sunk deep in a red morocco chair with his book in his hand and his cat on his knee.

He had removed his best suit and, out of habit, had changed into old grey trousers and a disreputable but becoming velvet coat. For about an hour after Richard Dakers left (Anelida having refused to see him), Octavius had been miserable. Then she had come down, looking pale but familiar, saying she was sorry she'd been tiresome. She had kissed the top of his head and made him an omelette for his supper and had settled in her usual Monday night place on the other side of the fireplace behind a particularly large file in which she was writing up their catalogue. Once, Octavius couldn't resist sitting up high in order to look at her and as usual she made a hideous face at him and he made one back at her, which was a private thing they did on such occasions. He was reassured but not entirely so. He had a very deep affection for Anelida, but he was one of those people in whom the distress of those they love begets a kind of compassionate irritation. He liked Anelida to be gay and dutiful and lovely to look at; when he suspected that she had been crying he felt at once distressed and helpless and the sensation bored him because he didn't understand it.

When Alleyn rang the bell Anelida answered it. He saw, at once, that she had done her eyes up to hide the signs of tears.

Many of Octavius's customers were also his friends and it was not unusual for them to call after hours. Anelida supposed that Alleyn's was that sort of visit and so did Octavius, who was delighted to see him. Alleyn sat down between them, disliking his job.

"You look so unrepentantly cosy and Dickensian," he said, "both of you, that I feel like an interloper."

"My dear Alleyn, I do hope your allusion is not to that other and unspeakable little Nell and her drooling grandparent. No, I'm sure it's not. You are thinking of *Bleak House*, perhaps, and your fellow-investigator's arrival at his friend's fireside. I seem to remember, though, that his visit ended uncomfortably in an arrest. I hope you've left *your* manacles at the Yard."

Alleyn said, "As a matter of fact, Octavius, I *am* here on business, though not, I promise, to take either of you into custody."

"Really? How very intriguing! A bookish reference perhaps? Some malefactor with a flair for the collector's item?"

"I'm afraid not," Alleyn said. "It's a serious business, Octavius, and indirectly it concerns you both. I believe you were at Miss Mary Bellamy's birthday party this evening, weren't you?"

Anelida and her uncle both made the same involuntary movement of their hands. "Yes," Octavius said. "For a short time. We were."

"When did you arrive?"

"At seven. We were asked," Octavius said, "for six-thirty, but Anelida informed me it is the 'done thing' nowadays to be late."

"We waited," Anelida said, "till other people had begun to stream in."

"So you kept an eye on the earlier arrivals?"

"A bit. I did. They were rather intimidating."

"Did you by any chance see anybody go in with a bunch of Parma violets?"

Octavius jerked his leg. "Damn you, Hodge," he ejaculated and added mildly, "He makes bread on one's thigh. Unconscionable feline, be gone."

He cuffed the cat and it leapt indignantly to the floor.

Alleyn said, "I know you left early. I believe I know why."

"Mr. Alleyn," Anelida said. "What's happened? Why are you talking like this?"

Alleyn said, "It *is* a serious matter."

"Has Richard . . . ?" she began and stopped. "What are you trying to tell us?"

"He's all right. He's had a shock but he's all right."

"My dear Alleyn . . ."

"Unk," she said, "we'd better just listen."

And Alleyn told them, carefully and plainly, what had

happened. He said nothing of the implications.

"I wonder," he ended, "that you haven't noticed the comings and goings outside."

"Our curtains are drawn, as you see," Octavius said. "We had no occasion to look out. Had we, Nelly?"

Anelida said, "This will hurt Richard more than anything else that has ever happened to him." And then with dismay, "I wouldn't see him when he came in. I turned him away. He won't forgive me and I won't forgive myself."

"My darling child, you had every cause to behave as you did. She was an enchanting creature but evidently not always prettily behaved," Octavius said. "I always think," he added, "that one does a great disservice to the dead when one praises them inaccurately. *Nil nisi*, if you will, but at least let the *bonum* be authentic."

"I'm not thinking of her!" she cried out. "I'm thinking of Richard."

"Are you, indeed, my pet?" he said uncomfortably.

Anelida said, "I'm sorry, Mr. Alleyn. This is bad behaviour, isn't it? You must put it down to the well-known hysteria of theatre people."

"I put it down to the natural result of shock," Alleyn said, "and believe me, from what I've seen of histrionic behaviour, yours is in the last degree conservative. You must be a beginner."

"How right you are!" she said and looked gratefully at him.

The point had been reached where he should tell them of the implications and he was helped by Octavius, who said, "But why, my dear fellow, are you concerned in all this? Do the police in cases of accident..."

"That's just it," Alleyn said. "They do. They have to make sure."

He explained why they had to make sure. When he said that he must know exactly what had happened in the conservatory, Anelida turned so pale that he wondered if she, too, was going to faint. But she waited for a moment, taking herself in hand, and then told him, very directly, what had happened.

Timon Gantry, Montague and Richard had been talking

to her about her reading the leading role in *Husbandry in Heaven*. Mary Bellamy had come in, unnoticed by them, and had heard enough to make her realize what was afoot.

"She was very angry," Anelida said steadily. "She thought of it as a conspiracy and she accused me of—of—" Her voice faltered but in a moment she went on. "She said I'd been setting my cap at Richard to further my own ends in the theatre. I don't remember everything she said. They all tried to stop her, but that seemed to make her more angry. Kate Cavendish and Bertie Saracen had come in with Mr. Templeton. When she saw them she attacked them as well. It was something about another new production. She accused them, too, of conspiracy. I could see Unk on the other side of the glass door, like somebody you want very badly in a nightmare and can't reach. And then Mr. Templeton went out and spoke to him. And then I went out. And Unk behaved perfectly. And we came home."

"Beastly experience," Alleyn said. "For both of you."

"Oh horrid," Octavius agreed. "And *very* puzzling. She was, to meet, you know, so perfectly enchanting. One is quite at a loss...!" He rumpled his hair.

"Poor Unky!" Anelida said.

"Was Colonel Warrender in the conservatory?"

"That is Templeton's cousin, isn't it? One sees the likeness," said Octavius. "Yes, he was. He came into the hall and tried to say something pleasant, poor man."

"So did the others," Anelida said. "I'm afraid I wasn't as responsive as I ought to have been. I—we just walked out."

"And Richard Dakers walked out after you?"

"Yes," she said. "He did. And I went off to my room and wouldn't see him. Which is so awful."

"So what did he do?" Alleyn asked Octavius.

"Do? Dakers? He was in a great taking-on. I felt sorry for him. Angry, you know, with *her*. He said a lot of hasty, unpleasant things which I feel sure he didn't mean."

"What sort of things?"

"Oh!" Octavius said. "It was, as far as I recollect, to the effect that Mrs. Templeton had ruined his life. All very extravagant and ill-considered. I was sorry to hear it."

"Did he say what he meant to do when he left here?"

"Yes, indeed. He said he was going back to have it out with her. Though how he proposed to do anything of the sort in the middle of a party, one can't imagine. I went to the door with him, trying to calm him down, and I saw him go into the house."

"And that was the last you saw of him?"

"In point of fact, yes. The telephone rang at that moment. It's in the back room as you'll remember. I answered it and when I returned here I thought for a moment he had done so, too. I suppose because he was so much in my mind."

Anelida made a small ejaculation, but her uncle went on:

"A ludicrous mistake. It was dark in here by then—very—and he was standing in silhouette against the windows. I said, 'My dear chap, what now?' or something of that sort, and he turned and then, of course, I saw it was Colonel Warrender, you know."

"What had *he* come for?" Anelida asked rather desperately.

"Well, my dear, I suppose on behalf of his cousin and to repeat his vicarious apologies and to attempt an explanation. I felt it much better to make as little of the affair as possible. After all we don't *know* Warrender and in any case it was really nothing to do with him. He meant very well, no doubt. I was, I hope, perfectly civil, but I got rid of him in a matter of seconds."

"Yes," Alleyn said. "I see. To sidetrack for a moment, I suppose you're by way of being an authority on Victorian tinsel pictures, aren't you? Do you go in for them? I seem to remember..."

"How *very* odd!" Octavius exclaimed. "My dear fellow, I sold one this morning to young Dakers, as a birthday present for—oh, well, there you are!—for his guardian."

"Madame Vestris?"

"You saw it then? Charming, isn't it?"

"Yes," Alleyn said. "Charming."

Anelida had been watching Alleyn, as he was well aware, very closely. She now asked him the question he had expected.

"Mr. Alleyn," Anelida said. "Do you think it was not an accident?"

He gave her the inevitable answer. "We don't know. We're not sure."

"But what do you believe? In your heart? I must know. I won't do anything silly or make a nuisance of myself. Do you believe she was murdered?"

Alleyn said, "I'm afraid I do, Anelida."

"Have you told Richard?"

"Not in so many words."

"But he guessed?"

"I don't know," Alleyn said carefully, "what he thought. I've left him to himself for a little."

"Why?"

"He's had a very bad shock. He fainted."

She looked steadily at him and then with a quick collected movement rose to her feet.

"Unk," she said, "don't wait up for me and don't worry."

"My dear girl," he said, in a fluster, "what do you mean? Where are you going?"

"To Richard," she said. "Where else? Of course to Richard."

chapter six

On the Scent

WHEN ANELIDA RANG the bell at 2 Pardoner's Place, it was answered, almost at once, by a policeman.

She said, "It's Miss Lee. I've been talking to Superintendent Alleyn. He knows I'm here and I think is probably coming himself in a moment. I want to speak to Mr. Richard Dakers."

The policeman said, "I see, Miss. Well, now, if you'll wait a moment I'll just find out whether that'll be all right. Perhaps you'd take a chair."

"No, thank you. I want to see him at once, please."

"I'll ascertain..." he had begun rather austerely when Alleyn himself arrived.

"Sir?"

"Yes, all right. Is Mr. Dakers still in the drawing-room? Good." Alleyn looked at Anelida. "Come along," he said. She lifted her chin and went to him.

She was in a state of mind she had never before experienced. It was as if her thoughts and desires and behaviour had been abruptly simplified and were governed by a single intention. She knew that somewhere within herself she must be afraid, but she also knew that fear, as things had turned out, was inadmissible.

She followed Alleyn across the hall. He said, "Here you are," and opened a door. She went from the hall into the drawing-room.

Immediately inside the door was a tall leather screen. She walked round it and there, staring out of a window, was Richard. Anelida moved a little towards him and halted. This gave her time to realize how very much she liked the shape of his head and at once she felt an immense tenderness for him and even a kind of exultation. In a second, she would speak his name, she would put herself absolutely on his side.

"Richard," she said.

He turned. She noticed that his face had bleached, not conventionally, over the cheekbone, but at the temples and down the jaw-line.

"Anelida?"

"I had to come. I'm trying to make up for my bad behaviour. Here, you see, I am."

He came slowly to her and when he took her hands in his, did so doubtfully. "I can't believe my luck," he said. "I thought I'd lost you quite irrevocably. Cause enough, God knows."

"On the contrary, I assure you."

He broke into an uncertain smile. "The things you say! Such grand phrases!" His hands tightened on hers. "You know what's happened, don't you? About Mary?"

"Yes. Richard, I'm so terribly sorry. And what a hopeless phrase *that* is!"

"I shouldn't let you stay. It's not the place for you. This is a nightmare of a house."

"Do you want me? Am I any good, being here?"

"I love you." He lifted her hands to his face. "Ah no! Why did I tell you! This isn't the time."

"Are you all right now—to talk, I mean? To talk very seriously?"

"I'm all right. Come over here."

They sat together on the sofa, Richard still holding her

hands. "He told us you fainted," said Anelida.

"Alleyn? Has he been worrying you?"

"Not really. But it's because of what he did say that I'm here. And because—Richard, when I wouldn't see you and you went away—did you come back here?"

"Yes," he said. "I did."

"Did you see her?"

He looked down at their clasped hands. "Yes."

"Where?"

"In her room. Only for a few minutes. I—left her there."

"Was anyone else with you?"

"Good God, no!" he cried out.

"And then? Then what?"

"I went away. I walked for heaven knows how long. When I came back—it was like this."

There was a long silence. At last Richard said very calmly, "I know what you're trying to tell me. They think Mary has been murdered and they wonder if I'm their man. Isn't it?"

Anelida leant towards him and kissed him. "That's it," she said. "At least, I think so. We'll get it tidied up and disposed of in no time. But I think that's it."

"It seems," he said, "so fantastic. Too fantastic to be frightening. You mustn't be frightened. You must go away, my darling heart, and leave me to—to do something about it."

"I'll go when I think it'll make things easier for you. Not before."

"I love you so much. I should be telling you how much, not putting this burden upon you."

"They may not leave me with you for long. You must remember exactly what happened. Where you went. Who may have seen you. And Richard, you must tell them what she was doing when you left."

He released her hands and pressed the palms of his own to his eyes. "She was laughing," he said.

"Laughing? They'll want to know why, won't they? What you both said to make her laugh."

"Never!" he said violently. "Never!"

"But—they'll ask you."

"They can ask and ask and ask again. Never!"

"You must!" she said desperately. "Think! It's what one always reads—that innocent people hold out on the police and muddle everything up and put themselves in the wrong. Richard, think what they'll find out anyway! That she spoke as she did to me, that you were angry, that you said you'd never forgive her. Everyone in the hall heard you. Colonel Warrender..."

"He!" Richard said bitterly. "He won't talk. He daren't."

"What do you mean?"

"It doesn't matter."

"Oh!" she cried out. "You are frightening me! What's going to happen when they ask you about it? What'll they think when you won't tell them!"

"They can think what they like." He got up and began to walk about the room. "Too much has happened. I can't get it into perspective. You don't know what it's like. I've no right to load it on to you."

"Don't *talk* like that," Anelida said desperately. "I love you. It's my right to share."

"You're so young."

"I've got all the sense I'm ever likely to have."

"Darling!"

"Never mind about me! You needn't tell me anything you don't want to. It's what you're going to say to them that matters."

"I will tell you—soon—when I can."

"If it clears you they won't make any further to-do about it. That's all they'll worry about. Clearing it up. You must tell them what happened. Everything."

"I can't."

"My God, *why*?"

"Have you any doubts about me? Have you!"

She went to him. "You must know I haven't."

"Yes," he said. "I can see that."

They stared at each other. He gave an inarticulate cry and suddenly she was in his arms.

Gracefield came through the folding doors from the dining-room.

"Supper is served, sir," he said.

Alleyn rose from his comfortable seclusion behind the screen, slipped through the door into the hall, shut it soundlessly behind him and went up to their office.

2

"I've been talking," Mr. Fox remarked, "to a press photographer and the servants."

"And I," Alleyn said sourly, "have been eavesdropping on a pair of lovers. How low can you get? Next stop, with Polonius behind the arras in a bedroom."

"All for their good, I daresay," Fox observed comfortably.

"There is that. Fox, that blasted playwright is holding out on us. And on his girl for a matter of that. But I'm damned if I like him as a suspect."

"He seems," Fox considered, "a very pleasant young fellow."

"What the devil happened between him and Mary Bellamy when he came back? He won't tell his girl. He merely says the interview ended in Miss Bellamy laughing. We've got the reports from those two intensely prejudiced women, who both agree he looked ghastly. All right. He goes out. There's this crash Florence talked about. Florence goes down to the half-landing and Ninn hears a spray being used. Templeton comes out from the drawing-room to the foot of the stairs. He calls up to Florence to tell her mistress they're waiting for her. Florence goes up to the room and finds her mistress in her death throes. Dakers returns two hours after the death, comes up to his room, writes a letter and tries to go away. End of information. Next step: confront him with the letter?"

"Your reconstruction of it?"

"Oh," Alleyn said. "I fancy I can lay my hands on the original."

Fox looked at him with placid approval and said nothing.

"What did you get from your press photographer? And

which photographer?" Alleyn asked.

"He was hanging about in the street and said he'd something to tell me. Put-up job to get inside, of course, but I thought I'd see what it was. He took a picture of deceased with Mr. Dakers in the background at twenty to eight by the hall clock. He saw them go upstairs together. Gives us an approximate time for the demise, for what it's worth."

"About ten minutes later. What did you extract from the servants?"

"Not a great deal. It seems the deceased wasn't all that popular with the staff, except Florence, who was hers, as the cook put it, body and soul. Gracefield held out on me for a bit, but he's taken quite a liking to you, sir, and I built on that with good results."

"What the hell have you been saying?"

"Well, Mr. Alleyn, you know as well as I do what snobs these high-class servants are."

Alleyn didn't pursue the subject.

"There was a dust-up," Fox continued, "this morning with Miss Cavendish and Mr. Saracen. Gracefield happened to overhear it." He repeated Gracefield's account, which had been detailed and accurate.

"According to Anelida Lee this row was revived in the conservatory," Alleyn muttered. "What were they doing here this morning?"

"Mr. Saracen had come to do the flowers, about which Gracefield spoke very sarcastically, and Miss Cavendish had brought the deceased that bottle of scent."

"What!" Alleyn said. "Not the muck on her dressing-table? Not Formidable? *This morning?*"

"That's right."

Alleyn slapped his hand down on Richard's desk and got up. "My God, what an ass I've been!" he said and then, sharply, "Who opened it?"

"She did. In the dining-room."

"And used it? Then?"

"Had a bit of a dab, Gracefield said. He happened to be glancing through the serving-hatch at the time."

"What became of it after that?"

"Florence took charge of it. I'm afraid," Fox said, "I'm

not with you, Mr. Alleyn, in respect of the scent."

"My dear old boy, think! Think of the bottle."

"Very big," Fox said judiciously.

"Exactly. Very big. Well then. . .?"

"Yes. Ah, yes," Fox said slowly and then, "Well, I'll be staggered!"

"And so you jolly well should. This could blow the whole damn case wide open again."

"Will I fetch them?"

"Do. And call on Florence, wherever she is. Get the whole story, Fox. Tactfully, as usual. Find out when the scent was decanted into the spray and when she used it. Watch the reactions, won't you? And see if there's anything in the Plumtree stories: about Richard Dakers's parentage and Florence being threatened with the sack."

Fox looked at his watch. "Ten o'clock," he said. "She may have gone to bed."

"That'll be a treat for you. Leave me your notes. Away you go."

While Fox was on this errand, Alleyn made a plot, according to information, of the whereabouts of Charles Templeton, the four guests, the servants and Richard Dakers up to the time when he himself arrived on the scene. Fox's spadework had been exhaustive, as usual, and a pretty complicated pattern emerged. Alleyn lifted an eyebrow over the result. How many of them had told the whole truth? Which of them had told a cardinal lie? He put a query against one name and was shaking his head over it when Fox returned.

"Bailey's finished with them," Fox said and placed on Richard's desk the scent-spray, the empty Formidable bottle and the tin of Slaypest.

"What'd he find in the way of dabs?"

"Plenty. All sorts, but none that you wouldn't expect. He's identified the deceased's. Florence says she and Mr. Templeton and Colonel Warrender all handled the exhibit during the day. She says the deceased got the Colonel to operate the spray on her, just before the party. Florence filled it from the bottle."

"And how much was left in the bottle?"

"She thinks it was about a quarter-full. She was in bed," Fox added in a melancholy tone.

"That would tally," Alleyn muttered. "No sign of the bottle being knocked over and spilling, is there?"

"None."

Alleyn began to tap the Slaypest tin with his pencil. "About half-full. Anyone know when it was first used?"

"Florence reckons, a week ago. Mr. Templeton didn't like her using it and tried to get Florence to make away with it."

"Why didn't she?"

"No chance according to her. She went into a great taking-on and asked me if I was accusing her of murder."

"*Did* she get the sack, this morning?"

"When I asked her she went up like a rocket bomb, the story being that Mrs. Plumtree has taken against her and let out something that was told in confidence."

Alleyn put his head in his hands. "Oh *Lord*!" he said.

"You meet that kind of thing," Mr. Fox observed, "in middle-age ladies. Florence says that when Miss Bellamy or Mr. Templeton was out of humour, she would make out she was going to sack Florence, but there was nothing in it. She says she only told Mrs. Plumtree as a joke. I kind of nudged in a remark about Mr. Dakers's parentage, but she wasn't having any of that. She turned around and accused me of having a dirty mind and in the next breath had another go at Mrs. Plumtree. All the same," Mr. Fox added primly, "I reckon there's something in it. I reckon so from her manner. She appears to be very jealous of anybody who was near the deceased and that takes in Mr. Templeton, Mr. Dakers, Mrs. Plumtree and the Colonel."

"Good old Florrie," Alleyn said absent-mindedly.

"You know, sir," Fox continued heavily, "I've been thinking about the order of events. Take the latter part of the afternoon. Say, from when the Colonel used the scent. What happened after *that*, now?"

"According to himself he went downstairs and had a quick one with Mrs. Templeton in the presence of the servants while Templeton and Dakers were closeted in the study. All this up to the time when the first guests began to come in. It looks good enough, but it's not cast iron."

"Whereas," Fox continued, "Florence and Mrs. Plumtree went upstairs. Either of them could have gone into Mrs. Templeton's room, and got up to the odd bit of hanky-panky, couldn't they, now?"

"The story is that they were together in their parlour until they went downstairs to the party. They're at daggers-drawn. Do you think that if one of them had popped out of the parlour the other would feel disposed to keep mum about it?"

"Ah. There is that, of course. But it might have been forgotten."

"Come off it, Foxkin."

"The same goes for Mr. Templeton and Mr. Dakers. They've said, independently of each other, that they were together in the study. I don't know how you feel about that one, Mr. Alleyn, but I'm inclined to accept it."

"So am I. Entirely."

"If we do accept all this, we've got to take it that the job was fixed after the guests began to arrive. Now, up to the row in the conservatory the three gentlemen were all in the reception rooms. The Colonel was in attendance on the deceased. Mr. Templeton was also with her receiving the guests and Mr. Dakers was on the lookout for his young lady."

"What's more, there was a press photographer near the foot of the stairs, a cinematographer half-way up, and a subsidiary bar at the foot of the backstairs with a caterer's man on duty throughout. He saw Florence and Ninn and nobody else go up. What's that leave us in the way of a roaring-hot suspect?"

"It means," Fox said, "either that one of those two women fixed it then..."

"But when? You mean before they met on the landing and tried to listen in on the famous scene?"

"I suppose I do. Yes. While the photograph was being taken."

"Yes?"

"Alternatively someone else went up before that."

"Again, when? It would have to be after the cinema unit moved away and before Mrs. Templeton left the conservatory and came out into the hall where she was photographed with Dakers glowering in the background. And it would have to be before she took him upstairs."

"Which restricts you to the entrance with the birthday cake and the speeches. I reckon someone could have slipped upstairs then."

"The general attention being focused on the speakers and the stairs being clear? Yes. I agree with you. So far. But, see here, Fox; this expert didn't do the trick as simply as that, I'm inclined to think there was one more visit at least, more likely that there were two more, one before and one after the death. Tidying up, you know. If I'm right, there was a certain amount of tidying up."

"My God," Fox began with unwonted heat, "what are you getting at, Mr. Alleyn? It's tough enough as it is, d'you want to make it more difficult? What's the idea?"

"If it's any good it's going to make it easier. Much easier."

Alleyn stood up.

"You know, Br'er Fox," he said, "I can see only one explanation that really fits. Take a look at what's offering. Suicide? Leave her party, go up to her bedroom and spray herself to death? They all scout the notion and so do I. Accident? We've had it: the objection being the inappropriateness of the moment for her to horticult and the nature of the stains. Homicide? All right. What's the jury asked to believe? That she stood stock-still while her murderer pumped a deluge of Slaypest into her face at long and then at short range? Defending counsel can't keep a straight face over that one. But if, by any giddy chance, I'm on the right track, there's an answer that still admits homicide. Now, listen, while I check over and see if you can spot a weakness."

Mr. Fox listened placidly to a succinct argument, his gaze resting thoughtfully the while on the tin, the bottle, and the scent-spray.

"Yes," he said when Alleyn had finished. "Yes. It adds up, Mr. Alleyn. It fits. The only catch that I can see rests in the little difficulty of our having next-to-nothing to substantiate the theory."

Alleyn pointed a long finger at the exhibits. "We've got those," he said, "and it'll go damn hard if we don't rake up something else in the next half hour."

"Motive?"

"Motive unknown. It may declare itself. Opportunity's our bird, Fox. Opportunity, my boy."

"What's the next step?"

"I rather fancy shock tactics. They're all cooped up in the dining-room, aren't they?"

"All except Mr. Templeton. He's still in the study. When I looked in they were having supper. He'd ordered it for them. Cold partridge," Mr. Fox said rather wistfully. "A bit of a waste, really, as they didn't seem to have much appetite."

"We'll see if we can stimulate it," Alleyn said grimly, "with these," and waved his hand at the three exhibits.

3

Pinky Cavendish pushed her plate away and addressed herself firmly to her companions.

"I feel," she said, "completely unreal. It's not an agreeable sensation." She looked round the table. "Is there any reason why we don't say what's in all our minds? Here we sit, pretending to eat: every man-jack of us pea-green with worry but cutting the whole thing dead. I can't do with it. Not for another second. I'm a loquacious woman and I want to talk."

"Pinky," Timon Gantry said. "Your sense of timing! Never quite successfully co-ordinated, dear, is it?"

"But, *actually*," Bertie Saracen plaintively objected, "I do so feel Pinky's dead right. I mean we *are* all devastated and for my part, at least, terrified; but there's no *real* future, is there, in maintaining a *charnel-house* decorum? It can't improve anything, or can it? And it's so excessively wearing. Dicky, dear, you won't misunderstand me, will you? The hearts, I promise you, are utterly in their right place which, speaking for myself, is in the boots."

Richard, who had been talking in an undertone to Anelida, looked up. "Why not talk," he said, "if you can raise something that remotely resembles normal conversation."

Warrender darted a glance at him. "Of course," he said.

"Entirely agree." But Richard wouldn't look at Warrender.

"Even abnormal conversation," Pinky said, "would be preferable to strangulated silence."

Bertie, with an air of relief, said, "Well then, everybody, let's face it. We're *not* being herded together in a"—he swallowed—"in a communual cell just out of constabular whimsy. Now *are* we?"

"No, Bertie," Pinky said, "we are not."

"Under hawklike supervision," Bertie added, "if Sergeant Philpott doesn't mind my mentioning it."

P.C. Philpott, from his post at the far end of the room, said, "Not at all, sir," and surreptitiously groped for his notebook.

"Thank you," Bertie said warmly. Gracefield and a maid came in and cleared the table in a deathly silence. When they had gone Bertie broke out again. "My God," he said. "Isn't it as clear as daylight that every one of us, except Anelida, is under suspicion for something none of us likes to mention?"

"I do," Pinky said. "I'm all for mentioning it, and indeed if I don't mention it I believe I'll go off like a geyser."

"No, you won't, dear," Gantry firmly intervened. He was sitting next to Pinky and looked down upon her with a cranelike tilt of his head. "You'll behave beautifully and not start any free-associating nonsense. This is not the time for it."

"Timmy darling, I'm sorry as sorry but I'm moved to defy you," Pinky announced with a great show of spirit. "In the theatre—never. Outside it and under threat of being accused of murder—yes. There!" she ejaculated. "I've said it! Murder. And aren't you all relieved?"

Bertie Saracen said at once, "Bless you, darling. Immeasurably."

Timon Gantry and Colonel Warrender simultaneously looked at the back of Philpott's head and then exchanged glances: two men, Anelida felt, of authority at the mercy of an uncontrollable situation.

"Very well, then," Pinky continued. "The police think Mary was murdered and presumably they think one of us murdered her. It sounds monstrous, but it appears to be true. The point is does anyone here agree with them?"

"I don't," Bertie said. He glanced at the serving-hatch and lowered his voice. "After all," he said uncomfortably, "we're not the only ones."

"If you mean the servants..." Richard said angrily.

"I don't mean anybody in particular," Bertie protested in a great hurry.

"—It's quite unthinkable."

"To my mind," Pinky said, "the whole thing's out of this world. I don't and can't and won't believe it of anybody in the house."

"Heah, heah," Warrender ejaculated, lending a preposterously hearty note to the conversation. "Ridiculous idea," he continued loudly. "Alleyn's behaving altogether too damn high-handedly." He looked at Richard, hesitated and with an obvious effort said, "Don't you agree?"

Without turning his head, Richard said, "He knows his own business, I imagine."

There was a rather deadly little silence broken by Timon Gantry.

"For my part," Gantry said, "I feel the whole handling of the situation is so atrociously hard on Charles Templeton."

A guilty look came into their faces, Anelida noticed, as if they were ashamed of forgetting Charles. They made sympathetic noises and were embarrassed.

"What I resent," Pinky said suddenly, "is being left in the dark. *What* happened? *Why* the mystery? *Why not* accident? All we've been told is that poor Mary died of a dose of pest-killer. It's hideous and tragic and we're all shocked beyond words, but if we're being kept here under suspicion"—she brought her clenched fist down on the table—*"we've a right to know why!"*

She had raised her not inconsiderable voice to full projection point. None of them had heard the door from the hall open.

"Every right," Alleyn said, coming forward. "And I'm sorry that the explanation has been so long delayed."

The men had half-risen, but he lifted his hand and they sat back again. Anelida, for all her anxiety, had time to reflect that he was possessed of an effortless authority before which even Gantry, famous for this quality, became merely one of a controllable group. The attentive silence that descended upon them was of exactly the same kind as that which Gantry himself commanded at rehearsals. Even Colonel Warrender, though he raised his eyebrows, folded his arms and looked uncommonly portentous, found nothing to say.

"I think," Alleyn said, "that we will make this a round-the-table discussion." He sat in the vacant chair at the end of the table. "It gives one," he explained with a smile at Pinky Cavendish, "a spurious air of importance. We shall need five more chairs, Philpott."

P.C. Philpott placed them. Nobody spoke.

Fox came in from the hall bringing Florence and Old Ninn in his wake. Old Ninn was attired in a red flannel gown. Florence had evidently redressed herself rather sketchily and covered the deficiencies with an alpaca overall. Her hair was trapped in a tortuous system of tin curlers.

"Please sit down," Alleyn said. "I'm sorry about dragging you in again. It won't, I hope, be for long."

Florence and Ninn, both looking angry and extremely reluctant and each cutting the other dead, sat on opposite sides of the table, leaving empty chairs between themselves and their nearest neighbours.

"Where's Dr. Harkness, Fox?"

"Back in the conservatory, I believe, sir. We thought it better not to rouse him."

"I'm afraid we must do so now."

Curtains had been drawn across the conservatory wall. Fox disappeared behind them. Stertorous, unlovely and protesting noises were heard and presently he re-appeared with Dr. Harkness, now bloated with sleep and very tousled.

"Oh torment!" he said in a thick voice. "Oh hideous condition!"

"Would you," Alleyn asked, "be very kind and see if you think Mr. Templeton is up to joining us? If there's any doubt about it, we won't disturb him. He's in the study."

"Very well," said Dr. Harkness, trying to flatten his hair with both hands. "Never, never, never, any of you, chase up four whiskies with three glasses of champagne. Don't *do* it!" he added furiously as if somebody had shown signs of taking this action. He went out.

"We'll wait," Alleyn said composedly, "for Mr. Templeton," and arranged his papers.

Warrender cleared his throat. "Don't like the look of that sawbones," he said.

"Poor pet," Bertie sighed. "And yet I almost wish I were in his boots. A pitiable but *not* unenviable condition."

"Bad show!" Warrender said. "Fellar's on duty."

"Are you true?" Gantry asked suddenly, gazing at Warrender with a kind of devotion.

"I beg your pardon, sir?"

Gantry clasped his hands and said ecstatically, "One would never dare! Never! And yet people say one's productions tend towards caricature! You shall give them the lie in their teeth, Colonel. In your own person you shall refute them."

"I'm damned if I know what you're talking about, Gantry, but if you're trying to be abusive..."

"'No abuse,'" Alleyn quoted unexpectedly. He was reading his notes. "'No abuse in the world: no, faith, boys, none'."

They stared at him. Gantry, thrown off his stride, looked round the table as if calling attention to Alleyn's eccentricity. Bertie leant towards him. "Formidable!" he murmured, indicating Alleyn.

"*What!*" Pinky ejaculated. "*What* did you say, dear?"

"Formidable!" Bertie repeated. "I said 'formidable.' Why? Oh God! Sorry!"

Warrender made some sort of exclamation.

"I was talking about Mr. Alleyn, dear," Bertie explained. "I said he was formidable."

"Oh!" Pinky said. "That! Sorry!"

"A misunderstanding," Alleyn remarked to his notes. "But don't let it put you off the scent. We're coming to that in a minute."

Pinky, greatly disconcerted, had opened her mouth to reply but was prevented by the appearance of Charles Templeton. He had come in with Dr. Harkness. He was a bad colour, seemed somehow to have shrunk and walked like the old man he actually was. But his manner was contained and he smiled faintly at them.

Alleyn got up and went to him. "He's all right," Dr. Harkness said. "He'll do. Won't you, Charles?"

"I'll do," Charles repeated. "Much better."

"Would you rather sit in a more comfortable chair?" Alleyn suggested. "As you see, we are making free with your dining-room table."

"Of course. I hope you've got everything you want. I'll join you."

He took the nearest chair. Richard had got up and now, gripping Charles's shoulders, leant over him. Charles turned his head and looked up at him. During that moment, Alleyn thought, he saw a resemblance.

Richard said, "Are you well enough for all this?"

"Yes, yes. Perfectly."

Richard returned to his place, Dr. Harkness and Fox took the two remaining seats, and the table was full.

Alleyn clasped his hands over his papers, said, "Well, now," and wishing, not for the first time, that he could find some other introductory formula, addressed himself to his uneasy audience.

Anelida thought, "Here we all sit like a committee meeting and the chairman thinks one of us is a murderer." Richard, very straight in his chair, looked at the table. When she stirred a little he reached for her hand, gripped it and let it go.

Alleyn was talking.

". . . I would like to emphasize that until the pathologist's report comes in, there can be no certainty, but in the meantime I think we must try to arrive at a complete pattern of events. There are a number of points still to be settled and to that end I have kept you so long and asked you to come here. Fox?"

Fox had brought a small case with him. He now opened it, produced the empty scent bottle and laid it on the table.

"Formidable," Alleyn said and turned to Pinky. "Your birthday present, wasn't it, and the cause, I think, of your misunderstanding just now with Mr. Saracen."

Pinky said angrily, "What have you done with the scent? Sorry," she added. "It doesn't matter, of course. It's only that—well, it was full this morning."

"When you gave it to Miss Bellamy? In this room?"

"That's right."

Alleyn turned to Florence. "Can you help us?"

"I filled her spray from it," Florence said mulishly.

"That wouldn't account for the lot, Florry," Pinky pointed out.

"Was the spray empty?" Alleyn asked.

"Just about. She didn't mind mixing them."

"And how much was left in the bottle?"

"*He* asked me all this," Florence said, jerking her head at Fox.

"And now I do."

"About that much," she muttered, holding her thumb and forefinger an inch apart.

"About a quarter. And the spray was full?"

She nodded.

Fox, with the expertise of a conjuror, produced the scent-spray and placed it by the bottle.

"And only about 'that much,'" Alleyn pointed out, "is now in the spray. So we've got pretty well three-quarters of this large bottle of scent to account for, haven't we?"

"I fail utterly," Warrender began, "to see what you think you're driving at."

"Perhaps you can help. I understand, sir, that you actually used this thing earlier in the day."

"Not on myself, God damn it!" Warrender said and then shot an uneasy glance at Charles Templeton.

Gantry gave a snort of delight.

"On Miss Bellamy?" Alleyn suggested.

"Naturally."

"And did you happen to notice how much was left?"

"It was over three-quarters full. What!" Warrender demanded, appealing to Charles.

"I didn't notice," he said, and put his hand over his eyes.

"Do you mind telling me, sir, how you came to do this?"

"Not a bit. Why should I?" Warrender rejoined, and with every appearance of exquisite discomfort added, "She asked me to. Didn't she, Charles?"

He nodded.

Alleyn pressed for more detail and got an awkward

account of the scene with a grudging confirmation from Florence and a leaden one from Charles.

"Did you use a great deal of the scent?" he asked.

"Fair amount. She *asked* me to," Warrender angrily repeated.

Charles shuddered and Alleyn said, "It's very strong, isn't it? Even the empty bottle seems to fill the room if one takes the stopper out."

"Don't!" Charles exclaimed. But Alleyn had already removed it. The smell, ponderable, sweet and improper, was disturbingly strong.

"Extraordinary!" Gantry said. "She only wore it for an afternoon and yet—the association."

"*Will* you be quiet, sir!" Warrender shouted. "My God, what sort of a cad do you call yourself? Can't you see..." He made a jerky, ineloquent gesture.

Alleyn replaced the stopper.

"Did you, do you think," he asked Warrender, "use so much that the spray could then accommodate what was left in the bottle?"

"I wouldn't have thought so."

"No," said Florence.

"And even if it was filled up again, the spray itself now only contains about that same amount. Which means, to insist on the point, that somehow or another three-quarters of the whole amount of scent has disappeared."

"That's impossible," Pinky said bluntly. "Unless it was spilt."

"No," Florence said again. Alleyn turned to her.

"And the spray and bottle were on the dressing-table when you found Miss Bellamy?"

"Must of been. I didn't stop," Florence said bitterly, "to tidy up the dressing-table."

"And the tin of Slaypest was on the floor?"

Fox placed the tin beside the other exhibits and they looked at it with horror.

"Yes?" Alleyn asked.

"Yes," said Warrender, Harkness and Gantry together, and Charles suddenly beat with his hand on the table.

"Yes, yes, *yes*," he said violently. "My God, must we have all this!"

"I'm very sorry, sir, but I'm afraid we must."

"Look here," Gantry demanded, "are you suggesting that—what the hell are you suggesting?"

"I suggest nothing," Alleyn said. "I simply want to try and clear up a rather odd state of affairs. Can anybody offer an explanation?"

"She herself—Mary—must have done something about it. Knocked it over perhaps."

"Which?" Alleyn asked politely. "The bottle or the spray?"

"I don't know," Gantry said irritably. "How should I? The spray, I suppose. And then filled it up."

"There's no sign of a spill, as Florence has pointed out."

"I know!" Bertie Saracen began. "You think it was used as a sort of blind to—to . . ."

"To what, Mr Saracen?"

"Ah, no," Bertie said in a hurry. "I—thought—no, I was muddling. I don't know."

"I think I do," Pinky said and turned very white.

"Yes?" Alleyn said.

"I won't go on. I can't. It's not clear enough. Please."

She looked Alleyn straight in the eyes. "Mr. Alleyn," Pinky said. "If you prod and insist, you'll winkle out all sorts of odd bits of information about—about arguments and rows. Inside the theatre and out. Mostly inside. Like a good many other actresses, Mary did throw the odd temperament. She threw one," Pinky went on against an almost palpable surge of consternation among her listeners, "for a matter of that, this morning."

"*Pinky!*" Gantry warned her on a rising note.

"Timmy, why not? I daresay Mr. Alleyn already knows," she said wearily.

"How very wise you are," Alleyn exclaimed. "Thank you for it. Yes, we do know, in a piecemeal sort of way, as you've suggested, that there were ructions. We *have* winkled them out. We know, for instance, that there was a difference of opinion, on professional grounds, here in this room. This morning. We know it was resurrected with other controversial matters during the party. We know that you and Mr. Saracen were involved and when I say that, I'm quite sure you're both much too sensible to suppose I'm suggesting anything more. Fox and I speak only of facts. We'll be nothing but grateful if you can help us discard as many as possible of the awkward load of facts that we've managed to accumulate."

"All this," Gantry said, "sounds mighty fine. We're on foreign ground, Pinky, and may well make fools of ourselves. You watch your step, my girl."

"I don't believe you," she said, and still looking full at Alleyn, "What do you want to know?"

"First of all, what your particular row was about."

She said, "All right with you, Bertie?"

"Oh Christmas!" he said. "I suppose so."

"You're a fool, Bertie," Timon Gantry said angrily. "These things can't be controlled. You don't know where you'll fetch up."

"But then you see, Timmy dear, I never do," Bertie rejoined with a sad little giggle.

Gantry rounded on Pinky Cavendish. "You might care to remember that other people are involved."

"I don't forget, Timmy, I promise you." She turned to Alleyn. "This morning's row," she said, "was because I told Mary I was going to play the lead in a new play. She felt I was deserting her. Later on, during the party when we were all"—she indicated the conservatory—"in there, she brought it up again."

"And was still very angry?"

Pinky looked unhappily at Charles. "It was pretty hot while it lasted. Those sorts of dusts-up always were, with Mary."

"And you were involved, Mr. Saracen?"

"Not 'alf!" Bertie said and explained why.

"And you, Mr. Gantry?"

"Very well—yes. In so far as I am to produce the comedy."

"But you copped it both ways, Timmy," Bertie pointed out with some relish. "You were involved in the other one, too. About Dicky's 'different' play and Anelida being asked to do the lead. She was angrier about that than anything. She was livid."

"Mr. Alleyn knows," Anelida said and they looked uneasily at her.

"Never mind, dear," Gantry said rather bossily. "None of this need concern you. Don't get involved."

"She *is* involved," Richard said, looking at her. "With me. Permanently, I hope."

"Really?" Pinky cried out in her warmest voice and beamed at Anelida. "How lovely! Bertie! Timmy! Isn't that lovely! Dicky, *darling*! Anelida!"

They made enthusiastic noises. It was impossible, Anelida found, not to be moved by their friendliness, but it struck her as quite extraordinary that they could switch so readily to this congratulatory vein. She caught a look of—what? Surprise? Resignation? in Alleyn's eye and was astounded when he gave her the faintest shadow of a wink.

"Delightful though it is to refresh ourselves with this news," he said, "I'm afraid I must bring you back to the matter in hand. How did the row in the conservatory arise?"

Pinky and Bertie gave him a look in which astonishment mingled with reproach.

Richard said quickly, "Mary came into the conservatory while we were discussing the casting of my play, *Husbandry in Heaven*. I should have told her—warned her. I didn't and she felt I hadn't been frank about it."

"I'm sorry, but I shall have to ask you exactly what she said."

He saw at once that Pinky, Saracen and Gantry were going to refuse. They looked quickly at one another and Gantry said rather off-handedly, "I imagine none of us remembers in any detail. When Mary threw a temperament she said all sorts of things that everybody knew she didn't mean."

"Did she, for instance, make threats of any sort?"

Gantry stood up. "For the last time," he said, "I warn you all that you're asking for every sort of trouble if you let yourselves be led into making ill-considered statements about matters that are entirely beside the point. For the last time I suggest that you consider your obligations to your profession and your careers. Keep your tongues behind your teeth or, by God, you'll regret it."

Bertie, looking frightened, said to Pinky, "He's right, you know. Or isn't he?"

"I suppose so," she agreed unhappily. "There is a limit—I suppose. All the same..."

"If ever you've trusted yourselves to my direction," Gantry said, "you do so now."

"All right." She looked at Alleyn. "Sorry."

Alleyn said, "Then I must ask Colonel Warrender and Mr. Templeton. Did Miss Bellamy utter threats of any sort?"

Warrender said, "In my opinion, Charles, this may be a case for a solicitor. One doesn't know what turn things may take. Meantime, wait and see, isn't it?"

"Very well," Charles said. "Very well."

"Mr. Dakers?" Alleyn asked.

"I'm bound by the general decision," Richard said, and Anelida, after a troubled look at him, added reluctantly:

"And I by yours."

"In that case," Alleyn said, "there's only one thing to be done. We must appeal to the sole remaining witness."

"Who the hell's that!" Warrender barked out.

"Will you see if you can get him, Fox? Mr. Montague Marchant," said Alleyn.

4

On Pinky and Bertie's part little attempt was made to disguise their consternation. It was obvious that they desired, more than anything else, an opportunity to consult together. Gantry, however, merely folded his arms, lay back in his chair and looked at the ceiling. He might have been waiting to rise in protest at a conference of Actors' Unity. Warrender, for his part, resembled a senior member at a club committee meeting. Charles fetched a heavy sigh and rested his head on his hand.

Fox went out of the room. As he opened the door into the hall a grandfather clock at the foot of the stairs was striking eleven. It provoked an involuntary exclamation from the persons Alleyn had brought together round the table. Several of them glanced in despair at their watches.

"In the meantime," Alleyn said, "shall we try to clear up the position of Mr. Richard Dakers?"

160

Anelida's heart suddenly thudded against her ribs as if drawing attention to its disregarded sovereignty. She had time to think: "I'm involved, almost without warning, in a monstrous situation. I'm committed, absolutely, to a man of whom I know next to nothing. It's a kind of dedication and I'm not prepared for it." She turned to look at Richard and, at once, knew that her allegiance, active or helpless, was irrevocable. "So this," Anelida thought in astonishment, "is what it's like to be in love."

Alleyn, aware of the immediate reactions, saw Old Ninn's hands move convulsively in her lap. He saw Florence look at her with a flash of something that might have been triumph and he saw the colour fade unevenly from Warrender's heavy face.

He went over the ground again up to the time of Richard's final return to the house.

"As you will see," he said, "there are blank passages. We don't know what passed between Mr. Dakers and Miss Bellamy in her room. We do know that, whatever it was, it seemed to distress him. We know he then went out and walked about Chelsea. We know he returned. We don't know why."

"I wanted," Richard said, "to pick up a copy of my play."

"Good. Why didn't you say so before?"

"I clean forgot," he said and looked astonished.

"Do you now remember what else you did?"

"I went up to my old study to get it."

"And did you do anything else while you were there?"

There was no answer. Alleyn said, "You wrote a letter, didn't you?"

Richard stared at him with a sort of horror. "How do you—why should you...?" He made a small desperate gesture and petered out.

"To whom?"

"It was private. I prefer not to say."

"Where is it now? You've had no opportunity to post it."

"I—haven't got it."

"What have you done with it?"

"I got rid of it." Richard raised his voice. "I hope it's destroyed. It had nothing whatever to do with all this. I've told you it was private."

"If that's true I can promise you it will remain so. Will you tell me—in private—what it was about?"

Richard looked at him, hesitated, and then said, "I'm sorry. I can't."

Alleyn drew a folded paper from his pocket. "Will you read this, if you please? Perhaps you would rather take it to the light."

"I can... All right," Richard said. He took the paper, left the table and moved over to a wall lamp. The paper rustled as he opened it. He glanced at it, crushed it in his hand, strode to the far end of the table and flung it down in front of Warrender.

"Did you *have* to do this?" he said. "My God, what sort of a man are you!" He went back to his place beside Anelida.

Warrender, opening and closing his hands, sheet-white and speaking in an unrecognizable voice, said, "I don't understand. I've done nothing. What do you mean?"

His hand moved shakily towards the inside pocket of his coat. "No! It's not... It can't be."

"Colonel Warrender," Alleyn said to Richard, "has not shown me the letter. I came by its content in an entirely different way. The thing I have shown you is a transcription. The original, I imagine, is still in his pocket."

Warrender and Richard wouldn't look at each other. Warrender said, "Then how the hell..." and stopped.

"Evidently," Alleyn said, "the transcription is near enough to the original. I don't propose at the moment to make it generally known. I will only put it to you that when you, Mr. Dakers, returned the second time, you went to your study, wrote the original of this letter and subsequently, when you were lying on the sofa in the drawing-room, passed it to Colonel Warrender, saying, for my benefit, that you had forgotten to post it for him. Do you agree?"

"Yes."

"I suggest that it refers to whatever passed between you and Mrs. Templeton when you were alone with her in her room a few minutes before she died and that you wished to make Colonel Warrender read it. I'm still ready to listen to any statement you may care to make to me in private."

To Anelida the silence seemed interminable.

"Very well," Alleyn said. "We shall have to leave it for the time being."

None of them looked at Richard. Anelida suddenly and horribly remembered something she had once heard Alleyn tell her uncle. "You always know, in a capital charge, if the jury are going to bring in a verdict of guilty: they never look at the accused when they come back." With a sense of doing something momentous she turned, looked Richard full in the face and found she could smile at him.

"It'll be all right," he said gently.

"All right!" Florence said bitterly. "It doesn't strike me as being all right, and I wonder you've the nerve to say so!"

As if Florence had put a match to her, Old Ninn exploded into fury. "You're a bad girl, Floy," she said, trembling very much and leaning across the table. "Riddled through and through with wickedness and jealousy and always have been."

"Thank you very much, I'm sure, Mrs. Plumtree," Florence countered with a shrill outbreak of laughter. "Everyone knows where your favour lies, Mrs. Plumtree, especially when you've had a drop of port wine. You wouldn't stop short of murder to back it up."

"Ninn," Richard said, before she could speak, "for the love of Mike, darling, shut up."

She reached out her small knotted hands to Charles Templeton. "You speak for him, sir. Speak for him."

Charles said gently, "You're making too much of this, Ninn. There's no need."

"There shouldn't be the need!" she cried. "And *she* knows it as well as I do." She appealed to Alleyn. "I've told you. *I've told you.* After Mr. Richard came out I heard her. That wicked woman, there, knows as well as I do." She pointed a gnarled finger at the spray-gun. "We heard her using that thing after everyone had warned her against it."

"How do you know it was the spray-gun, Ninn?"

"What else could it have been?"

Alleyn said, "It might have been her scent, you know."

"If it was! If it was, that makes no difference."

"I'm afraid it would," Alleyn said. "If the scent-spray had been filled up with Slaypest."

chapter seven

Re-entry of Mr. Marchant

THE SCENT-SPRAY, the bottle and the Slaypest tin had assumed star-quality. There they stood in a neat row, three inarticulate objects, thrust into the spotlight. They might have been so many stagehands, yanked out of their anonymity and required to give an account of themselves before an unresponsive audience. They met with a frozen reception.

Timon Gantry was the first to speak. "Have you," he asked, "any argument to support your extraordinary assumption?"

"I have," Alleyn rejoined, "but I don't propose to advance it in detail. You might call it a *reductio ad absurdum*. Nothing else fits. One hopes," he added, "that a chemical analysis of the scent-spray will do something to support it. The supposition is based on a notion that while Mrs. Templeton had very little reason, after what seems to have been a stormy interview, to deluge her plants and herself with insecticide, she may more reasonably be pictured as taking up her scent-spray, and using that."

"Not full on her face," Bertie said unexpectedly. "She'd never use it on her face. Not directly. Not after she was made-up. Would she, Pinky? Pinky—would she?"

But Pinky was not listening to him. She was watching Alleyn.

"Well, anyway," Bertie said crossly. "She wouldn't."

"Oh yes she would, Mr. Saracen," Florence said tartly. "And did. Quite regular. Standing far enough off to get the fine spray only, which was what she done, as the Colonel and Mr. Templeton will bear me out, this afternoon."

"The point," Alleyn said, "is well taken, but it doesn't, I think, affect the argument. Shall we leave it for the time being? I'm following, by the way, a very unorthodox line over this inquiry and I see no reason for not telling you why. Severally, I believe you will all go on withholding information that may be crucial. Together I have hopes that you may find these tactics impracticable." And while they still gaped at him he added, "I may be wrong about this, of course, but it does seem to me that each of you, with one exception, is most mistakenly concealing something. I say mistakenly because I don't for a moment believe that there has been any collusion in this business. I believe that one of you, under pressure of an extraordinary emotional upheaval, has acted in a solitary and an extraordinary way. It's my duty to find out who this person is. So let's press on, shall we?" He looked at Charles. "There's a dictionary of poisons in Mr. Dakers's former study. I believe it belongs to you, sir."

Charles lifted a hand, saw that it trembled, and lowered it again. "Yes," he said. "I bought it a week ago. I wanted to look up plant sprays."

"Oh my goodness me!" Bertie ejaculated and stared at him. There was a general shocked silence.

"This specific spray?" Alleyn asked, pointing to the Slaypest.

"Yes. It gives the formula. I wanted to look it up."

"For God's sake, Charles," Warrender exclaimed, "why the devil can't you make yourself understood?" Charles said nothing and he waved his hands at Alleyn. "He was worried about the damned muck!" he said. "Told Mary. Showed it..."

"Yes?" Alleyn said as he came to a halt. "Showed it to whom?"

"To me, blast it! We'd been trying to persuade her not to use the stuff. Gave it to me to read."

"Did you read it?"

"'Course I did. Lot of scientific mumbo-jumbo but it showed how dangerous it was."

"What did you do with the book?"

"*Do* with it? I dunno. Yes, I do, though. I gave it to Florence. Asked her to get Mary to look at it. Didn't I, Florence?"

"I don't," said Florence, "remember anything about it, sir. You might have."

"Please try to remember," Alleyn said. "Did you, in fact, show the book to Mrs. Templeton?"

"Not me. She wouldn't have given me any thanks." She turned round in her chair and looked at Old Ninn. "I remember now. I showed it to Mrs. Plumtree. Gave it to her."

"Well, Ninn? What did you do with the book?"

Old Ninn glared at him. "Put it by," she said. "It was unwholesome."

"Where?"

"I don't recollect."

"In the upstairs study?"

"Might have been. I don't recollect."

"So much for the book," Alleyn said wryly and turned to Warrender. "You, sir, tell us that you actually used the scent-spray, lavishly, on Mrs. Templeton before the party. There were no ill-effects. What did you do after that?"

"Do? Nothing. I went out."

"Leaving Mr. and Mrs. Templeton alone together?"

"Yes. At least..." His eyes slewed round to look at her. "There was Florence."

"No, there wasn't If you'll pardon my mentioning it, sir," Florence again intervened. "I left, just after you did, not being required any further."

"Do you agree?" Alleyn asked Charles Templeton. He drew his hand across his eyes.

"I? Oh yes. I think so."

"Do you mind telling me what happened then? Between

you and your wife?"

"We talked for a moment or two. Not long."

"About?"

"I asked her not to use the scent. I'm afraid I was in a temper about it." He glanced at Pinky. I'm sorry, Pinky, I just—didn't like it. I expect my taste is hopelessly old-fashioned."

"That's all right, Charles. My God," Pinky added in a low voice, "I never want to smell it again, myself, as long as I live."

"Did Mrs. Templeton agree not to use it again?"

"No," he said at once. "She didn't. She thought me unreasonable."

"Did you talk about anything else?"

"About nothing that I care to recall."

"Is that final?"

"Final," Charles said.

"Did it concern, in some way, Mr. Dakers and Colonel Warrender?"

"Damn it!" Warrender shouted. "He's said he's not going to tell you, isn't it!"

"It did concern them," Charles said.

"Where did you go when this conversation ended?"

"I went downstairs to my study. Richard came in at about that time and was telephoning. We stayed there until the first guests arrived."

"And you, Colonel Warrender? Where were you at this time? What did you do when you left the bedroom?"

"Ah—I was in the drawing-room. She—ah—Mary—came in. She wanted a re-arrangement of the tables. Gracefield and the other fella did it and she and I had a drink."

"Did she seem quite herself, did you think?"

"Rather nervy. Bit on edge."

"Why?"

"Been a trying day, isn't it?"

"Anything in particular?"

He glanced at Richard. "No," he said. "Nothing else."

Fox returned. "Mr. Marchant will be here in about a quarter of an hour, sir," he said.

There were signs of consternation from Pinky, Bertie and Timon Gantry.

"Right." Alleyn got up, walked to the far end of the table and picked up the crumpled paper that still lay where Richard had thrown it down. "I must ask Colonel Warrender and Mr. Dakers to give me a word or two in private. Perhaps we may use the study."

They both rose with the same abrupt movement and followed him from the room, stiffly erect.

He ushered them into the study and turned to Fox who had come into the hall.

"I'd better take this one solus, I think, Fox. Will you get the exhibits sent at once for analysis. Say it's first priority and we're looking for a trace of Slaypest in the scent-spray. They needn't expect to find more than a trace, I fancy. I want the result as soon as possible. Then go back to the party in there. See you later."

In Charles Templeton's study, incongruously friendly and comfortable, Warrender and Richard Dakers faced Alleyn, still not looking at each other.

Alleyn said, "I've asked you in here, without witnesses, to confirm or deny the conclusion I have drawn from the case-history, as far as it goes. Which is not by any means all the way. If I'm wrong, one or both of you can have a shot at knocking me down or hitting me across the face or performing any other of the conventional gestures. But I don't advise you to try."

They stared at him apparently in horrified astonishment.

"Well," he said, "here goes. My idea, such as it is, based on this business of the letter, which, since you seem to accept my pot shot at it, runs like this."

He smoothed out the crumpled sheet of paper. "It's pieced together, by the way," he said, "from the impression left on the blotting-paper." He looked at Richard. "The original was written, I believe, by you to Mrs. Templeton when you returned, finally, to the house. I'm going to read this transcription aloud. If it's wrong anywhere, I hope you'll correct me."

Warrender said, "There's no need."

"Perhaps not. Would you prefer to show me the original?"

With an air of diffidence that sat very ill on him, Warrender appealed to Richard. "Whatever you say," he muttered.

Richard said, "Very well! Go on. Go on. Show him."

Warrender put his hand inside his coat and drew out an envelope. He dropped it on Charles Templeton's desk, crossed to the fireplace and stood there with his back turned to them.

Alleyn picked up the envelope. The word "Mary" was written on it in green ink. He took out the enclosure and laid his transcription beside it on the desk. As he read it through to himself the room seemed monstrously quiet. The fire settled in the grate. A car or two drove past and the clock in the hall told the half-hour.

"I've come back," Alleyn read, *"to say that it would be no use my pretending I haven't been given a terrible shock and that I can't get it sorted out, but I'm sure it will be better if we don't meet. I can't think clearly now, but at least I know I'll never forgive your treatment of Anelida this afternoon. I should have been told everything from the beginning. R."*

He folded the two papers and put them aside. "So they do correspond," he said. "And the handwriting is Mr. Dakers's."

Neither Richard nor Warrender moved or spoke.

"I think," Alleyn said, "that when you came back for the last time, you went up to your study and wrote this letter with the intention of putting it under her door. When you were about to do so you heard voices in the room, since two of my men were working there. So you came downstairs and were prevented from going out by the constable on duty. It was then that you came into the room where I was interviewing the others. The letter was in your breast pocket. You wanted to get rid of it and you wanted Colonel Warrender to know what was in it. So you passed it to him when you were lying on the sofa in the drawing-room. Do you agree?"

Richard nodded and turned away.

"This evening," Alleyn went on, "after Mr. Dakers left the Pegasus Bookshop, you, Colonel Warrender, also paid a call on Octavius Browne. Dusk had fallen but you were standing in the window when Octavius came in and seeing you against it he mistook you for his earlier visitor, who he thought must have returned. He was unable to say why he made this mistake, but I think I can account for it. Your heads are very much the same shape. The relative angles and distances from hairline to the top of the nose, from there to the tip and from the tip to the chin are almost identical. Seen in silhouette with the other features obliterated, your profiles must be strikingly alike. In full-face the resemblance disappears. Colonel Warrender has far greater width and a heavier jawline."

"In these respects," he said, "Mr. Dakers, I think, takes after his mother."

2

"Well," Alleyn said at last, after a long silence, "I'm glad, at least, that it seems I am not going to be knocked down."

Warrender said, "I've nothing to say. Unless it's to point out that, as things have come about, I've had no opportunity to speak to"—he lifted his head—"to my son."

Richard said, "I don't want to discuss it. I should have been told from the beginning."

"Whereas," Alleyn said, "you were told, weren't you, by your mother this afternoon. You went upstairs with her when you returned from the Pegasus and she told you then."

"Why!" Warrender cried out. "Why, why, *why*?"

"She was angry," Richard said. "With me." He looked at Alleyn. "You've heard or guessed most of it, apparently. She thought I'd conspired against her."

"Yes?"

"Well—that's all. That's how it was."

Alleyn waited. Richard drove his hands through his hair. "All right!" he cried out. "All right! I'll tell you. I suppose I've got to, haven't I? She accused me of ingratitude and disloyalty. I said I considered I owed her no more than I had already paid. I wouldn't have said that if she hadn't insulted Anelida. Then she came quite close to me and—it was horrible—I could see a nerve jumping under her cheek. She kept repeating that I owed her everything—everything, and that I'd insulted her by going behind her back. Then I said she'd no right to assume a controlling interest in either my friendships or my work. She said she had every right. And then it all came out. Everything. It happened because of our anger. We were both very angry. When she'd told me, she laughed as if she'd scored with the line of climax in a big scene. If she hadn't done that I might have felt some kind of compassion or remorse or something. I didn't. I felt cheated and sick and empty. I went downstairs and out into the streets and walked about trying to find an appropriate emotion. There was nothing but a sort of faint disgust." He moved away and then turned to Alleyn. "But I didn't murder my"—he caught his breath—"my brand-new mother. I'm not, it appears, that kind of bastard."

Warrender said, "For God's sake, Dicky!"

"Just for the record," Richard said, "*were* there two people called Dakers? A young married couple, killed in a car on the Riviera? Australians, I've always been given to understand."

"It's—it's a family name. My mother was a Dakers."

"I see," Richard said. "I just wondered. It didn't occur to you to marry her, evidently." He stopped short and a look of horror crossed his face. "I'm sorry! I'm sorry!" he cried out. "Forgive me, Maurice, it wasn't I who said that."

"My dear chap, of course I wanted to marry her. She wouldn't have it! She was at the beginning of her career. What could I give her? A serving ensign on a very limited allowance. She—naturally—she wasn't prepared to throw up her career and follow the drum."

"And—Charles?"

"He was in a different position. Altogether."

"Rich? Able to keep her in the style to which she would like to become accustomed?"

"There's no need," Warrender muttered, "to put it like that."

"Poor Charles!" Richard said and then suddenly, "Did he know?"

Warrender turned a painful crimson. "No," he said. "It was—it was all over by then."

"Did he believe in the Dakers story?"

"I think," Warrender said after a pause, "he believed everything Mary told him."

"Poor Charles!" Richard repeated, and then turned on Alleyn. "He's not going to be told? Not now! It'd kill him. There's no need—is there?"

"None," Alleyn said, "that I can see."

"And you!" Richard demanded of Warrender.

"Oh for God's sake, Dicky!"

"No. Naturally. Not you."

There was a long silence.

"I remember," Richard said at last, "that she once told me it was you who brought them together. What ambivalent roles you both contrived to play. Restoration comedy at its most elaborate."

Evidently they had forgotten Alleyn. For the first time they looked fully at each other.

"Funny," Richard said. "I have wondered if Charles was my father. Some pre-marital indiscretion, I thought it might have been. I fancied I saw a likeness—the family one, of course. You and Charles are rather alike, aren't you? I must say I never quite believed in the Dakers. But why did it never occur to me that she was my mother? It really was very clever of her to put herself so magnificently out of bounds."

"I don't know," Warrender exclaimed, "what to say to you. There's nothing I can say."

"Never mind."

"It need make no difference. To your work. Or to your marrying."

"I really don't know how Anelida will feel about it. Unless..."He turned, as if suddenly aware of him, to Alleyn. "Unless, of course, Mr. Alleyn is going to arrest me for matricide, which will settle everything very neatly, won't it?"

"I shouldn't," Alleyn said, "depend upon it. Suppose you set about clearing yourself if you can. Can you?"

"How the hell do I know? What am I supposed to have done?"

"It's more a matter of finding out what you couldn't have done. Where did you lunch? Here?"

"No. At the Garrick. It was a business luncheon."

"And after that?"

"I went to my flat and did some work. I'd got a typist in."

"Until when?"

"Just before six. I was waiting for a long-distance call from Edinburgh. I kept looking at the time because I was running late. I was meant to be here at six to organize the drinks. At last I fixed it up for the call to be transferred to this number. As it was I ran late and Mary—and she was coming downstairs. The call came through at a quarter to seven just as I arrived."

"Where did you take it?"

"Here in the study. Charles was there. He looked ill and I was worried about him. He didn't seem to want to talk. I kept getting cut off. It was important, and I had to wait. She—wasn't very pleased about that. The first people were arriving when I'd finished."

"So what did you do?"

"Went into the drawing-room with Charles and did my stuff."

"Had you brought her some Parma violets?"

"I? No. She hated violets."

"Did you see them in her room?"

"I didn't go up to her room. I've told you—I was here in the study."

"When had you last been in her room?"

"This morning."

"Did you visit it between then and the final time when you returned from the Pegasus and this disturbing scene took place?"

"I've told you. How could I? I . . ." His voice changed. "I was with Anelida until she left and I followed her into the Pegasus."

"Well," Alleyn said after a pause, "if all this is provable, and I don't see why it shouldn't be, you're in the clear."

Warrender gave a sharp outcry and turned quickly, but Richard said flatly, "I don't understand."

"If our reading of the facts is the true one, this crime was to all intents and purposes committed between the time (somewhere about six o'clock) when Mrs. Templeton was sprayed with scent by Colonel Warrender and the time fixed by a press photographer at twenty-five minutes to eight, when she returned to her room with you. She never left her room and died in it a few minutes after you had gone."

Richard flinched at the last phrase but seemed to have paid little attention to the earlier part. For the first time, he was looking at his father, who had turned his back to them.

"Colonel Warrender," Alleyn said, "why did you go to the Pegasus?"

Without moving he said, "Does it matter? I wanted to get things straight. With the gel."

"But you didn't see her?"

"No."

"Maurice," Richard said abruptly.

Colonel Warrender faced him.

"I call you that still," Richard went on. "I suppose it's not becoming, but I can't manage anything else. There are all sorts of adjustments to be arranged, aren't there? I know I'm not making this easy for either of us. You see one doesn't know how one's meant to behave. But I hope in time to do better: you'll have to give me time."

"I'll do that," Warrender said unevenly.

He made a slight movement as if to hold out his hand, glanced at Alleyn and withdrew it.

"I think," Alleyn said, "that I should get on with my job. I'll let you knew when we need you."

And he went out, leaving them helplessly together.

In the hall he encountered Fox.

"Peculiar party in there," he said. "Boy meets father. Both heavily embarrassed. They manage these things better in France. What goes on at your end of the table?"

"I came out to tell you, sir. Mr. Templeton's come over very poorly again, and Dr. Harkness thinks he's had about as much as he can take. He's lying down in the drawing-room, but as soon as he can manage it the doctor wants to get him into bed. The idea is to make one up in his study and save the stairs. I thought the best thing would be to let those two—Florence and Mrs. Plumtree—fix it up. The doctor'll help him when the time comes."

"Yes. All right. What a hell of a party this is, by and large. All right. But they'll have to bung the mixed-up playwright and his custom-built poppa out of it. Where? Into

175

mama-deceased's boudoir, I suppose. Or they can rejoin that goon-show round the dining-room table. *I* don't know. Nobody tells me a thing. What else?"

"None of them will own up to knowing anything about the Parma violets. They all say she had no time for violets."

"Blast and stink! Then who the devil put them on her dressing-table? The caterer in a fit of frustrated passion? Why the devil should we be stuck with a bunch of Parma violets wilting on our plates."

Like Scheherazade, Fox discreetly fell silent.

"Pardon me, sir, but did I hear you mention violets?"

It was Gracefield, wan in the countenance, who had emerged from the far end of the hall.

"You did indeed," Alleyn said warmly.

"If it is of any assistance, sir, a bunch of violets was brought in immediately prior to the reception. I admitted the gentleman myself, sir, and he subsequently presented them to madam on the first floor landing."

"You took his name, I hope, Gracefield?"

"Quite so, sir. It was the elderly gentleman from the bookshop. The name is Octavius Browne."

3

"And what the merry hell," Alleyn ejaculated when Gracefield had withdrawn, "did Octavius think he was up to, prancing about with violets at that hour of the day? Damnation, I'll have to find out, and Marchant's due any minute. Come on."

They went out at the front door. Light still glowed behind the curtains at the Pegasus.

"You hold the fort here, Fox, for five minutes. Let them get Templeton settled down in the study, and if Marchant turns up, keep him till I'm back. Don't put him in with that horde of extroverts in the dining-room. Save him up. What a go!"

He rang the bell and Octavius opened the door.

"You again!" he said. "How late! I thought you were Anelida."

"Well, I'm not and I'm sorry it's late, but you'll have to let me in."

"Very well," Octavius said, standing aside. "What's up, now?"

"Why," Alleyn asked, as soon as the door was shut, "did you take violets to Mrs. Templeton?"

Octavius blushed. "A man with a handcart," he said, "went past the window. They came from the Channel Islands."

"I don't give a damn where they came from. It's where they went to that matters. When did the cart go past?"

Octavius, disconcerted and rather huffy, was bustled into telling his story. Anelida had sent him downstairs while she got ready for the party. He was fretful because they'd been asked for half-past six and it was now twenty-five to seven and he didn't believe her story of the need to arrive late. He saw the handcart with the Parma violets and remembered that in his youth these flowers had been considered appropriate adjuncts to ladies of the theatre. So he went out and bought some. He then, Alleyn gathered, felt shy about presenting them in front of Anelida. The door of Miss Bellamy's house was open. The butler was discernible in the hall. Octavius mounted the steps. "After all," he said, "one preferred to give her the opportunity of attaching them in advance if she chose to do so."

He was in the act of handing them over to Gracefield when he heard a commotion on the first landing and a moment later Miss Bellamy shouted out at the top of her voice, "Which only shows how wrong you were. You can get out whenever you like, my friend, and the sooner the better."

For a moment Octavius was extremely flustered, imagining that he himself was thus addressed, but the next second she appeared above him on the stairs. She stopped short and gazed down at him in astonishment. "A vision," Octavius said. "Rose-coloured or more accurately, geranium, but with the air, I must confess, of a Fury."

This impression, however, was almost at once dissipated. Miss Bellamy seemed to hesitate, Gracefield murmured an explanation which Octavius himself elaborated. "And then, you know," he said, "suddenly she was all graciousness. Overwhelmingly so. She"—he blushed again—"asked me to come up and I went. I presented my little votive offering. And

177

then, in point of fact, she invited me into her room: a pleasing and Gallic informality. I was not unmoved by it. She laid the flowers on her dressing-table and told me she had just given an old bore the sack. Those were her words. I gathered that it was somebody who had been in her service for a long period. What did you say?"

"Nothing. Go on. You interest me strangely."

"Do I? Well. At that juncture there were sounds of voices downstairs—the door, naturally, remained open—and she said, 'Wait a moment, will you?' And left me."

"Well?" Alleyn said after a pause.

"Well, I did wait. Nothing happened. I bethought me of Nelly, who would surely be ready by now. Rightly or wrongly," Octavius said, with a sidelong look at Alleyn, "I felt that Nelly would be not entirely in sympathy with my impulsive little *sortie* and I was therefore concerned to return before I could be missed. So I went downstairs and there *she* was, speaking to Colonel Warrender in the drawing-room. They paid no attention to me. I don't think they saw me. Warrender, I thought, looked very much put out. There seemed nothing to do but go away. So I went. A curious and not unintriguing experience."

"Thank you, Octavius," Alleyn said, staring thoughtfully at him. "Thank you very much. And now I, too, must leave you. Good-night."

As he went out he heard Octavius saying rather fretfully that he supposed he might as well go to bed.

A very grand car had drawn up outside Miss Bellamy's house and Mr. Montague Marchant was climbing out of it. His blond head gleamed, his overcoat was impeccable and his face exceedingly pale.

"Wait," he said to his chauffeur.

Alleyn introduced himself. The anticipated remark was punctually delivered.

"This is a terrible business," said Mr. Marchant.

"Very bad," Alleyn said. "Shall we go in?"

Fox was in the hall.

"I just don't quite understand," Marchant said, "why I've been sent for. Naturally, we—her management—want to give every assistance but at the same time..." He waved his pearly gloves.

Alleyn said, "It's simple. There are one or two purely business matters to be settled and it looks as if you are our sole authority."

"I should have thought..."

"Of course you would," Alleyn rejoined. "But there is some need for immediate action. Miss Bellamy has been murdered."

Marchant unsteadily passed his hand over the back of his head. "I don't believe you," he said.

"You may as well, because it happens to be true. Would you like to take your coat off? No? Then, shall we go in?"

Fox said, "We've moved into the drawing-room, sir, it being more comfortable. The doctor is with Mr. Templeton but will be coming in later."

"Where's Florence?"

"She helped Mrs. Plumtree with the bed-making and they're both waiting in the boudoir in case required."

"Right. In here, if you will, Mr. Marchant. I'll just have a look at the patient and then I'll join you."

He opened the door. After a moment's hesitation, Marchant went through and Fox followed him.

Alleyn went to the study, tapped on the door and went in.

Charles was in bed, looking very drawn and anxious. Dr. Harkness sat in a chair at a little distance, watching him. When he saw Alleyn he said, "We can't have any further upsets."

"I know," Alleyn rejoined and walked over to the bed. "I've only come in to inquire," he said.

Charles whispered, "I'm sorry about this. I'm all right. I could have carried on."

"There's no need. We can manage."

"There you are, Charles," Harkness said. "Stop fussing."

"But I want to know, Harkness! How can I stop fussing! My God, what a thing to say! I want to know what they're thinking and saying. I've a right to know. Alleyn, for God's sake tell me. You don't suspect—anyone close to her, do you? I can stand anything but that. Not—not the boy?"

"As things stand," Alleyn said, "there's no case against him."

"Ah!" Charles sighed and closed his eyes. "Thank God for that." He moved restlessly and his breath came short. "It's all these allusions and hints and evasions..." he began excitedly. "Why can't I be told things! Why not? Do you suspect *me*! Do you? Then for Christ's sake let's have it and be done with it."

Harkness came over to the bed. "This won't do at all," he said and to Alleyn, "Out."

"Yes, of course," Alleyn said and went out. He heard Charles panting, "But I *want* to talk to him," and Harkness trying to reassure him.

When Marchant went into the drawing-room Timon Gantry, Colonel Warrender, Pinky Cavendish and Bertie Saracen were sitting disconsolately in armchairs before a freshly tended fire. Richard and Anelida were together at some remove from the others and P.C. Philpott attended discreetly in the background. When Marchant came in, Pinky and Bertie made a little dash at him and Richard stood up. Marchant kissed Pinky with ritual solemnity, squeezed Bertie's arm, nodded at Gantry, and advanced upon Richard with soft extended hand.

"Dear boy!" he said. "What can one say! Oh my *dear* Dicky!"

Richard appeared to permit, rather than return, a long pressure of his hand. Marchant added a manly grip of his shoulder and moved on to acknowledge, more briefly, Anelida and Colonel Warrender. His prestige was unmistakable. He said any number of highly appropriate things. They listened to him dolefully and appeared to be relieved when at last Alleyn came in.

Alleyn said, "Before going any further, Mr. Marchant, I think I should make it quite clear that any questions I may put to you will be raised with the sole object of clearing innocent persons of suspicion and of helping towards the solution of an undoubted case of homicide. Mary Bellamy has been murdered; I believe by someone who is now in this house. You will understand that matters of personal consideration or professional reticence can't be allowed to obstruct an investigation of this sort. Any attempt to withhold information may have disastrous results. On the other hand information that turns out to be irrelevant, as yours, of course, may, will be entirely wiped out. Is that understood?"

Gantry said, "In my opinion, Monty, we should take legal advice."

Marchant looked thoughtfully at him.

"You are at liberty to do so," Alleyn said. "You are also at liberty to refuse to answer to any or all questions until the arrival of your solicitor. Suppose you hear the questions and then decide."

Marchant examined his hands, lifted his gaze to Alleyn's face and said, "What are they?"

There was a restless movement among the others.

"First. What exactly was Mrs. Templeton's, or perhaps in this connection I should say Miss Bellamy's, position in the firm of Marchant & Company?"

Marchant raised his eyebrows. "A leading and distinguished artist who played exclusively for our management."

"Any business connection other than that?"

"Certainly," he said at once. "She had a controlling interest."

"Monty!" Bertie cried out.

"Dear boy, an examination of our shareholders list would give it."

"Has she held this position for some time?"

"Since 1956. Before that it was vested in her husband, but he transferred his holdings to her in that year."

"I had no idea he had financial interests in the theatre world."

"These were his only ones, I believe. After the war we were in considerable difficulties. Like many other managements we were threatened with a complete collapse. You may say that he saved us."

"In taking this action was he influenced by his wife's connections with the Management?"

"She brought the thing to his notice, but fundamentally I should say he believed in the prospect of our recovery and expansion. In the event he proved to be fully justified."

"Why did he transfer his share to her, do you know?"

"I don't know, but I can conjecture. His health is precarious. He's—he was—a devoted husband. He may have been thinking of death duties."

"Yes, I see."

Marchant said, "It's so warm in here," and unbuttoned his

overcoat. Fox helped him out of it. He sat down, very elegantly and crossed his legs. The others watched him anxiously.

The door opened and Dr. Harkness came in. He nodded at Alleyn and said, "Better, but he's had as much as he can take."

"Anyone with him?"

"The old nurse. He'll settle down now. No more visits, mind."

"Right."

Dr. Harkness sat heavily on the sofa and Alleyn turned again to Marchant.

"Holding, as you say, a controlling interest," he said, "she must have been a power to reckon with, as far as other employees of the Management were concerned."

The lids drooped a little over Marchant's very pale eyes. "I really don't think I follow you," he said.

"She was, everyone agrees, a temperamental woman. For instance, this afternoon, we are told, she cut up very rough indeed. In the conservatory."

The heightened tension of his audience could scarcely have been more apparent if they'd begun to twang like bow-strings, but none of them spoke.

"She would throw a temperament," Marchant said coolly, "if she felt the occasion for it."

"And she felt the occasion in this instance?"

"Quite so."

"Suppose, for the sake of argument, she had pressed for the severance of some long-standing connection with your management? Would she have carried her point?"

"I'm afraid I don't follow that either."

"I'll put it brutally. If she'd demanded that you sign no more contracts with, say, Mr. Gantry or Mr. Saracen or Miss Cavendish, would you have had to toe the line?"

"I would have talked softly and expected her to calm down."

"But if she'd stuck to it?" Alleyn waited for a moment and then took his risk. "Come," he said. "She did issue an ultimatum this afternoon."

Saracen scrambled to his feet. "There!" he shouted.

"What did I tell you! Somebody's blown the beastly gaff and now we're to suffer for it. I *said* we should talk first, ourselves, and be frank and forthcoming and see how right I was!"

Gantry said, "For God's sake hold your tongue, Bertie."

"What do we get for holding our tongues?" He pointed to Warrender. "We get an outsider giving the whole thing away with both hands. I bet you, Timmy. I bet you anything you like."

"Utter balderdash!" Warrender exclaimed. "I don't know what you think you're talking about, Saracen."

"Oh pooh! You've told the Inspector or Commander or Great Panjandrum or whatever he is. You've *told* him."

"On the contrary," Gantry said, "you've told him yourself. You *fool*, Bertie."

Pinky Cavendish, in what seemed to be an agony of exasperation, cried out, "Oh *why*, for God's sake, can't we all admit we're no good at this sort of hedging! I can! Freely *and* without prejudice to the rest of you, if that's what you're all afraid of. And what's more, I'm going to. Look here, Mr. Alleyn, this is what happened to me in the conservatory. Mary accused me of conspiring against her and told Monty it was either her or me as far as the Management was concerned. Just that. And if it really came to the point I can assure you it'd be her and not me. You know, Monty, and we *all* know, that with her name and star-ranking, Mary was worth a damn sight more than me at the box-office *and* in the firm. All right! This very morning you'd handed me my first real opportunity with the Management. She was well able, if she felt like it, to cook my goose. But I'm no more capable of murdering her than I am of taking her place with her own particular public. And when you hear an actress admit that kind of thing," Pinky added, turning to Alleyn, "you can bet your bottom dollar she's talking turkey."

Alleyn said, "Produce this sort of integrity on the stage, Miss Cavendish, and nobody will be able to cook your goose for you." He looked round at Pinky's deeply perturbed audience, "Has anybody got anything to add to this?" he added.

After a pause, Richard said, "Only that I'd like to endorse

what Pinky said and to add that, as you and everybody else know, I was just as deeply involved as she. More so."

"Dicky darling!" Pinky said warmly. "No! Where you are now! Offer a comedy on the open market and watch the managements bay like ravenous wolves."

"Without Mary?" Marchant asked of nobody in particular.

"It's quite true," Richard said, "that I wrote specifically for Mary."

"Not always. And no reason," Gantry intervened, "why you shouldn't write now for somebody else." Once again he bestowed his most disarming smile on Anelida.

"Why not indeed!" Pinky cried warmly and laid her hand on Anelida's.

"Ah!" Richard said, putting his arm about her. "That's another story. Isn't it, darling?"

Wave after wave of unconsidered gratitude flowed through Anelida. "These are my people," she thought. "I'm in with them for the rest of my life."

"The fact remains, however," Gantry was saying to Alleyn, "that Bertie, Pinky, and Richard all stood to lose by Mary's death. A point you might care to remember."

"Oh lawks!" Bertie said. "*Aren't* we all suddenly generous and noble-minded! Everybody loves everybody! Safety in numbers, or so they say. Or do they?"

"In this instance," Alleyn said, "they well might." He turned to Marchant. "Would you agree that, with the exception of her husband, yourself and Colonel Warrender, Miss Bellamy issued some kind of ultimatum against each member of the group in the conservatory?"

"Would I?" Marchant said easily. "Well, yes. I think I would."

"To the effect that it was either they or she and you could take your choice?"

"More or less," he murmured, looking at his fingernails.

Gantry rose to his enormous height and stood over Marchant.

"It would be becoming in you, Monty," he said dangerously, "if you acknowledged that as far as I enter into

184

the picture the question of occupational anxiety does not arise. I choose my managements; they do not choose me."

Marchant glanced at him. "Nobody questions your prestige, I imagine, Timmy. I certainly don't."

"Or mine, I hope," said Bertie, rallying. "The offers I've turned down for the Management! Well, I mean to say! Face it, Monty dear, if Mary *had* bullied you into breaking off with Dicky and Timmy and Pinky and me, you'd have been in a very pretty pickle yourself."

"I am not," Marchant said, "a propitious subject for bullying."

"No." Bertie agreed. "Evidently." And there followed a deadly little pause. "I'd be obliged to everybody," he added rather breathlessly, "if they wouldn't set about reading horrors of any sort into what was an utterly unmeaningful little observation."

"In common," Warrender remarked, "with the rest of your conversation."

"Oh but what a catty big Colonel we've got!" Bertie said.

Marchant opened his cigarette case. "It seems," he observed, "incumbent on me to point out that, unlike the rest of you, I am ignorant of the circumstances. After Mary's death, I left the house at the request of—he put a cigarette between his lips and turned his head slightly to look at Fox—"yes, at the request of this gentleman, who merely informed me that there had been a fatal accident. Throughout the entire time that Mary was absent until Florence made her announcement, I was in full view of about forty guests and those of you who had not left the drawing-room. I imagine I do not qualify for the star role." He lit his cigarette. "Or am I wrong?" he asked Alleyn.

"As it turns out, Monty," Gantry intervened, "you're dead wrong. It appears that the whole thing was laid on before Mary went to her room."

Marchant waited for a moment, and then said, "You astonish me."

"Fancy!" Bertie exclaimed and added in an exasperated voice, "I *do* wish, oh *how* I do wish, dearest Monty, that you would stop being a parody of your smooth little self and get down to tin-tacks (*why* tin-tacks, one wonders?) and admit that, like all the rest of us, you qualify for the homicide stakes."

"And what," Alleyn asked, "have you got to say to that, Mr. Marchant?"

An uneven flush mounted over Marchant's cheekbones. "Simply," he said, "that I think everybody has, most understandably, become overwrought by this tragedy and that, as a consequence, a great deal of nonsense is being bandied about on all hands. And, as an afterthought, that I agree with Timon Gantry. I prefer to take no further part in this discussion until I have consulted my solicitor."

"By all means," Alleyn said. "Will you ring him up? The telephone is over there in the corner."

Marchant leant a little further back in his chair. "I'm afraid that's quite out of the question," he said. "He lives in Buckinghamshire. I can't possibly call him up at this time of night."

"In that case you will give me your own address, if you please, and I shan't detain you any longer."

"My address is in the telephone book and I can assure you that you are not detaining me now nor are you likely to do so in the future." He half-closed his eyes. "I resent," he said, "the tone of this interview, but I prefer to keep observation—if that is the accepted police jargon—upon its sequel. I'll leave when it suits me to do so."

"You can't," Colonel Warrender suddenly announced in a parade-ground voice, "take that tone with the police, sir."

"Can't I?" Marchant murmured. "I promise you, my dear Colonel, I can take whatever tone I bloody well choose with whoever I bloody well like."

Into the dead silence that followed this announcement, there intruded a distant but reminiscent commotion. A door slammed and somebody came running up the hall.

"My *God*, what now!" Bertie Saracen cried out. With the exception of Marchant and Dr. Harkness they were all on their feet when Florence, grotesque in tin curling pins, burst into the room.

In an appalling parody of her fatal entrance she stood there, mouthing at them.

Alleyn strode over to her and took her by the wrist. "What is it?" he said. "Speak up."

And Florence, as if in moments of catastrophe she was in command of only one phrase, gabbled, "The doctor! Quick! For Christ's sake! Is the doctor in the house!"

chapter eight

Pattern Completed

CHARLES TEMPLETON lay face down, as if he had fallen forward, with his head toward the foot of the bed that had been made up for him in the study. One arm hung to the floor, the other was outstretched beyond the end of the bed. The back of his neck was empurpled under its margin of thin white hair. His pyjama jacket was dragged up, revealing an expanse of torso—old, white and flaccid. When Alleyn raised him and held him in a sitting position, his head lolled sideways, his mouth and eyes opened and a flutter of sound wavered in his throat. Dr. Harkness leant over him, pinching up the skin of his forearm to admit the needle. Fox hovered nearby. Florence, her knuckles clenched between her teeth, stood just inside the door. Charles seemed to be unaware of these four onlookers; his gaze wandered past them, fixed itself in terror on the fifth; the short person who stood pressed back against the wall in shadow at the end of the room.

The sound in his throat was shaped with great difficulty

into one word. "No!' it whispered. "No! No!"

Dr. Harkness withdrew the needle.

"What is it?" Alleyn said. "What do you want to tell us?"

The eyes did not blink or change their direction, but after a second or two they lost focus, glazed, and remained fixed. The jaw dropped, the body quivered and sank.

Dr. Harkness leant over it for some time and then drew back.

"Gone," he said.

Alleyn laid his burden down and covered it.

In a voice that they had not heard from him before, Dr. Harkness said, "He was all right ten minutes ago. Settled. Quiet. Something's gone wrong here and I've got to hear what it was." He turned on Florence. "Well?"

Florence, with an air that was half combative, half frightened, moved forward, keeping her eyes on Alleyn.

"Yes," Alleyn said, answering her look, "we must hear from you. You raised the alarm. What happened?"

"That's what I'd like to know!" she said at once. "I did the right thing, didn't I? I called the doctor. Now!"

"You'll do the right thing again, if you please, by telling me what happened before you called him."

She darted a glance at the small motionless figure in shadow at the end of the room and wetted her lips.

"Come on, now," Fox said. "Speak up."

Standing where she was, a serio-comic figure under her panoply of tin hair curlers, she did tell her story.

After Dr. Harkness had given his order, she and—again that sidelong glance—she and Mrs. Plumtree had made up the bed in the study. Dr. Harkness had helped Mr. Templeton undress and had seen him into bed and they had all waited until he was settled down, comfortably. Dr. Harkness had left after giving orders that he was to be called if wanted. Florence had then gone to the pantry to fill a second hot-water bottle. This had taken some time as she had been obliged to boil a kettle. When she returned to the hall she had heard voices raised in the study. It seemed that she had paused outside the door. Alleyn had a picture of her, a hot-water bottle under her arm, listening avidly. She had heard Mrs. Plumtree's voice but had been unable to distinguish any words. Then, she said, she had heard Mr. Templeton cry "No!" three times, just as he did before he died, only much louder; as if, Florence said, he was frightened. After that there had been a clatter and Mrs. Plumtree had suddenly become audible. She had shouted, Florence reported, at the top of her voice, "I'll put a stop to it," Mr. Templeton had given a loud cry and Florence had burst into the room.

"All right," Alleyn said. "And what did you find?"

A scene, it appeared, of melodrama. Mrs. Plumtree with the poker grasped and upraised, Mr. Templeton sprawled along the bed, facing her.

"And when they seen me," Florence said, "she dropped the poker in the hearth and he gasped 'Florrie, don't let 'er' and then he took a turn for the worse and I see he was very bad. So I said, 'Don't you touch 'im. Don't you dare,' and I fetched the doctor like you say. And God's my witness," Florence concluded, "if she isn't the cause of his death! As good as if she'd struck him down, ill and all as he was, and which she'd of done if I hadn't come in when I did and which she'd do to me now if it wasn't for you gentlemen."

She stopped breathless. There was a considerable pause. "Well!" she demanded. "Don't you believe it? All right, then. Ask her. Go on. Ask her!"

"Everything in its turn," Alleyn said. "That will do from you for the moment. Stay where you are." He turned to the short motionless figure in the shadows. "Come along," he said. "You can't avoid it, you know. Come along."

She moved out into the light. Her small nose and the areas over her cheekbones were still patched with red, but otherwise her face was a dreadful colour. She said, automatically, it seemed, "You're a wicked girl, Floy."

"Never mind about that," Alleyn said. "Are *you* going to tell me what happened?"

She looked steadily up into his face. Her mouth was shut like a trap, but her eyes were terrified.

"Look here, Ninn," Dr. Harkness began very loudly. Alleyn raised a finger and he stopped short.

"Has Florence," Alleyn asked, "spoken the truth? I mean as to facts. As to what she saw and heard when she came back to this room?"

She nodded, very slightly.

"You had the poker in your hand. You dropped it when she came in. Mr. Templeton said, 'Florrie, don't let her.' That's true, isn't it?"

"Yes."

"And before she came in you had said, very loudly, to Mr. Templeton 'I'll put a stop to it'? Did you say this?"

"Yes."

"What were you going to put a stop to?"

Silence.

"Was it something Mr. Templeton had said he would do?"

She shook her head.

For a lunatic second or two Alleyn was reminded of a panel game on television. He saw the Plumtree face in close-up; tight-lipped, inimical, giving nothing away, winning the round.

He looked at Fox. "Would you take Florence into the hall? You too, Dr. Harkness, if you will?"

"I'm not going," Florence said. "You can't make me."

"Oh yes, I can," Alleyn rejoined tranquilly, "but you'd be very foolish to put it to the test. Out you go, my girl."

Fox approached her. "You keep your hands off me!" she said.

"Now, now!" Fox rumbled cosily. He opened the door. For a moment she looked as if she would show fight and then, with a lift of her chin, she went out. Fox followed her.

Dr. Harkness said, "There are things to be done. I mean..." He gestured at the covered form on the bed.

"I know. I don't expect to be long. Wait for me in the hall, will you, Harkness?"

The door shut behind them.

For perhaps ten seconds Alleyn and that small, determined and miserable little woman looked at each other.

Then he said, "It's got to come out, you know. You've been trying to save him, haven't you?"

Her hands moved convulsively, and she looked in terror at the bed.

"No, no," Alleyn said. "Not there. I'm not talking about him. You didn't care about him. You were trying to shield the boy, weren't you? You did what you did for Richard Dakers."

She broke into a passion of weeping and from then until the end of the case he had no more trouble with Ninn.

2

When it was over he sent her up to her room.

"Well," he said to Fox, "now for the final and far from delectable scene. We should, of course, have prevented all this, but I'm damned if I see how. We couldn't arrest on what we'd got. Unless they find some trace of Slaypest in the scent-spray my reading of the case will never be anything but an unsupported theory."

"They ought to be coming through with the result before long."

"You might ring up and see where they've got to."

Fox dialled a number. There was a tap at the door and Philpott looked in. He stared at the covered body on the bed.

"Yes," Alleyn said. "A death. Mr. Templeton."

"By violence, sir?"

"Not by physical violence. Heart disease. What is it, Philpott?"

"It's the lot in there, sir. They're getting very restive, especially Mr. Dakers and the Colonel. Wondering what was wrong with"—he looked again at the bed—"with him, sir."

"Yes. Will you ask Mr. Dakers and Colonel Warrender to go into the small sitting-room next door. I'll be there in a moment. Oh, and Philpott, I think you might ask Miss Lee to come too. And you may tell the others they will have very little longer to wait."

"Sir," said Philpott and withdrew.

Fox was talking into the telephone. "Yes. Yes. I'll tell him. He'll be very much obliged. Thank you."

He hung up. "They were just going to ring. They've found

an identifiable trace inside the bulb of the scent-spray."

"Have they indeed? That provides the complete answer."

"So you were right, Mr. Alleyn."

"And what satisfaction," Alleyn said wryly, "is to be had out of that?"

He went to the bed and turned back the sheet. The eyes, unseeing, still stared past him. The imprint of a fear, already nonexistent, still disfigured the face. Alleyn looked down at it for a second or two. "What unhappiness!" he said and closed the eyes.

"He had a lot to try him," Fox observed with his customary simplicity.

"He had indeed, poor chap."

"So did they all, if it comes to that. She must have been a very vexing sort of lady. There'll have to be a p.m., Mr. Alleyn."

"Yes, of course. All right. I'll see these people next door."

He re-covered the face and went out.

Dr. Harkness and Florence were in the hall, watched over by a Yard reinforcement. Alleyn said, "I think you'd better come in with me, if you will, Harkness." And to Florence, "You'll stay where you are for the moment, if you please."

Harkness followed him into the boudoir.

It had been created by Bertie Saracen in an opulent mood and contrasted strangely with the exquisite austerity of the study. "Almost indecently *you*, darling!" Bertie had told Miss Bellamy and, almost indecently, it was so.

Its present occupants—Richard, Anelida and Warrender—were standing awkwardly in the middle of this room, overlooked by an enormous and immensely vivacious portrait in pastel of Mary Bellamy. Charles, photographed some twenty years ago, gazed mildly from the centre of an occasional table. To Alleyn there was something atrociously ironic in this circumstance.

Richard demanded at once: "What is it? What happened? Is Charles...?"

"Yes," Alleyn said. "It's bad news. He collapsed a few minutes ago."

"But...? You don't mean...?"

"I'm afraid so."

Richard said, "Anelida! It's Charles. He means Charles has died. Doesn't he?"

"Why," she said fiercely, "must these things happen to you. *Why!*"

Dr. Harkness went up to him. "Sorry, old boy," he said, "I tried but it was no good. It might have happened any time during the last five years, you know."

Richard stared blankly at him. "My God!" he cried out. "You can't talk like that!"

"Steady, old chap. You'll realize, when you think it over. Any time."

"I don't believe you. It's because of everything else. It's because of Mary and . . ." Richard turned on Alleyn. "You'd no right to subject him to all this. It's killed him. You'd no right. If it hadn't been for you it needn't have happened."

Alleyn said very compassionately, "That may be true. He was in great distress. It may even be that for him this was the best solution."

"How dare you say that!" Richard exclaimed and then, "What do you mean?"

"Don't you think he'd pretty well got to the end of his tether? He'd lost the thing he most valued in life, hadn't he?"

"I—I want to see him."

Alleyn remembered Charles's face. "Then you shall," he promised, "presently."

"Yes," Harkness agreed quickly. "Presently."

"For the moment," Alleyn said, turning to Anelida, "I suggest that you take him up to his old room and give him a drink. Will you do that?"

"Yes," Anelida said. "That's the thing." She put her hand in Richard's. "Coming?"

He looked down at her. "I wonder," he said, "what on earth I should do without you, Anelida."

"Come on," she said, and they went out together.

Alleyn nodded to Harkness and he too went out.

An affected little French clock above the fireplace cleared its throat, broke into a perfect frenzy of silvery chimes and then struck midnight. Inspector Fox came into the room and shut the door.

Alleyn looked at Maurice Warrender.

"And now," he said, "there must be an end to equivocation. I must have the truth."

"I don't know what you mean," said Warrender, and could scarcely have sounded less convincing.

"I wonder why people always say that when they know precisely what one does mean. However, I'd better tell you. A few minutes ago, immediately after Charles Templeton died, I talked to the nanny, Mrs. Plumtree, who had been alone with him at the moment of his collapse. I told her that I believed she had uttered threats, that she had acted in this way because she thought Templeton was withholding information which would clear your son from suspicion of murder and that under the stress of this scene, Templeton suffered the heart attack from which he died. I told her your son was in no danger of arrest and she then admitted the whole story. I now tell you, too, that your son is in no danger. If you have withheld information for fear of incriminating him, you may understand that you have acted mistakenly."

Warrender seemed to be on the point of speaking but instead turned abruptly away and stood very still.

"You refused to tell me of the threats Mrs. Templeton uttered in the conservatory and I got them, after great difficulty it's true, from the other people who were there. When I asked you if you had quarrelled with Charles Templeton you denied it. I believe that, in fact, you *had* quarrelled with him and that it happened while you were together in the study before I saw you for the first time. For the whole of that interview you scarcely so much as looked at each other. He was obviously distressed by your presence and you were violently opposed to rejoining him there. I must ask you again. Had you quarrelled?"

Warrender muttered, "If you call it a quarrel."

"Was it about Richard Dakers?" Alleyn waited. "I think it was," he said, "but of course that's mere speculation and open, if you like, to contradiction."

Warrender squared his shoulders. "What's all this leading up to?" he demanded. "An arrest?"

"Surely you've heard of the usual warning. Come, sir, you did have a scene with Charles Templeton and I believe it was about Richard Dakers. Did you tell Templeton you were the father?"

"I did not," he said quickly.

"Did he know you were the father?"

"Not... We agreed from the outset that it was better that he shouldn't know. That nobody should know. Better on all counts."

"You haven't really answered my question, have you? Shall I put it this way? Did Templeton learn for the first time, this afternoon, that Dakers is your son?"

"Why should you suppose anything of the sort?"

"Your normal relationship appears to have been happy, yet at this time, when one would have expected you all to come together in your common trouble, he showed a vehement disinclination to see Dakers—or you."

Warrender made an unexpected gesture. He flung out his hands and lifted his shoulders. "Very well," he said.

"And *you* didn't tell him." Alleyn walked up to him and looked him full in the face. "She told him," he said. "Didn't she? Without consulting you, without any consideration for you or the boy. Because she was in one of those tantrums that have become less and less controllable. She made you spray that unspeakable scent over her in their presence, I suppose to irritate him. You went out and left them together. And she broke the silence of thirty years and told him."

"You can't possibly know."

"When she left the room a minute or two later she shouted at the top of her voice: 'Which only shows how wrong you were. You can get out whenever you like, my friend, and the sooner the better.' Florence had gone. You had gone. She was speaking to her husband. Did she tell you?"

"Tell *me*! What the hell..."

"Did she tell you what she'd said to Templeton?"

Warrender turned away to the fireplace, leant his arm on the shelf and hid his face.

"All right!" he stammered. "All right! What does it matter, now. All right."

"Was it during the party?"

He made some kind of sound, apparently in assent.

"Before or after the row in the conservatory?"

"After." He didn't raise his head and his voice sounded as if it didn't belong to him. "I tried to stop her attacking the girl."

197

"And that turned her against you? Yes, I see."

"I was following them, the girl and her uncle, and she whispered it. 'Charles knows about Dicky.' It was quite dreadful to see her look like that. I—I simply walked out—I..." He raised his head and looked at Alleyn. "It was indescribable."

"And your great fear after that was that she would tell the boy?"

He said nothing.

"As, of course, she did. Her demon was let loose. She took him up to her room and told him. They were, I daresay, the last words she spoke."

Warrender said, "You assume—you say these things—you..." and was unable to go on. His eyes were wet and bloodshot and his face grey. He looked quite old. "I don't know what's come over me," he said.

Alleyn thought he knew.

"It's not much cop," he said, "when a life's preoccupation turns out to have been misplaced. It seems to me that a man in such a position would rather see the woman dead than watch her turning into a monster."

"Why do you say these things to me. *Why!*"

"Isn't it so?"

With a strange parody of his habitual mannerism he raised a shaking hand to his tie and pulled at it.

"I understand," he said. "You've been very clever, I suppose."

"Not very, I'm afraid."

Warrender looked up at the beaming portrait of Mary Bellamy. "There's nothing left," he said. "Nothing. What do you want me to do?"

"I must speak to Dakers and then to those people in there. I think I must ask you to join us."

"Very well," Warrender said.

"Would you like a drink?"

"Thank you. If I may."

Alleyn looked at Fox who went out and returned with a tumbler and the decanter that Alleyn had seen on the table between Warrender and Charles at his first encounter with them.

"Whisky," Fox said. "If that's agreeable. Shall I pour it out, sir?"

Warrender took it neat and in one gulp. "I'm very much obliged to you," he said and straightened his back. The ghost of a smile distorted his mouth. "One more," he said, "and I shall be ready for anything, isn't it?"

Alleyn said, "I am going to have a word with Dakers before I see the others."

"Are you going to—to tell him?"

"I think it best to do so, yes."

"Yes. I see. Yes."

"When you are ready, Fox," Alleyn said and went out.

"He'll make it as easy as possible, sir," Fox said comfortably. "You may be sure of that."

"Easy!" said Warrender, and made a sound that might have been a laugh. "Easy!"

3

The persons sitting in the drawing-room were assembled there for the last time. In a few weeks Mary Bellamy's house would be transformed into the West End offices of a new venture in television, and a sedan chair, for heaven knows what reason, would adorn the hall. Bertie Saracen's decor, taken over in toto, would be the background for the frenzied bandying about of new gimmicks and Charles Templeton's study a waiting-room for disengaged actors.

At the moment it had an air of stability. Most of its occupants, having exhausted each in his or her own kind their capacity for anxiety, anger or compassion, had settled down into apathy. They exchanged desultory remarks, smoked continuously and occasionally helped themselves, rather self-consciously, to the drinks that Gracefield had provided. P.C. Philpott remained alert in his corner.

It was Dr. Harkness who, without elaboration, announced Charles Templeton's death and that indeed shook them into a state of flabbergasted astonishment. When Richard came in, deathly pale, with Anelida, they all had to pull themselves together before they found anything at all to say to him. They did, indeed, attempt appropriate remarks, but it was clear to Anelida that their store of consolatory offerings was spent. However heartfelt their sympathy, they were obliged to fall back on their technique in order to express it. Pinky Cavendish broke into this unreal state of affairs by suddenly giving Richard a kiss and saying warmly, "It's no good, darling. There really is just literally nothing we can say or do, but we wish with all our hearts that there was, and Anelida must be your comfort. There!"

"Pinky," Richard said unevenly, "you really are no end of a darling. I'm afraid I can't—I can't . . . I'm sorry. I'm just not reacting much to anything."

"Exactly," Marchant said. "How well one understands. The proper thing, of course, would be for one to leave you to yourself, which unfortunately this Yard individual at the moment won't allow."

"He *did* send to say it wouldn't be long now," Bertie pointed out nervously.

"Do you suppose," Pinky asked, "that means he's going to arrest somebody?"

"Who can tell! Do you know *what*?" Bertie continued very rapidly and in an unnatural voice. "I don't mind betting every man jack of us is madly wondering what all the others think about him. Or her. I know I am. I keep saying to myself, '*Can* any of them think I darted upstairs instead of into the loo, and did it!' I suppose it's no use asking you all for a frank opinion is it? It would be taking an advantage."

"*I* don't think it of you," Pinky said at once. "I promise you, darling."

"Pinky! Nor I of you. Never for a moment. And I don't believe it of Anelida or Richard. Do you?"

"Never for a moment," she said firmly. "Absolutely not."

"Well," Bertie continued, inspired by Pinky's confidence, "I should like to know if any of you *does* suppose it might be me." Nobody answered. "I can't help feeling immensely gratified," Bertie said. "Thank you. Now. Shall I tell you which of you I think *could—just—*under *frightful* provocation—do something violent all of a sudden?"

"Me, I suppose," Gantry said. "I'm a hot-tempered man."

"Yes. Timmy dear, you! But *only* in boiling hot blood with one blind swipe, not really meaning to. And that doesn't seem to fit the bill at all. One wants a calculating iceberg of a person for this job, doesn't one?"

There followed a period of hideous discomfort, during which nobody looked at anybody else.

"An idle flight of speculation, I'm afraid, Bertie," said Marchant. "Would you be very kind and bring me a drink?"

"But of course," said Bertie, and did so.

Gantry glanced at Richard and said, "Obviously there's no connection—apart from the shock of Mary's death having precipitated it—between Charles's tragedy—and hers." Nobody spoke and he added half-angrily, "Well, *is* there! Harkness—you were there."

Dr. Harkness said quickly, "I don't know what's in Alleyn's mind."

"Where's that momumental, that superb old ham, the Colonel? Why's he gone missing all of a sudden?" Gantry demanded. "Sorry, Dicky, he's a friend of yours, isn't he?"

"He's . . . Yes," Richard said after a long pause. "He is. I think he's with Alleyn."

"Not," Marchant coolly remarked, "under arrest, one trusts."

"I believe not," Richard said. He turned his back on Marchant and sat beside Anelida on the sofa.

"Oh lud!" Bertie sighed, "how *wearing* has been this long, long day and how frightened in a vague sort of way I continue to feel. Never mind. *Toujours l'audace.*"

The handle of the door into the hall was heard to turn. Everybody looked up. Florence walked round the leather screen. "If you'll just wait, Miss," the constable said and retired. Philpott cleared his throat.

Richard said, "Come in, Floy. Come and sit down."

She glanced stonily at him, walked into the farthest corner of the room and sat on the smallest chair. Pinky looked as if she'd like to say something friendly to her, but the impulse came to nothing and a heavy silence again fell upon the company.

It was broken by the same sound and a heavier tread. Bertie half-rose from his seat, gave a little cry of frustration and sank back again as Colonel Warrender made his entry, very erect and looking at no one in particular.

"We were just talking about you," said Bertie fretfully.

Richard stood up. "Come and join us," he said, and pushed a chair towards the sofa.

"Thank you, old boy," Warrender said awkwardly, and did so.

Anelida leant towards him and after a moment's hesitation put her hand on his knee. "I intend," she said under her breath, "to bully Richard into marrying me. Will you be on my side and give us your blessing?"

He drew his brows together and stared at her. He made an unsuccessful attempt to speak, hit her hand painfully hard with his own and ejaculated, "Clumsy ass. Hurt you, isn't it? Ah—Bless you."

"O.K.," said Anelida and looked at Richard. "Now, you see, darling, you're sunk."

There was a sound of masculine voices in the hall, Pinky said, "Oh *dear*!" and Gantry, "Ah, for God's sake!" Marchant finished his drink quickly and P.C. Philpott rose to his feet. So, after a mulish second or two, did Florence.

This time it was Alleyn who came round the leather screen.

There was only one place in the room from which he could take them all in at one glance and that was the hearthrug. Accordingly, he went to it and stood there like the central figure in some ill-assembled conversation piece.

"I'm sorry," he said, "to have kept you hanging about. It was unavoidable and it won't be for much longer. Until a short time ago you were still, all of you, persons of importance. From the police point of view, I mean, of course. It was through you that we hoped to assemble the fragments and fit them into their pattern. The pattern is now complete and our uncomfortable association draws to its end. Tomorrow there will be an inquest and you will be required, most of you, to appear at it. The coroner's jury will hear your evidence and mine and one can only guess at what they will make of it. But you have all become too far involved for me to use any sort of evasion. Already some of you are suspecting others who are innocent. In my opinion this is one of those cases where the truth, at any cost, is less damaging in the long run, to vague, festering conjecture. For you all must know," Alleyn went on, "you *must* know even if you won't acknowledge it..."—his glance rested fleetingly on Richard—"that this has been a case of homicide."

He waited. Gantry said, "I don't accept that," but without much conviction.

"You will, I think, when I tell you that the Home Office analyst has found a trace of Slaypest in the bulb of the scent-spray."

"Oh," Gantry said faintly, as if Alleyn had made some quite unimportant remark. "I see. That's different."

"It's conclusive. It clears up all the extraneous matter. The professional rows, the threats that you were all so reluctant to admit, the evasions and half-lies. The personal bickerings and antagonisms. They were all tidied away by this single fact."

Marchant, whose hands were joined in front of his face, lifted his gaze for a moment to Alleyn. "You are not making yourself particularly clear," he said.

"I hope to do so. This one piece of evidence explains a number of indisputable facts. Here they are. The scent-spray was harmless when Colonel Warrender used it on Mrs. Templeton. At some time before she went up to her room with Mr. Dakers, enough Slaypest was transferred to the scent-spray to kill her. At some time after she was killed the scent-spray was emptied and washed out and the remaining scent from the original bottle was poured into it. I think there were two, possibly three, persons in the house at that time who could have committed these actions. They are all familiar with the room and its appointments and surroundings. The presence of any one of them in her room would, under normal circumstances, have been unremarkable."

A voice from outside the group violently demanded, "Where is she? Why hasn't she been brought down to face it?" And then, with satisfaction, "Has she been taken away? *Has* she?"

Florence advanced into the light.

Richard cried out, "What do you mean, Floy? Be quiet! You don't know what you're saying."

"Where's Clara Plumtree?"

"She will appear," Alleyn said, "if the occasion arises. And you had better be quiet, you know."

For a moment she looked as if she would defy him, but seemed to change her mind. She stood where she was and watched him.

"There is, however," Alleyn said, "a third circumstance. You will all remember that after the speeches you waited down here for Mrs. Templeton to take her part in the ceremony of opening the presents. Mr. Dakers had left her in her room, passing Florence and Mrs. Plumtree on his way downstairs. Mrs. Plumtree had then gone to her room, leaving Florence alone on the landing. Mr. Templeton went from here into the hall. From the foot of the stairs he saw Florence on the landing and called up to her that you were all waiting for her mistress. He then rejoined the party here. A minute or so later Florence ran downstairs into this room and, after a certain amount of confused ejaculation, made it known that her mistress was desperately ill. Mr. Templeton rushed upstairs. Dr. Harkness, after a short delay, followed. With Florence, Colonel Warrender and Mr. Gantry hard on his heels.

"They found Mrs. Templeton lying dead on the floor of her room. The overturned tin of Slaypest lay close beside her right hand. The scent-spray was on the dressing-table. That has been agreed to, but I am going to ask for a further confirmation."

Dr. Harkness said, "Certainly. That's how it was."

"You'd make a statement on oath to that effect?"

"I would." He looked at Gantry and Warrender. "Wouldn't you?"

They said uneasily that they would.

"Well, Florence?" Alleyn asked.

"I said before: I didn't notice. I was too upset."

"But you don't disagree?"

"No," she admitted grudgingly.

"Very well. Now, you will see, I think, all of you, that the whole case turns on this one circumstance. The tin of Slaypest on the floor. The scent-spray and the empty bottle on the dressing-table."

"Isn't it awful?" Pinky said suddenly. "I know it must be childishly obvious, but I just can't bring myself to think."

"Can't you?" Gantry said grimly. "I can."

"Not having been involved in the subsequent discussions," Marchant remarked to nobody in particular, "the nicer points must be allowed, I hope, to escape me."

"Let me bring you up to date," Alleyn said. "There was poison in the scent-spray. Nobody, I imagine, will suggest that she put it there herself or that she used the Slaypest on herself. The sound of a spray in action was heard a minute or so before she died. By Ninn—Mrs. Plumtree."

"So she says," Florence interjected.

Alleyn went on steadily, "Mrs. Templeton was alone in her room. Very well. Having used the lethal scent-spray, did she replace it on the dressing-table and put the Slaypest on the floor?"

Florence said, "What did I tell you? Clara Plumtree! After I went. Say she *did* hear the thing being used. She done it! She went in and fixed it all. What did I tell you!"

"On your own evidence," Alleyn said, "and on that of Mr. Templeton, you were on the landing when he called up to you. You returned at once to the bedroom. Do you think that in those few seconds, Mrs. Plumtree, who moves very slowly, could have darted into the room, re-arranged the scent-spray, and Slaypest, darted out again and got out of sight?"

"She could've hid in the dressing-room. Like she done afterwards when she wouldn't let me in."

Alleyn said: "I'm afraid that won't quite do. Which brings me to the fourth point. I won't go into all the pathological details, but there is clear evidence that the spray was used in the normal way—at about arm's length and without undue pressure—and then at very close quarters and with maximum pressure. Her murderer, finding she was not dead, made sure that she would die. Mrs. Plumtree would certainly not have had an opportunity to do it. There is only one person who could have committed that act and the three other necessary acts as well. Only one."

"*Florence!*" Gantry cried out.

"No. Not Florence. Charles Templeton."

4

The drawing-room now seemed strangely deserted. Pinky Cavendish, Montague Marchant, Dr. Harkness, Bertie Saracen and Timon Gantry had all gone home. Charles Templeton's body had been carried away. Old Ninn was in her bed. Florence had retired to adjust her resentments and nurse her heartache as best she could. Mr. Fox was busy with routine arrangements. Only Alleyn, Richard, Anelida and Warrender remained in the drawing-room.

Richard said, "Ever since you told me and all through that last scene with them, I've been trying to see why. Why *should* he, having put up with so much for so long, do such a monstrous thing? It's—it's... I've always thought him—he was so..." Richard drove his fingers through his hair. "Maurice! You knew him. Better than any of us."

Warrender, looking at his clasped hands, muttered unhappily, "What's that word they use nowadays? Perfectionist?"

"But what do you... Yes. All right. He was a perfectionist, I suppose."

"Couldn't stand anything that wasn't up to his own standard. Look at those T'ang figures. Little lady with a flute and little lady with a lute. Lovely little creatures. Prized them more than anything else in the house. But when the parlour-maid or somebody knocked the end off one of the little lute pegs, he wouldn't have it. Gave it to me, by God!" said Warrender.

Alleyn said, "That's illuminating, isn't it?"

"But it's one thing to feel like that and another to—No!" Richard exclaimed, "it's a nightmare. You can't reduce it to that size. It's irreducible. Monstrous!"

"It's happened," Warrender said flatly.

"Mr. Alleyn," Anelida suggested, "would you tell us what you think? Would you take the things that led up to it out of their background and put them in order for us? Might that help, do you think, Richard?"

"I think it might, darling. If anything can."

"Well," Alleyn said, "shall I try? First of all, then, there's her personal history. There are the bouts of temperament that have increased in severity and frequency—to such a degree that they have begun to suggest a serious mental condition. You're all agreed about that, aren't you? Colonel Warrender?"

"I suppose so. Yes."

"What was she like thirty years ago, when he married her?"

Warrender looked at Richard. "Enchanting. Law unto herself. Gay. Lovely." He raised his hand and let it fall. "Ah, well! There it is. Never mind."

"Different? From these days?" Alleyn pursued.

"My God, yes!"

"So the musician's lute was broken? The perfect had become imperfect?"

"Very well. Go on."

"May we think back to yesterday, the day of the party? You must tell me if I'm all to blazes but this is how I see it. My reading, by the way, is pieced together from the statements Fox and I have collected from all of you and from the servants, who, true to form, knew more than any of you might suppose. Things began to go wrong quite early, didn't they? Wasn't it in the morning that she learnt for the first time that her..." He hesitated for a moment.

"It's all right," Richard said. "Anelida knows. Everything. She says she doesn't mind."

"Why on earth should I?" Anelida asked of the world at large. "We're not living in the reign of King Lear. In any case, Mr. Alleyn's talking about *Husbandry in Heaven* and me and how your mama didn't much fancy the idea that you'd taken up with me and still less the idea of my reading for the part."

"Which she'd assumed was written for her. That's it," Alleyn said. "That exacerbated a sense of being the victim of a conspiracy, which was set up by the scene in which she learnt that Miss Cavendish was to play the lead in another comedy and that Gantry and Saracen were in the 'plot.' She was a jealous, aging actress, abnormally possessive."

"But not always," Richard protested. "Not anything like always."

"Getting more so," Warrender muttered.

"Exactly. And perhaps because of that her husband, the perfectionist, may have transferred his ruling preoccupation from her to the young man whom he believed to be his son and on whom she was loath to relinquish her hold."

"But *did* he?" Richard cried out. "Maurice, did he think that?"

"She'd—let him assume it."

"I see. And in those days, as you've told us, he believed everything she said. I understand now," Richard said to Alleyn, "why you agreed that there was no need to tell him about me. He already knew, didn't he?"

"She herself," Alleyn went on, "told Colonel Warrender, after the flare-up in the conservatory, that she had disillusioned her husband."

"Did Charles," Richard asked Warrender, "say anything to you afterwards? Did he?"

"When we were boxed up together in the study. He hated my being there. It came out. He was..." Warrender seemed to search for an appropriate phrase. "I've never seen a man so angry," he said at last. "So sick with anger."

"Oh God!" Richard said.

"And then," Alleyn continued, "there was the row over the scent. He asked her not to use it. She made you, Colonel Warrender, spray it lavishly over her, in her husband's presence. You left the room. You felt, didn't you, that there was going to be a scene?"

"I shouldn't have done it. She could always make me do what she wanted," Warrender said. "I knew at the time but—isn't it?"

"Never mind," Richard said, and to Alleyn, "Was it then she told him?"

"I think it was at the climax of this scene. As he went out she was heard to shout after him, 'Which only shows how wrong you were. You can get out whenever you like, my friend, and the sooner the better.' She was not, as the hearer supposed, giving a servant the sack, she was giving it to him."

"And half an hour later," Richard said to Anelida, "there he was—standing beside her, shaking hands with her friends. I thought, when I was telephoning, he looked ill. I told you. He wouldn't speak."

"And then," Anelida said to Alleyn, "came the scene in the conservatory."

"Exactly. And, you see, he knew she had the power to make good her threats. Hard on the heels of the blow she had dealt him, he had to stand by and listen to her saying what she did say to all of you."

"Richard," Anelida said, "can you see? He'd loved her and he was watching her disintegrate. Anything to stop it!"

"I can see, darling, but I can't accept it. Not that."

"To put it very brutally," Alleyn said, "the treasured possession was not only hideously flawed, but possessed of a devil. She reeked of the scent he'd asked her not to wear. I don't think it would be too much to say that at that moment it symbolized for him the full horror of his feeling for her."

"D'you mean it was then he did it?" Warrender asked.

"Yes. Then. It must have been then. During all the movement and excitement just before the speeches. He went upstairs, emptied out some of the scent and filled up the atomizer with Slaypest. He returned during the speeches. As she left the drawing-room she came face to face with him. Florence heard him ask her not to use the scent."

Warrender gave an exclamation. "Yes?" Alleyn asked.

"Good God, d'you mean it was a—kind of gamble? If she did as he'd asked—like those gambles on suicide? Fella with a revolver. Half live, half blank cartridges."

"Exactly that. Only this time it was a gamble in murder." Alleyn looked at them. "It may seem strange that I tell you in detail so much that is painful and shocking. I do so because I believe that it is less damaging in the long run to know rather than to doubt."

"Of course it is," Anelida said quickly. "Richard, my dear, isn't it?"

"Yes," Richard said. "I expect it is. Yes, it is."

"Well, then," Alleyn said, "immediately after he'd spoken to her, you came in. The photographs were taken and you went upstairs together. You tackled her about her treatment of Anelida, didn't you?"

"It would be truer to say she attacked me. But, yes—we were both terribly angry. I've told you."

"And it ended in her throwing your parentage in your teeth?"

"It ended with that."

"When you'd gone she hurled your birthday present into the bathroom where it smashed to pieces. Instead of at once returning downstairs she went through an automatic performance. She powdered her face and painted her mouth. And then—well, then it happened. She used her scent-spray, holding it at arm's length. The windows were shut. It had an immediate effect, but not the effect he'd anticipated."

"What d'you mean?" Warrender asked.

"You've read the dictionary of poisons he bought. You may remember it gives a case of instant and painless death. But it doesn't always act in that way."

"He thought it would?"

"Probably. In this case, she became desperately ill. Florence came in and found her so. Do you remember what Charles Templeton said when Florence raised the alarm?"

Warrender thought for a moment. "Yes. I do. He said 'My God, not *now!*' I thought he meant 'Not a temperament at this juncture.'"

"Whereas he meant 'Not *now*. Not so soon.' He then rushed upstairs. There was some delay in getting Harkness under way, wasn't there?"

"Tight. Bad show. I put ice down his neck."

"And by the time you all arrived on the scene, the Slaypest was on the floor and the atomizer on the dressing-table. And she was dead. He had found her as Florence had left her. Whether she'd been able to say anything that showed she knew what he'd done is a matter of conjecture. Panic, terror, a determination to end it at all costs—we don't know. He *did* end it as quickly as he could and by the only means he had."

There was a long silence. Anelida broke it. "Perhaps," she said, "if it hadn't happened as it did, he would have changed his mind and not let it happen."

"Yes. It's possible, indeed. As it was he had to protect himself. He had to improvise. It must have been a nightmare. He'd had a bad heart-turn and had been settled down in his dressing-room. As soon as he was alone; he went through the communicating door, emptied the atomizer into the lavatory, washed it out as best he could and poured in what was left of the scent."

"But how do you *know*?" Richard protested.

"As he returned, Old Ninn came into the dressing-room. She took it for granted he had been in the bathroom for the obvious reason. But later, when I developed my theory of the scent-spray, she remembered. She suspected the truth, particularly as he had smelt of Formidable. So strongly that when Florence stood in the open doorway of the dressing-room she thought it was Ninn, and that she had been attempting to do the service which Florence regarded as her own right."

"My poor old Ninn!" Richard cried.

"She, as you know, was not exactly at the top of her form. There had been certain potations, hadn't there? Florence, who in her anger and sorrow, was prepared to accuse anybody of anything, made some very damaging remarks about you."

"There's no divided allegiance," Richard said, "about Floy."

"Nor about Ninn. She was terrified. Tonight she went into the study after Templeton had been put to bed there and told him that if there was any chance of suspicion falling on you, she would tell her story. He was desperately ill but he made some kind of attempt to get at her. She made to defend herself. He collapsed and died."

Richard said, "One can't believe these things of people one has loved. For Charles to have died like that."

"Isn't it better?" Alleyn asked. "It *is* better. Because, as you know, we would have gone on. We would have brought him to trial. As it is, it's odds on that the coroner's jury will find it an accident. A rider will be added pointing out the dangers of indoor pest-killers. That's all."

"It is better," Anelida said, and after a moment, "Mightn't one say that he brought about his own retribution?" She turned to Richard and was visited by a feeling of great tenderness and strength. "We'll cope," she said, "with the future. Won't we?"

"I believe we will, darling," Richard said. "We must, mustn't we?"

Alleyn said, "You've suffered a great shock and will feel it for some time. It's happened and can't be forgotten. But the hurt *will* grow less."

He saw that Richard was not listening to him. He had his

arm about Anelida and had turned her towards him.

"You'll do," Alleyn said, unheeded.

He went up to Anelida and took her hand. "True," he said. "Believe me. He'll be all right. To my mind he has nothing to blame himself for. And that," Alleyn said, "is generally allowed to be a great consolation. Good-night."

5

Miss Bellamy's funeral was everything that she would have wished.

All the Knights and Dames, of course, and the Management and Timon Gantry, who had so often directed her. Bertie Saracen who had created her dresses since the days when she was a bit-part actress. Pinky Cavendish in floods, and Maurice, very Guardee, with a stiff upper lip.

Quite insignificant people, too: her old Ninn with a face like a boot and Florence with a bunch of primroses. Crowds of people whom she herself would have scarcely remembered, but upon whom, as a columnist in a woman's magazine put it, she had at some time bestowed the gift of her charm. And it was not for her fame, the celebrated clergyman pointed out in his address, that they had come to say goodbye to her. It was, quite simply, because they had loved her.

And Richard Dakers was there, very white and withdrawn, with a slim, intelligent-looking girl beside him.

Everybody.

Except, of course, her husband. It was extraordinary how little he was missed. The lady columnist could not, for the life of her, remember his name.

Charles Templeton had, as he would have wished, a private funeral.

NGAIO MARSH

BESTSELLING PAPERBACKS BY A "GRAND MASTER" OF THE MYSTERY WRITERS OF AMERICA.

___ 07534-5	ARTISTS IN CRIME	$2.95
___ 07105-6	CLUTCH OF CONSTABLES	$2.50
___ 06715-6	DEATH AND THE DANCING FOOTMAN	$2.50
___ 06166-2	DEATH IN ECSTASY	$2.50
___ 07503-5	DEATH OF A FOOL	$2.95
___ 06716-4	DEATH OF A PEER	$2.50
___ 07506-X	DIED IN THE WOOL	$2.95
___ 07447-0	ENTER A MURDERER	$2.95
___ 07074-2	FINAL CURTAIN	$2.50
___ 07549-3	GRAVE MISTAKE	$2.95
___ 07502-7	HAND IN GLOVE	$2.95
___ 06820-9	KILLER DOLPHIN	$2.50
___ 06821-7	LAST DITCH	$2.50
___ 07359-8	LIGHT THICKENS	$2.95
___ 07535-3	A MAN LAY DEAD	$2.95

Prices may be slightly higher in Canada.

NGAIO MARSH

____ 07627-9	BLACK AS HE'S PAINTED	$2.95
____ 07507-8	NIGHT AT THE VULCAN	$2.95
____ 07606-6	OVERTURE TO DEATH	$2.95
____ 07505-1	PHOTO FINISH	$2.95
____ 07504-3	WHEN IN ROME	$2.95
____ 07440-3	DEAD WATER	$2.95
____ 07851-4	THE NURSING HOME MURDER	$2.95
____ 06179-4	SPINSTERS IN JEOPARDY	$2.50
____ 07443-8	TIED UP IN TINSEL	$2.95
____ 06012-7	VINTAGE MURDER	$2.50
____ 07501-9	A WREATH FOR RIVERA	$2.95
____ 07700-3	DEATH AT THE BAR	$2.95
____ 07735-6	SINGING IN THE SHROUDS	$2.95

Prices may be slightly higher in Canada.
